Female, Nude

Rhiannon Lucy Cosslett

TINDER
PRESS

Copyright © Rhiannon Lucy Cosslett 2026

The right of Rhiannon Lucy Cosslett to be identified as
the Author of the Work has been asserted by her in accordance
with the Copyright, Designs and Patents Act 1988.

Epigraph from Carol Ann Duffy's *Standing Female Nude* is reproduced with
permission of Rogers, Coleridge and White Ltd., on behalf of Carol Ann Duffy.
Copyright © Carol Ann Duffy

First published in 2026 by Tinder Press
An imprint of Headline Publishing Group Limited

1

Apart from any use permitted under UK copyright law, this
publication may only be reproduced, stored, or transmitted, in any form,
or by any means, with prior permission in writing of the publishers or,
in the case of reprographic production, in accordance with the terms
of licences issued by the Copyright Licensing Agency.

All characters in this publication are fictitious and any resemblance
to real persons, living or dead, is purely coincidental.

Cataloguing in Publication Data is available from the British Library

Hardback ISBN 978 1 0354 1381 2

Typeset in Scala by CC Book Production

Printed and bound in Great Britain by Clays Ltd, Elcograf S.p.A.

Headline's policy is to use papers that are natural, renewable and
recyclable products and made from wood grown in sustainable forests.
The logging and manufacturing processes are expected to conform
to the environmental regulations of the country of origin.

Headline Publishing Group Limited
An Hachette UK Company
Carmelite House
50 Victoria Embankment
London EC4Y 0DZ

The authorised representative in the EEA is Hachette Ireland,
8 Castlecourt Centre, Dublin 15, D15 XTP3, Ireland
(email: info@hbgi.ie)

www.headline.co.uk
www.hachette.co.uk

For Sarah and her sister Lucy

'Each morning a vision came to me.
   Gradually I understood that these were naked glimpses of my soul.
   I called them Nudes.'

– 'The Glass Essay', Ann Carson

'Living *in* a female body is different from looking *at* it, as a man. Even the Venus of Urbino menstruated, as women know and men forget.'

– Lisa Tickner

'When it's finished
he shows me proudly, lights a cigarette. I say
Twelve francs and get my shawl. It does not look like me.'

– 'Standing Female Nude', Carol Ann Duffy

Paula Modersohn-Becker,
Self-Portrait at 6th Wedding Anniversary, 1906

In my hand, there is a postcard that I bought when I was nineteen and slipped inside my tatty copy of Ways of Seeing. *I hold it by the top right-hand corner between my thumb and forefinger, and as I do it trembles slightly, because I am breathing too quickly. I am wondering whether to send it, or to make a phone call instead.*

The glossy card is a reproduction of your self-portrait from 1906. It was painted on your thirtieth birthday, six years after your wedding day. Your eyes confront me from your tilted face, not solemn exactly, but peacefully authoritative as you cradle your rounded belly. Your breasts are simply a fact.

You wanted to be pregnant, but you weren't when you painted this. You were just trying it on, as one might a costume. Seeing how it fit. I think you wanted it desperately, but you feared it, too.

You had left your husband and gone to Paris to be an artist. Maybe, like me, you were often struck with terror at all the art you hadn't made. Maybe that made you want to burn down your life.

I bought the postcard in a museum gift shop. Since I was a little girl, I have collected postcards of paintings. I always wanted to hold on to the meaning for as long as I could after leaving the gallery, to absorb the magic, somehow.

The nudes we studied at university were mannered and bloodless. I'd had no idea that you existed, until I saw your painting on that Interrail trip, at a loose end in a small German city while the others slept off their hangovers. The first known nude self-portrait by a female painter. My vision cracked open.

I stood in front of you, eager to absorb every detail. What did I notice? Aside from your breasts, it was your mannish, artist's hands. The flesh of your arms, the flushes of pink there and in your face. A refutation of idealised perfection. Here is a woman's body as seen by a woman.

I know better, now, than to be surprised at your omission from the syllabus. I look at the postcard as I stand, shaking, in a half-unpacked spare room, the same age as you were when you died: thirty-one.

I wonder how many great artists the world has lost to childbirth. I think you would have found a way to be a mother and to carry on making art, had you lived. You had been planning to leave your husband for good, to raise the baby on your own.

You died eighteen days after giving birth, the first time they let you stand up. They wove roses through your hair and walked you through to hold your daughter. Your final words were, 'What a pity.'

I decide that your painting means too much to part with. I put you down gently, and go to pick up the phone.

First day, morning

During my first night on the island, I dreamed that a baby slipped smoothly from my vagina, and, without making a sound, slithered its way up my body – cord still attached – towards my right nipple, which it clamped in its mouth and began to suck.

The surprise arrival of the baby, owing to the complete absence of any pregnancy, meant that my dream-self produced no milk, nor did I have anywhere to put the infant. In the end, Greg and I placed it in a cardboard Amazon box. Its showing up was a shock, but not an altogether unpleasant one. When I awoke, damp and babyless at dawn, I was bemused by how bereft I felt.

The villa was still with sleep as I gently closed the door and took the path down to the sea, where the annoyance I had felt about being awake so early after a long journey began to dissipate. It's hard to cry and swim at the same time, and the bay, which was empty, looked so disarmingly beautiful in the dawn light that I soon forgot everything about the dream. Behind me was a long stretch of golden sand fringed with scented Aleppo pines, empty of buildings with the exception of a small, shuttered taverna that would remain closed for another five hours. The beach itself was fringed with cliffs that rose sharply from the water, the liquid glistening around their feet the clearest I had ever seen. The land behind the beach, which was dotted with olive groves, was also steep. Among these groves stood the house belonging to Alessia's father.

I swam towards the horizon. The sun was rising steadily, bathing the whitewashed monastery in light. Perched on a rocky peninsula that swung around to shelter the bay, the monastery ventured its presence almost humbly, its domed roofs not squat exactly, but lacking the urge to tower and impose that other religious buildings projected. Instead, it watched the cove's activities unfold with quiet complacency, its bells silent. The monks had long gone.

I paused and now, out of my depth but able to see every detail of the sea floor, began to tread water, my breath beating in my ears. I was making little splashing sounds with my fingers, but it was at the noise of a much louder splash that I turned, and saw a man's dark head bobbing in the surf bordering the rocks below the church. I raised my hand in greeting but his head remained still, and something about his own presumed solitude stopped me from making a sound. Instead, I made my way back to shore unnoticed, and climbed the path and then the steps towards the house, dripping without my towel.

On the terrace, Helena was a ringleted goddess on a Doric stone bench, drinking an espresso and tapping out a message on her phone, her gel nails making a plasticky clicking sound against the screen.

She looked up. 'Early morning swim?'

I nodded.

'Gorgeous day for it. You'll laugh at me, but I'm having a fucking nightmare trying to work out what headpiece to wear.' Helena went into the pocket of her silk dressing gown and pulled out a packet of Karelia slim cigarettes, then started tapping its base against her palm.

I wondered why it was that people did that.

'My mother wants me to wear this hideous antique wax orange-blossom thing that belonged to my granny. Mum wore it when she married Dad, and she's managed to dig it out of the attic, but I want something more like this – look. We're rowing about it.'

I looked at the freeze-dried flower crown on the screen, and then back at this woman whom I had known for more than a decade. She was, undeniably, a woman, but all the same I struggled to see her as one, owing not only to her slightness but also to the image of her at eighteen that was fixed in my memory, in leggings and a hooded sweatshirt emblazoned with her classmates' names, hair swept to one side. A woman whose aim in life, stolen from Joni Mitchell, had been to wreck her stockings in some jukebox dive. A woman who could roll a three-skin joint with one hand, whose sharp sense of comic timing left men in bars who worked in finance in the dust, who had written her thesis on reconciling the domestic in the fiction of Virginia Woolf, and who, in an excoriating speech, had berated the men in the students' union for what she dubbed their 'predatory sense of entitlement'.

A flower crown. It comes for us all, in the end.

Privately thinking that the wax headpiece sounded prettier, I sat down next to Helena and reached over to tuck a strand of hair behind her ear. 'Stop worrying about it. At least for now. It's your hen. You're supposed to enjoy it.'

'I wish people would stop calling it my *hen*. I hate the word. Like we're dumpy little featherbrains going cluck, cluck, cluck.'

'Sorry. What should we say instead? Bachelorette party?'

'Too American. And four doesn't make a party.'

I'd wondered about that. Was it that there were only three women living whom Helena actually liked, or was she being deliberately selective? One thing I had come to understand about Helena, and which had become much more apparent since she became successful, was how much she liked Nice Things: things that were not only expensive, but which in and of themselves seemed to speak of her inner character. Leather-bound diaries and silk pyjamas, hand-painted ceramics, mid-century furniture. In contrast to this carefully curated self-image, a squealing crowd of tipsy women lacked a certain chic.

'I'd better go and deflate the giant penis,' I said.

Inside, most of the house was still dark and shuttered, but the fact that everything was painted white meant that the light from the French windows leading on to the terrace was enough to guide my way back to my bedroom, dripping water from the ends of my hair on to the marble floors. I marvelled at the size of my bed, my only foreign holiday prior to this having been a post-exams trip to Mallorca: five sixteen-year-old girls crammed into a tiny apartment decorated in varying shades of brown, the smell of the drains in the adjacent bathroom infesting the nylon curtains and the bedspreads on which we lolled, eating cheesy corn snacks as we waited for whoever's turn it was to finish vomiting. I had lost touch with those girls since going to university.

In contrast, everything in the villa had been selected with taste so impeccable it was almost offensive. In each room, blue-and-white woven rugs broke up the pearlescent white of the floors, while handmade but unfolksy *objets d'art* dotted the otherwise minimalist shelves, giving pops of colour. The windows were framed with long white curtains cut from gauzy muslin, which I imagined would bathe the rooms in dreamy sunlight when the shutters were opened. The linen on the bed was also white, and on the wall behind it was a pen-and-ink line drawing of a seated female nude, possibly by Matisse. Possibly even an original. Alessia's father was a gallery owner in Athens.

We had arrived the night before in darkness, so I had not really seen the exterior of the villa until the morning, but as Alessia had showed us around, I'd had one of those moments where I felt suddenly outside myself. Now, standing there in that perfect room, I wondered how I had got here. It wasn't a smug feeling, more one of wonderment at how life could turn out, how shocked my younger self would be to see it. To go from watching European films about people in holiday villas to actually staying in one.

I showered, put on a white cheesecloth shirt, and went in search of breakfast.

I came upon Alessia in the open-plan living area, wearing a dress of striking Klein blue that was obviously chosen to complement the shutters that she was in the process of throwing open. She looked up at me.

'Did you sleep OK?'

'Great, thanks. I had a dip in the sea. The beach is so beautiful. I can't believe how clear the water is here.'

'This is my favourite place in the world.' Alessia smiled, and stepped back from the window. 'There's coffee.'

We went through another set of French doors on to the rear terrace and sat down at a large circular table with a mosaic top. It had been laid with pastries, breads and jams, as well as a pot of coffee and a jug of orange juice. The remains of two breakfasts had been stacked neatly to one side, and Iris had decamped to the padded wooden sunbeds that lined the edge of the swimming pool. The heat of the sun was making itself known even at this early hour, giving the air a heaviness and a lethargy that was deceptive for a place so near the sea. It could be that the closeness was owed to the valley's sharp sides, how they loomed over the solitary villa, cradling it in a way that didn't feel entirely benevolent.

As Alessia busied herself with breakfast, I murmured a greeting to the other women and was met with silence. Both she and Helena appeared to be asleep. Iris hadn't spoken to me at all on the flight, having put in her headphones as soon as she sat down. Lying next to her was a hardback edition of a much-hyped novel that had been obscenely popular that summer, about people in the publishing industry sleeping with one another. Iris, who was lying on her front, had probably been trying to gauge if she recognised any of her friends and colleagues – or, indeed, herself – among the thinly disguised characters.

I frowned at the back of her exposed neck. The polar opposite of a rainbow goddess, she was named for Iris Murdoch, who had been a friend of her mother's. It wasn't that I hated Iris – we'd been in each other's enforced company for too long for that. It was more that she gave me a feeling of inadequacy. This came less from her statuesque Nordic looks and more from her cultural capital and bitchy attitude, which strongly suggested that she had sized you up and found you wanting. After many years of trying to form a bond, I had long accepted that I lacked the qualities she needed in a friend, and had all but stopped trying.

Sometimes, I wondered if Iris's coldness was a defence mechanism. On the topic of her job, as an editor at a well-known literary publisher, she was brittle to a degree that spilled over into unpleasantness, perhaps owing to the fact she had not won her status entirely on merit.

For example, in the airport bookshop the day before:

Iris: I can't find the *LRB* anywhere. You'd think they'd stock it at an international airport.
Me: What's the *LRB*?

Iris: The *London Review of Books*.
Me: Oh. Don't you get it free at work?
Iris, settling for the *New Yorker*: What makes you think we have a budget? Don't you ever listen?

I offered her an aspartame smile. She stalked off towards the self-checkouts while I stood there, holding in one hand an introduction to Greek mythology written by a television celebrity, and in the other the sandwiches that Greg, who hated the thought of me overspending at the airport, had made for me that morning and wrapped tenderly in foil. I knew perfectly well what *LRB* stood for.

Perhaps I did hate her. Looking back at that time now, I can see that I was fraying at the edges. Afterwards, they would say that I was having an episode, would collectively pick over the holiday for signs as they sat with their glasses of Picpoul. As my therapist said, it was easier to diagnose madness than to designate such an act a reasonable response to events. Had I not seemed a bit off from that first day? A little outside the rest of the group?

But then, that had always been the case.

Iris's disdain for me had been obvious from the first time we met at university, when she and Alessia had spent the entire evening talking about people they knew in the art world (Iris's father was on the board of a museum, and Alessia's was a wealthy collector who, at the time, was looking into starting a gallery). As they spoke, I chewed on my straw.

It wasn't the rudeness of it that bothered me. It was the fact that I allowed it to make me feel small. I had shrugged off Eleanor Roosevelt's advice and consented to feeling inferior. I had signed on the dotted line. I often used to feel that way in those days, when people were half-rubble, still trying to assemble their makeshift identities into something more concrete. I had first been drawn to these women because their ease and their confidence were qualities I lacked. I'd thought that Iris would grow out of her standoffishness, but she didn't. This perturbed me. I had come to like myself more as the years went on, which had made our acquaintance even more uneasy. And yet, when other people commented on Iris's rudeness, I found myself apologising on her behalf, telling them: 'She's different once you get to know her.'

It was a lie. She was the same.

The clink of the metal moka pot on china behind me called me to the table. Alessia was buttering the toast she would proceed to half-eat, humming a tune under her breath.

I sat.

'What's the plan for today?'

'Lounge here for the morning, then head down to the taverna for lunch.'

We had five days before the men would arrive.

'It's only five days.'

This was how I had put it to Greg, when I had asked him to fly out to Greece for the second half of the holiday, along with the rest of the plus-ones.

'It won't be that bad.'

Greg pushed his glasses up his nose and set aside the device he'd been scrolling on. I was leaning on the door frame, chewing my lip.

He was quiet.

'It's not really my idea of a good time, Soph,' he said, eventually.

He had never liked the girls, but the group's male contingent were even worse.

'I have nothing in common with them'. His voice came out in a whine, and I was momentarily embarrassed. 'I never know what to talk about.'

'You're being chippy,' I said. 'You're always chippy around people with money.'

He had retorted that it was better than being in awe of people with money. But he had relented.

I both was and wasn't looking forward to his arrival. Our relationship was in its sixth year and I was supposed to be deciding whether or not I wanted to have a baby, but I already felt as though I was melting. We all were. I could see my female friends dissolving before my eyes, their borders merging with the backgrounds of what had slowly and imperceptibly become our lives. The shift had been discombobulating. In our early twenties, despite the differences in our origins, it had been easy to pretend that we were all the same, that our destinies intersected. We all lived the same scrappy, ersatz existences in shared flats and thrift-shop clothes, working on various creative projects, sticky-taped together through bar and temp work. Then the money started making itself known. There had been hints of it before, of course – tabs settled with the wave of a hand, long periods spent interning without pay, trips to Bali – but now it seemed flagrant, undeniable. Its rude presence stood in the corner of the room like an ugly ornament, there, but not quite as flagrant as the prospect of a baby.

In many ways, Greg was the perfect man with whom to do it. He was gainfully employed, kind and relatively stable. He came from a fairly normal family and had several sisters, the result being that he treated women as human beings as opposed to strange creatures with mysterious bodily functions and opaque desires, sirens from a different school. He was tall and attractive, and didn't seem to be losing his hair. He was intelligent, too, though not obnoxiously so, and funny without ever being cruel.

I met him because we worked at the same art gallery. I had seen him around and admired the way he looked in his coat, which was a black trench with epaulettes that made him look vaguely French. He had an angular face and the sort of pale, Celtic skin that made him look as though he could be on drugs, or at least had had some acquaintance with them in the past, but despite looking it, he wasn't pretentious. There was an easy openness to his manner that endeared him to everyone. He smiled a lot and made witty jokes about the artists whose work we displayed. When I had started working in the gallery shop, we only really exchanged pleasantries for the first few weeks, or nodded at one another in the staff room or the smoking stairwell, until he came in to buy a birthday card.

'Do you think it's what he would have wanted?'

I stood at the till, baffled by this gnomic statement. 'Who?'

'Edvard Munch. Imagine: he's walking on this fjord at sunset, experiencing this agonising moment of existential pain. The sky is orange and seems to be splitting open, and he feels his whole identity fracturing. So he paints that feeling and calls it *The Scream*. Do you think he ever thought, while he was making it, 'One day, this howl of anguish at the human condition will end up as a felt finger-puppet in a gallery shop, priced five-ninety-nine?"'

I stared at him as he waggled the finger on which he had placed said puppet, grinning. His eyes were a surprising pale blue, and I held his gaze for a beat too long to show him that I'd noticed, then said:

'It's a common misconception that the face in the painting depicts the scream of the title. In fact the subject is covering his ears because it felt to Munch as though the entire sky was screaming. The scream is what he is *hearing*, not what he is doing. It's two-fifty for the card, please. I take it you don't want the finger-puppet.'

Later, at parties, he would tell people that that was the moment that he fell in love with me, and I went along with it. It made a neat little story, showing as it did that he was a feminist new man who relished a correction from an intelligent woman – one whom, he was to discover, had a first-class degree in fine art, though she was criminally underemployed in a shop. As though most artists don't end up in retail.

In truth, he had looked momentarily put out as I put the

card in its paper bag and handed it to him, our fingers grazing. It might be that he'd felt a charge then.

Perhaps I am not being fair to him. He was a good man, in the main part, and he would certainly dispute the idea that he'd felt threatened.

I'd say that words, however wittily arranged, are all very well. Sometimes I think that he only fell in love with me when he found out what else I could do with my mouth.

Francesca Woodman, From Space², Providence, Rhode Island, 1976

I found you in my teenage years, thinking I heard the cry of one unhappy soul to another. I read that you were the Plath of photography, unaware then of the persistent cataloguing of female pain into something non-threatening and manageable, the stripping away of all its righteous cadences, its fury, its wit.

In this tiny photograph, taken when you were eighteen, floral shards obscure your face and groin. We see only your navel, and your feet, looking as though they are travelling out of the wall into our dimension – or maybe dissolving out of it, away from us.

'Am I in the picture? Am I getting in or out of it? I could be a ghost, an animal or a dead body, not just this girl standing on the corner . . . ?' you once wrote.

I used to look at my body in the bathroom mirror, admiring its youthful proportions, a ghostly echo with the same skinny frame as yours. The body that men want; the body of a child with breasts.

I knew this already and could not help but find it pleasing. You were always trying to make your body disappear, to conceal or contort it. Like me, you loved gothic fiction, perhaps identified with its confined heroines, their shimmering madness, captured in the spectral blur of the long exposure.

You liked mirrors, too. You were thirteen when you stood in front of the camera lens for the first time. What was that child thinking? What drew her to capture the fleeting presence of her body in the world?

You – the child of artists – used nudity like a much more mature photographer; we are not used to such sexual confidence in so young a woman. You used to sneak into the natural history museum in Florence after everyone went home and experiment with shooting. You seemed to like abandoned places.

I look at your self-portraits and I feel myself enter the empty rooms of your heart: the peeling wallpaper, the bare floorboards, the derelict structures in which you shot. The tension between these decaying surroundings and your eroticised body makes objectification a battle for the eye.

People view all your work through the prism of your death, yet there is so much playful humour there. You're messing around, having a laugh, making fun of the male gaze. While the teenager in me was drawn to your sadness, the woman in me is drawn to your sense of irony.

It was only years after you threw yourself from a Lower East Side window at the age of twenty-two that the world started taking notice. You're now considered one of the twentieth century's great photographers. There is a psychic risk in being an artist, your father said.

You had created, in total, ten thousand negatives.

First day, afternoon

Lying by the pool, looking at the gap between Iris's legs as she rubbed cream into her milky skin, I wondered why I always seemed to be in a game of measuring up. I had looked at those legs and envied them, and then, as my eyes were drawn to her face, I'd had an automatic thought: 'Tiny eyes; almost piggy.'

This appraisal was a comfort blanket, a method of psychological reassurance that I had developed from a young age, to make the beauty, talent or achievement of other women manageable. She may have a beautiful face, but her body is all out of proportion. She may have won a prize, but her teeth are crooked. And so on.

Sunlight danced on the surface of the water. Helena was talking about how she could neither afford to lose weight nor gain it in the months coming up to her wedding, because she had already bought her dress, and as it was a sample which fitted perfectly, she was hoping to avoid alterations. She was comparing notes with Alessia on her chosen method of deprivation, and as she did so I continued to look at Iris, my eyes sweeping up and down her body, appraising her concave stomach, her round, retroussé breasts, her linear arms, which did not bloat unflatteringly when she held them against the sides of her body. I lamented female objectification, and would never view a life model this way, yet outside of the studio, I looked at women more ruthlessly than most men ever would.

I scanned their forms for imperfections as a restorer might hunt for chips in stone, and would often find many that were to my satisfaction. Yet sometimes there were women with no discernible flaws, who adhered so rigidly to conventional beauty standards that they did not seem real. Women like these had been mesmerising to me since puberty. They always affected naturalness and ignorance under our gazes, yet they always knew they were observed, just as every woman knows she is being observed all the time, is even observing herself.

I like women. I understand them. I swell with anger to hear of their exploitation, and feel pain at their sadnesses. But their triumphs pain me too. I do not know why their successes must feel like my own personal failures.

Were I to paint Iris – were she to stand in front of me, vulnerable and goose-fleshed in my cool, borrowed studio – her body would cease to be a threat, would instead be broken down into nothing more than a series of lines and curves inverted in the dark lenses of my pupils. To deconstruct a body in this way is not to have power over it – at least, I have never felt in my own art that I am claiming ownership of my models. But the act of observing becomes detached. The form becomes a fact, nothing more. I had been trying to transpose this way of seeing to the world at large. Or, to put it less academically: I was trying to become less bogged down by beauty.

Tuning back in to the conversation, I listened to Helena talking about her mother.

'She said that dresses in that style do not flatter our figure,' Helena was saying. She put emphasis on the 'our'. 'It has proven to me what I always thought, which is that she sees me as an extension of herself.'

'My mother definitely does that,' said Alessia. 'I feel that whenever she comments on my weight. It's her own self-loathing being projected on to me. Every time I visit her, she will place the fat beneath my arms between her thumb and her forefinger and then pinch it, and shake her head. Like this.' She demonstrated, using Helena.

'Mine couldn't care less what I look like,' said Iris. 'But she cried when I didn't get a first.'

'The mothers are not coming off well here,' said Helena, lighting a cigarette and shifting on her lounger.

I felt a need to defend my own. 'I think mine was always just glad that we were alive,' I said. 'If she ever went on a diet, she kept it well hidden.'

They went quiet, so I didn't elaborate on the fact that to starve myself, when the life she had gifted us was so fragile and precious, would have seemed to my mother a gross ingratitude.

The sun was rising higher in the sky and the air had become thick and still. We could hear the sea in the distance, but the olive groves around the villa were silent. The pool's clean lines beckoned, making me think inevitably of Hockney. I got up and walked to the other side, my feet dancing over the noon scorch of the marble. I glanced over at the others, but they were now deep in conversation, their heads bent slightly in listening poses. I wanted to draw them. I dove, swam two lengths of the pool, and climbed out to lie in the sun.

At one, we threw on our dresses and walked down to the taverna. The day-trippers had arrived on the beach, and the sea was dotted with bobbing heads; a throng wandered its way towards the monastery. It could almost have been a different place to the one in which the stranger and I swam earlier that morning. The taverna was bustling, but Alessia wound her way confidently towards a large table at the front. As we were about to sit, a grey-haired man who looked to be in his late seventies emerged from the darkness of the kitchen and embraced her. She said something to him in Greek, and a conversation followed. The rest of us stood smiling, but he gestured for us to sit, before disappearing and returning with two bronze-coloured carafes of wine.

Iris swilled a little wine in her glass, sipped, made a face, and adjusted her expression. At home she drank reds, shared the still lifes she took of glasses placed just so on the shaded tables of London institutions, Quo Vadis and Noble Rot, St. John for supper with her father. But to show disdain would be to insult Alessia, who had poured the wine and was raising a glass to Helena.

'What is it these hen parties say? "Same penis for ever"? To having the same penis for ever.' Then she grinned at me, and a look of complicity passed between us, because I knew that to her, this was a fate worse than death.

Iris rolled her eyes while we clinked.

'Well, this certainly beats the last hen party I went to,' I said, as the others looked at their menus.

I thought about my friend Tess's hen night at home, in the small provincial market town in which I'd grown up. How she'd worn a veil and a sash and had danced in the centre of our glittery rabble, flushed with alcohol and excitement as she sang 'Like a Prayer', and how I had moaned performatively to Helena about it having been tacky and retrograde. I loved Tess, had known her since our mothers gave birth in the same ward. She knew the things that had frightened me in my girlhood, had been at the beach that day and put her sticky, six-year-old hand in mine at the hospital when it had looked as though my little sister would not survive the accident. She understood that since leaving, I would always be somehow split between the person I was at home and the person I had become, and that it wasn't so much a question of playacting as it was that I wanted to be more than the girl with the ill sister, that I needed to construct a new identity, at least for a little while, before love and duty pulled me back again. It's a myth that we ever escape the places we are from.

'I say that, but it was great fun,' I added. Then, pointlessly: 'She has a son now.'

The others were looking at their menus. A waiter approached.

I looked up and with a start realised it was the man from the beach. His face flickered and I felt a beat, then another when I tilted my eyes up towards his.

'*Kalispera,*' I said. 'Can we have some tzatziki for the table, please? And a Greek salad.' I paused while I looked to the others for guidance, and Alessia looked up towards me and the waiter, and laughed.

'Ky.' Declarative, knowing.

He walked over to her as she stood up, and they kissed on both cheeks. His hand was on her arm and she was tracing her fingers over the hem of her dress, near the bust. It was clear to everyone that they had slept together. As they stood talking, I observed the curls of his hair, the strong line of his nose. His T-shirt was close-fitting enough to show that his torso was both wiry and muscular, like that of a climber.

Alessia finished the order and I watched the red tag on the back of his jeans retreating to the darkness of the restaurant's interior, then swiftly turned my head towards the bright sea, squinting.

'You never told me you'd had a waiter, Alessia,' said Helena. 'I couldn't have imagined it.'

'He's an old family friend,' Alessia said, waving her hand. 'I have known him since I was tiny. We have had the house my whole life, and they the restaurant.'

'It's his parents' restaurant?' I was playing with the tablecloth.

'Yes,' said Alessia. 'And yes, we have had a few nights together, over the years. When we were teenagers, mostly.

Helena, I am not sure what you are implying, about him being a waiter. In Greece, we do not have this bizarre class system that you British insist on. It is not looked down upon to work in a restaurant.'

'It was a joke', said Helena. 'We have a cliché about Greek waiters, is all.'

'The way you English speak about foreigners is always a stereotype,' Alessia said. 'This is the cause of the current problem.'

We had agreed not to talk about what was happening at home, the increasingly febrile climate. How a passing stranger had told Alessia, as she was strolling down the street on the phone to her father, to 'Speak English.' How, in ten days' time, when we flew home, we might be returning to a collapsed government.

'He is not just a waiter,' she continued, with sarcasm. 'He is an archaeologist in Athens. Since the crisis, he has returned every summer to help his parents. His mother is not well.'

'He's beautiful, whatever he does,' said Iris, to try and defuse the tension. 'You should have seen Sophie. She couldn't keep her eyes off him.'

They all looked at me and I gave a pretend leer, not realising that he was behind me with the appetisers. He put them down and retreated while the others tried not to laugh.

'You're practically a married woman,' said Helena.

'Don't be tedious,' I said. 'Just because I've been with Greg for six years doesn't mean that I've lost all appreciation for other men. Can we talk about something more interesting?'

'She's changing the subject.'

'I think we've hit a nerve.'

'Look,' I said. 'I'm happy with Greg. I love him. We live together. We are thinking of having a baby.' I poured another glass of wine, pretending not to notice their surprise. 'Lay off.'

None of these were untrue statements, but they were a distilled version of events. The essentials. I didn't know how to explain to the others that the thought of motherhood repelled me, that a part of me viewed it as an act of submission. Of lying on your back and opening your legs for a man, and then again and again for teams of doctors and specialists, and finally for a child. That marks a woman in the eyes of others. It is not that she hasn't always been perceived as a body – that is the sad rule of femininity – but with motherhood, the horrific truth of the body is made real in their minds, and after that she is tainted.

I thought of Tess limping from room to room in the aftermath of her birth, smelling of blood and piss and baby sick, the absorbent pad between her legs giving her a strange sort of waddle; her husband trying to arrange his face to imply that the way he saw her hadn't changed. And I thought of my mother, dabbing the drool from the corner of my sister's mouth, wiping her after she had been to the toilet. I thought often of the Frida Kahlo birth portrait, in which her mother lies, legs akimbo, in a bed in a pool of blood, her face covered with a sheet as though by a shroud. Her identity obliterated.

I feared this loss of self, that I would not accept it with the grace and humour of women like my mother and my friend, that I would battle and kick against it, might let the child down in ways myriad and irreversible. I knew that the woman had to have the strength to put her needs to one side, however much she might want to remain a person in the world. I knew what it was to care for a human who was more vulnerable, but my sister had never been inside my body. I had never, unlike Helena's mother, seen her as an extension of myself, had never poured all my own thwarted needs into keeping her alive.

    I mopped up some tzatziki with my bread and watched Ky taking an order from another table, admiring the triangle of his torso, the slope of his shoulders drawing my eye down to his muscular arms. I then turned to look at Helena, who had eaten everything on her plate except for the large block of feta that had been atop her salad, and now lay there, glistening, like wet marble waiting to be sculpted.

Fish had followed, then yoghurt with honey. Ky's father had come out and insisted that we try some of his wife's home-made raki, as I joked about how, if we were at home, none of us would have dreamed of touching alcohol distilled in a bathtub. We had left the restaurant after three and made our way in a dreamlike state back up towards the villa. We had all retired to our rooms to sleep, but I had found myself lying with my eyes open, unable to relax. I tried to read a little, but found I couldn't concentrate. I sent Greg a message saying that I missed him. I hung up my dresses in the wardrobe. My fingers tingled with restless anxiety.

Eventually, I must have drifted off, and I woke at dusk to a knock on the door. Alessia came in, wearing underwear and a T-shirt, and sat down on the end of the bed. I thanked her again for the holiday, but she brushed me off with a dismissive sound, and shifted closer towards me.

'I am sorry they teased you at lunch,' she said. 'I think it got to you a little.'

'Please,' I said, reaching for her hand. 'I'm used to it; it's fine.'

She rested her head on my shoulder, lifted it and smiled. I was struck by the perfect distance between her eyes.

'I want to draw you,' I said.

'You can. You can draw me this week, if you like.'

'Or better, paint. Just a portrait. I wouldn't want to make you feel uncomfortable.'

Alessia shrugged. 'I don't mind. I have always wanted a drawing of myself.'

I had seen Alessia in her underwear many times. We had danced in her kitchen like that one summer, drunk on orange wine. We had been in changing rooms in shops and yoga studios, tried on outfits before evenings out. I had even put her under the stream of the shower once, after she had taken so much cocaine that she had started panicking that her heart would stop. But to draw her naked would be different.

'Do you think Ky is attractive?'

'Objectively, of course.' I didn't mention that I had seen him swimming that morning.

'You can sleep with him, if you want.'

I started. 'I don't want to sleep with him. I don't even know him.'

'I don't care. I have not slept with him for at least three years. He is an interesting man. Intelligent, like you. I think you will have a lot in common.'

'Did you forget about Greg, my boyfriend, who is coming here in less than a week?'

'Please,' she said, echoing me with a raised eyebrow. 'I know what you want.'

And then she left, to salt the tomatoes in time for dinner.

Tracey Emin, I Could Feel You, 2014

It was love at first sight, that day in the gallery. I was just nineteen, newly released into the big city, free from responsibility and desperate to start living the big life I somehow believed I deserved. Those scrawled, frantic sketches of a woman (you?), nude, fingering yourself, legs spread, head thrown back, so defiant, so unapologetic. How did you find the courage to draw your naked body like this? There was something feral about your desire that was alien to me, back then. The black gouache descends into a tangle below your abdomen; what could be your hand blurs with the void of your sex. The painting hums with sensual aggression. Love isn't always gentle, you said once.

I was angry, in those days. I was starting to realise what we were up against. I remember a male student called you 'vile'; critics used terms such as 'hysterical' and 'overwrought', about work you had made about traumatic experiences. Your rape as a teenager. I look at your work and I see truth. Blood and flesh. Sometimes agony. I found you at just the right time.

'Art is a cathartic act for me,' you said. 'I kind of went off that idea for a long time. I wanted to be superior to the act of what I do, which is really stupid.'

I saw you again the winter before I went to Greece. I was older, had had my own fortnight of tears by then. The gallery was quiet; it was the middle of the afternoon. I walked from canvas to canvas, a witness – and a comrade. And I cried. I was overwrought. We had been arguing constantly about the question of a baby.

But I haven't done anything yet, I said. There is just so much to do.

You might feel differently about it when you're pregnant, he said. You might love it.

I've been pregnant before, I said to him. Before we met. I told you.

In the last room, How it Feels, *your 1996 film about your abortion. You tour the places in London that were the backdrop to it, this decision you made, to keep growing as an artist rather than growing a child. Later, you would say that you would have been no good as an artist had you had children. I do not believe this. But I do believe you when you say that the emotional pull would have been too powerful for you, that you would have loved them too much to be able to detach enough to make all the art you wanted.*

When I got home, I looked up I Could Feel You *again, studied the lustful angle of your thrown-back head, the scrawled suggestion of your nipples, and I thought: I don't want to die without having ever felt like that.*

Second day, morning

Dry mouth, dry heave, sharp pain between the eyebrows.

We had stayed up until the early hours, drinking. First the Greek rosé, then the Metaxa belonging to Alessia's father. We had danced drunkenly in the kitchen as we had in our early twenties, forming a circle as we mouthed along to Cyndi Lauper, briefly transported to those days of polyester party dresses and gold eyeshadow, false lashes that we would forget to remove before bed, leaving them to crawl down our cheeks like sluggish spiders as we slept. Even Iris seemed rejuvenated, freer, by midnight slurring her words and grabbing my hand for a moment at a key change, so that I remembered how much fun she could be, before she twirled and let it go.

I knew from the pain in my head that my hangover would be existential. Though I hadn't made the link yet, this post-drinking anxiety was something that had started happening: all the usual symptoms, complemented by a profound, deep-seated conviction that everyone I loved would die. In this anxious state, glaciers melted with nature-documentary speed, in perfect tandem with the time-lapse blossoming of tumours in my lungs, their petals unfurling with deadly intent. The oceans were rising, I would die of a terminal illness, my sister would have a seizure and never come to: I was convinced. Worst of all, I would never be a painter. Maybe I would die in the shop.

During these times, I would vow to stop drinking, but never did. Greg hated it when I got like this. Five years older, he had already worked it all out. He was always trying to get me to exercise, to eat and drink more healthily, to go to meditation. I had tried the latter once, but the loving-kindness meditation had proved too much. I succeeded in wishing loving kindness to almost every being on earth, visualising Iris when the tutor asked us to picture our enemies, remembering how she had once told me that, when she got to boarding school, having begged her mother not to send her away, she had cried for two weeks. I wished her loving kindness, no matter what, but I'm not sure I truly meant it. And when I came to zoom out and travel across the Atlantic, somehow landing on the White House, it became impossible. I just couldn't do it.

Greg had kept telling me to go back to the class, but I always made vague excuses. I didn't want to tell him that I thought there might be too much anger inside me.

'If you want to have a baby, you have to start looking after your body,' Greg would say.

I was technically a non-smoker then. My furry tongue that morning told me that the previous evening had been rife with technicalities, some of them class A. And yet, for some reason I had still set my alarm for dawn, which is how I found myself yet again making my way down to the shore before anyone else was awake.

Ky was there again. I could see his dark head bobbing next to the rocks, his back to me, just the suggestion of his bare shoulders. I wondered what Alessia had said to him about me, and was taken aback anew by her suggestion that I sleep with him. Alessia had never been faithful to any man, as long as I had known her. It was just one of those things: a habit for which you'd judge a stranger harshly, but in a friend would find yourself contorting to excuse. Her father had had a string of lovers; her mother, for some reason, had lived elsewhere. She had never seen commitment or fidelity, I'd protest. She'd had no model to work from. Greg would roll his eyes.

I took off my shirt and placed it and my towel under a nearby pine. Was I being deliberately quiet so as not to alert him to my presence? I couldn't say. He was a couple of hundred metres off, at the other side of the small bay, but near enough that, when he climbed out of the water, I could see that he was naked. I turned my head sharply, averting my eyes like a prudish character in a Victorian novel, then walked quickly to the east side of the beach. There, I spent a half-hour swimming close to the cliffs.

He was standing – dressed – on the terrace of the taverna when I came out. His longish hair was towel dry. I offered him a nervous smile, a glance he returned, and then he held up a small porcelain coffee cup and mimed drinking it with a quizzical look.

I nodded.

He walked into the darkened interior and I sat at one of the tables, looking out to sea. We hadn't exchanged a single word until he placed the hot coffee down in front of me, alongside some small pasties, and I said: '*Efcharistó.*'

'You speak more Greek than most English people,' he said.

'I could say the same of your English.'

'I studied in Norway for a year. None of the foreign students spoke Norwegian, so we all spoke English to each other.'

'It's good,' I said.

'Not as good as Alessia's.' He looked up at me. 'How long will you stay?'

'We have nine days. But the men are joining halfway through.'

'The men.' He smiled, and I found myself counting the creases around his eyes.

'The men.'

He stirred his coffee, the teaspoon clinking against the side of his cup. 'I hope I did not shock you just now. I did not know there would be someone else here so early.'

I shook my head. 'No. In a way, it felt appropriate.'

'I do not understand.'

'Well, in Greek mythology, a man always seems to be chancing upon a woman bathing naked.'

'You know Greek myths?'

'Not really. I'm playing catch-up.'

'Cat-chup?'

I laughed. 'I'm behind other people,' I explained. 'I am trying to learn. In England, only the good schools teach ancient history. I have been reading a lot. That's how I learned about Actaeon and Artemis. He disturbed the goddess bathing, and to punish him she turned him into a deer. He ends up being torn apart by his own hounds.'

'Do you know the story of Arethusa?'

'I don't.'

'The river-god, Alpheus, saw her bathing and decided to rape her. She tries to escape him by transforming into a spring, but he will not leave her alone. He is transformed into a river and follows her to Sicily.'

'See? It's always men who just happen to chance upon the women swimming naked,' I said.

'Not so. Or I know of one example of a woman watching a man. Like you.'

'Oh? Tell me.'

'Hermaphroditus. You have this word in English, yes?'

'Hermaphrodite?'

'Yes. He was the child of Hermes and Aphrodite. He was very handsome. When he was fifteen, he left the caves where he was raised, and went to the city of Caria. In the woods outside the walls, he found the nymph Salmacis in her pool . . .'

'So he discovered her bathing?'

'No, she lived in the pool. You should listen.' He placed his fingertips on the skin just up from my wrist, and his eyes met mine.

This is ridiculously erotic, I thought. If I told the others, they wouldn't believe it.

'Well, the minute she saw him, she wanted him, but he rejected her and she went away. After she had gone, he took off his clothes and got into the pool. He was swimming when she came and wrapped herself around him and forced him to kiss her.'

'Shocking.'

'Very. He was struggling, so she begged the gods that they should never be apart, and they blended them together into one being.'

'The hermaphrodite.'

'You are quick.'

'It's coming back to me, a bit. I'm an artist, and at college we studied a painting of this scene. We always used to laugh at it, because she is clinging on to him so much and his face looks so horrified. It's the role reversal, I guess.'

He was just sitting there, looking at me so intently that I almost turned away.

'So, you think I am like Salmacis? Watching you swimming before I pounce? I am hurt.' I was trying to flirt, but it sounded parodic.

'Yes. In this case, you are the deviant.'

'I think you mean pervert. What were you doing in Norway, anyway?'

'Mostly digging up Vikings.'

'Vikings. They were even worse than the Ancient Greeks.' We were still looking at each other.

'Maybe you're right,' I said. 'Maybe I was watching you.'

* * *

Alessia was waiting for me when I got back. I didn't see her until she was right in front of me, because I was looking at paintings of Hermaphroditus and Salmacis on my screen as I walked. It was possible to have the Francesco Albani painting I had told Ky about printed on a yoga mat. It's what he would have wanted, I thought, and then I pictured Greg and felt guilty.

Alessia beckoned me towards a whitewashed outbuilding on the other side of a small grove.

'How is this?' she said, opening the French windows to reveal a monastic white room containing very little furniture, save for a table, two chairs, and a daybed in the corner.

'The light is good,' I said. 'I don't have many materials. No easel. Only a sketchbook and pencils, some charcoal.'

'That will do, won't it?'

'I would rather paint.'

'I will ask Agatha to go to Artemonas for materials and an easel. There are some artists with galleries and studios there.'

'Thank you. I can—'

'Sophie.' Alessia paused. 'I can pay you, you know.'

'Oh – no . . . I don't . . .'

'Six hundred euro? Does that seem reasonable?'

'Very, but—'

'I would prefer it.'

I gestured in acquiescence. I needed the money. 'I'm nervous,' I said. 'In case you don't like it.'

'I know I will love it.'

I went to get my sketchbook. When I returned, Alessia

moved towards the bed in the corner, and pulled her shirt from over her head. She wasn't wearing a bra, but had on a pair of black bikini bottoms, which she wriggled to her ankles. I had seen her breasts before, at the Ponds. They were the sort of breasts men wrote poems about, comparing them to fruit. Her pubic hair was trimmed and dark.

'How should I stand?'

'Find a stance that is comfortable and natural, and that you can hold for a long period of time.'

Alessia experimented, then settled on an easy contrapposto: one leg slightly forward, bent gently at the knee, her hand resting lightly on that thigh, the other on her hip. I squinted and held my pencil at arm's length, proceeding to break her body down to a series of shapes, to trace the margins of her skin. I noted the inverted bow of her torso as it undulated into her hips, as though a sculptor had cut a perfect curve from the marble of her form. It reminded me a little of the *Rokeby Venus*, how the smooth line of her hip and that of her waist and lower back join to form almost a semi-circle in space. I thought of my own hips, and how the way flesh collected there meant their line undulated, then banished the image.

Though the department didn't do much on feminist art history, we had learned enough to understand that, in Western art, the female nude was a pinnacle of containment: a woman's body as a smooth, alabaster edifice within which fluids gushed and pooled, forbidden from breaking the surface. I didn't want to paint like that.

'If it weren't for your skin, you could be a classical statue,' I said.

'Is that a compliment?'

'Absolutely. They represented ideal women. Some were so beautiful they would drive men wild with lust. Did you know that in the Parthenon, one particular statue of Aphrodite was so magnetic that a man snuck into the temple where it stood and made love to it?'

'How do you make love to a statue?'

'I guess the guy rubbed himself up against it.'

'Poor Aphrodite. It's not her fault she's so hot.'

'Well, the man felt so ashamed, I think, that he threw himself from a cliff. There's still a stain.'

'Men are disgusting.'

'Ky told me this morning that I was a pervert,' I said, immediately regretting it.

Alessia raised an eyebrow. 'Why?'

'I was watching him swimming,' I said.

'He is very sexy,' she said. 'He looks how a man should look. Even though there is nothing between us now, I see this.'

I wanted to ask her what it was like, but it felt cheap, especially with her standing naked in front of me. The imaginative step was too slight.

'We got into a conversation about Greek mythology. He told me a story.'

'You've always liked it when men tell you things,' Alessia said.

It was true; she knew me. I did like it, especially when they told me things that I knew already. There was a sort of power in letting them go on, in knowing but staying silent. For a long time, this silent knowing would have been the only power women had. There must have been so many of us, over thousands and thousands of years, in the most harrowing and brutal of circumstances, watching silently, barely writing, barely painting, barely saying anything that was recorded, but knowing, nevertheless. Like the stains blossoming on our thighs, our arses, our stomachs: we knew.

A week after we first spoke, Greg went for a meeting at the National Gallery and sent me a photograph from the shop, via my work email. The subject was 'WHWHW', and the picture was of some Van Gogh hand soap.

'WHWHW??!' I replied.

'What He Would Have Wanted,' said Greg, attaching a photo of a Monet cushion.

Later that week, we had another masturbator in gallery two. I was coming back from lunch when I heard a commotion. I arrived in time to see Kev and Godwin from security manhandling a man in his thirties from the room as tourists gawped. The man himself looked disturbingly normal, like a photograph of the fiancé of someone you haven't seen since college, and not at all shamefaced.

'You'd think the internet would suffice,' said Greg, who was leaning up against the palatial through doors in an immaculate white shirt, his hair slightly tousled.

I became conscious of the sandwich crumbs down the front of my dress.

'I don't know,' I said, 'there's something rather quaint about it in this day and age.'

'There's nothing quaint about public wanking, Sophie. It was in front of one of the ghastly baroque orgies.'

I looked at his arms in the rolled-up sleeves of his shirt, and he saw me looking. 'You seem to have very low standards,' he said.

'So low you might even be in with a shot.'

He smiled again, then reached over and flicked some BLT remnants from my jumper, his fingers grazing just below my collarbone. 'When are you free?'

The number of masturbators was not something I had anticipated when I took the job. As Greg had implied, it felt like a crime that belonged in another era. To picture it was to see a man with a twirly moustache and a top hat, fiddling with himself under his umbrella, not some guy in a jumper with an iPhone in his pocket. Yet we caught several of these a month, nearly always in the vicinity of the tackiest paintings of naked women in our collection. They were almost always charged, and after that we heard no more of them. I often wondered what became of them, how they told their families what they were in court for. There was an understanding that almost every man on the planet had watched porn, but touching yourself up to a Rubens? There was something deviant about that.

'It's a shame we first met in the shop,' Greg said to me in the pub that evening. 'The events of today would have been quite the meet-cute.'

He was in his late twenties then, still young enough for me not to have to wonder why he was single and what might be wrong with him. A Cambridge-educated history of art graduate with an MA from the Courtauld, he had won one of the very few curatorial roles at the gallery, beating thousands of other applicants.

I was twenty-four, had completed my undergraduate degree and was trying to save money for a master's programme, painting in the evening and running a weekly life-drawing class, which, after I had paid the model, hardly left enough money for materials, let alone food.

'What sort of art do you make?' he asked, sipping his pint.

I was so attracted to him that I had to take him in piecemeal. I looked at the crinkles at the corners of his eyes, then at his forearms, with their constellations of freckles, rebuking myself for such a corny line of description. I wanted to tell him that in French they called them 'sun stains', but this too sounded clichéd. There seemed to be few ways of thinking about him that weren't. The lack of emotional range in all the songs on the radio suddenly began to make sense.

'I suppose you would call it semi-figurative,' I said nervously. 'It's not really working for me at the moment. I mean, it's good, I think, but it's not great. There's something missing. I'm just not quite there yet. The elements themselves are well done, but they never seem to coalesce. It would help if I had more time and energy . . .' I tailed off and fiddled with the corner of the beer mat.

'I'd like to see it sometime.'

We talked a little about family. He had grown up in Bristol. They had been comfortable. His parents were university lecturers, and he had three sisters, one of whom lived in Florence and worked for a buyer. I briefly mentioned that I also had a sister, but then changed the subject before he asked how old she was or what she did. It wasn't that I didn't want him to know, but I was never quite sure at what point it was best to bring up the accident. I knew from past experience that it changed the way men saw me, and I wasn't ready for that yet. For now, I could be anyone.

Frida Kahlo, Henry Ford Hospital, 1932

I went all the way to Mexico City to see your painting. It took me until my late forties to be able to afford this trip, but I did it. I had to.

The painting shows you bleeding out on to white sheets after your miscarriage, your body small and twisted as though in intense pain, your stomach rounded still. You painted your face in a way that's almost unbearable to look at. Your dead son is attached to you with an umbilical-like cord, hovering above you like a ghost, his face wearing the calm expression of a dreaming infant. Also attached to you via twisting red cords are a wilting orchid, a snail, a pelvis, an autoclave, a medical dummy. It is only a small painting, but I have to force myself to breathe at the rawness of it.

People still can't handle the reality of injured and disabled bodies; growing up with my little sister taught me that. People would rather look away, or couch difference in euphemism. When they write about your accident, they skirt around its brutality. They talk about the rail of the bus piercing your pelvis, your hip, your abdomen. They never say your vagina. Your uterus was punctured, causing lifelong agony, multiple miscarriages. When the tram and the bus you were on collided, the force of it blew off your clothes. A passenger had been carrying a tin of powdered gold, and this fell all over your red, bleeding body. An apt metaphor for what has been done to your art since, the pain you insisted we confront dusted over with something more shiny.

My whole life, my family have had to negotiate others' discomfort about the life and the body of a person we dearly love. Your willingness to depict your disabled body without shame, to show pride in it, was revolutionary.

I find it crass, but they put your self-portraits on cushions now. There are Frida egg cups, Frida socks, Frida mugs. To look you up online is to be confronted with a million poor, AI-generated pastiches. Little girls dress up as you, their mothers painting on to them your thick, black monobrow. This, you would have liked, I think. You spent your life in costume. It is a blessing and a curse to be rediscovered, reified. You are a feminist goddess, a rebel girl.

But they wouldn't put Henry Ford Hospital on a tote bag. Or the untitled lithograph you made that same year, in which the moon also weeps for your lost child. You are crying, but in your left hand you hold a palette, as if to say that you are still an artist even if you cannot be a mother. You seem to have reconciled yourself to it in a way that many couldn't, myself included: 'I lost three children and a series of other things that would have fulfilled my *horrible life ... My painting took the place of all of this. I think work is the best.'*

I still wonder at how you made the first depictions of abortion and miscarriage in Western art. Thousands and thousands of years, and no visual record at all, only blank, dark space where all that pain should be. Until you.

Second day, evening

We had eaten lunch at the villa – a simple salad of fresh tomatoes and red onion, swimming in olive oil, with crusty bread and cold white wine – and had spent the afternoon chatting desultorily on the sun loungers. I sat under a parasol while the others cooked themselves, turning like rotisserie chickens. When the heat became too much, they would take it in turns to float aimlessly around the pool, emerging to reapply suncream. Iris was reading a manuscript, having finished the buzzy novel and declared it pedestrian. Helena tip-tapped-tapped her screen, alternating between browsing for alarmingly specific wedding-related tat and arguing with her mother about place settings. White earbuds nestled in Alessia's hair and she nodded in time to her music. I lay, slightly removed, in the shade of an olive tree, protecting my Celtic skin, occasionally brushing away the stray leaves and small twigs that wove themselves into my hair every time the breeze shook the tree's branches.

I had taken to placing my phone in a large urn next to the French windows, realising that the time I was spending scrolling through ex-classmates' New York openings and Tuscan residencies was unhealthy. Since graduating, I had continued making art, but other than a couple of graduate group shows, none of it had been exhibited. When I looked at the canvas at the end of a long painting session, I was struck only by an absence of meaning. Meanwhile, those with whom I had studied seemed to be finding meaning everywhere – not to mention money. They were living in Brooklyn. Their art-school haircuts became art-world haircuts. They started wearing big abstract earrings. I longed for the world of the past, when no internet meant I didn't have to see it, or hear anything about it.

I walked over to the urn to check my phone, smiling at a photograph my mum had sent through of her and Rosie (*Miss you, darling girl, hope you are enjoying your holiday xxx*).

There was also a message from Greg, sent the day before.
– *How is it? Is Iris still being a bitch?*

I hadn't bothered to reply until now.
– *Always. Helena is obsessed with flower arrangements, and I'm painting Alessia in an outhouse. The sea is beautiful.*

I didn't understand why we were spending all our time by the pool when the most stunning beach was visible from where we sat. Every now and again, I would stand up and walk over to the white plaster wall and admire the light. The way it stood out against the background layers of sea and sky looked fake, like something from a holiday brochure or a tacky painting. In the distance, the monastery gleamed like a baby's tooth.

Around five, I decided to walk down to the beach. Alessia was sprawled on a lounger, her limbs bent and splayed like an insect's. The others had gone to their rooms to lie down. I threw on a white shirt and a hat and took the path down to the sea. On the beach, a few families lay on towels or played in the shallows, but it was fairly quiet. Although the monastery was listed as one of the island's leading tourist attractions, its size meant it took no more than ten minutes to look around, and aside from the beach and the taverna, there was little else to recommend the bay to visitors, wedged as it was between two hotspots replete with hotels and lined with restaurants where you could eat hand-rolled seafood pasta or fussy small plates of deconstructed moussaka.

I made my way over the rocks to the monastery, which was surrounded by a waist-high white wall not dissimilar to that at Alessia's family villa. It was more of a small church in a large courtyard than a monastery, really. There were about four other people admiring the views on the western side, looking back towards the bay. One was a woman, about my age, who was holding a small child by the arms as he or she lolloped in front of her. I could hear her speaking to it in a soft voice that wasn't English.

I was seeing babies and young children everywhere that summer. Of course, they were always there; I was only noticing them because I had them on my mind, because

Greg was asking for me to make a decision. In my second year at university, I had had an unplanned pregnancy followed by an abortion. It had been a simple decision made quickly and with no regret, a result of failed contraception during a one-night stand with a guy on the contemporary art course whose name I couldn't remember, but whose derivative installations I could. Afterwards, I walked out of the health centre to find a picture of his penis waiting for me on my phone as if to say, 'You made the right decision.'

That spring, too, I had found myself encountering pregnant women everywhere: on the sides of buses and billboards, serving me in restaurants, requiring my seat on the tube, as though the universe was determined to show me the path not taken, as though it wanted to force me to repent for skipping merrily towards an alternative future without a backward glance. But all it did was make me feel glad. I reflected that the child would be six now, the age at which I started to form coherent memories. The age I'd been when Rosie had her accident.

Though it was starting to be evening, the sun was as hot as ever; my fringe was wet beneath my hat. I reached the end of the courtyard, at the tip of the small peninsula, and looked down at the rocks below. There was a flat outcrop from which I had seen people swimming, and I decided to cool off.

Afterwards, as I made my way back towards the beach, my hair dripping and my shirt sticking to my wet bikini, I saw Ky leaning against the wall next to the taverna, smoking a cigarette. He raised his hand in greeting and walked over.

I was conscious that my wet hair, stringy and separated, showed more of my face than I was comfortable with; I hated my side profile and did my best to hide my chin behind my hair as much as possible. I stole a glance at myself in the window of a parked car.

'I saw you swimming in the distance, but I didn't want to come over in case you called me a pervert.' He was grinning.

'I wouldn't have minded.' I hardly knew what I was saying. 'We should swim together sometime.'

'Tomorrow morning, maybe,' he said. 'Alessia tells me that you are painting her picture.' He stood there looking at me for a while, as though sizing me up for my own portrait. He had spoken in the pretend casual tone of someone who wanted to know about it very much. I could tell he was thinking about her naked, and about me looking at her while she was.

'I am.'

'Have you painted from life before?'

'Of course I have. I studied art.'

'But it's different when it is a friend?'

When had they had this conversation, I wondered.

'She's very beautiful.'

'So are you.'

I laughed. 'Come on,' I said.

'What, your boyfriend doesn't tell you this?'

I didn't say anything. We just stood there, looking at each other.

'You are not beautiful like Alessia is. Or your tall blonde friend. You are soft.' He moved his hand in a sweeping curve.

It sounded as though he was calling me fat, but I didn't want to show weakness by pointing this out, so I made a dismissive noise. 'I'm not good at these conversations,' I said.

He shrugged and gave me a shy smile. 'Are you coming here for dinner?'

'No, I don't think so. I think we are cooking up at the house.'

'You like to smoke?' He mimed it by holding up two fingers to his pursed mouth and moving them backwards and forwards.

I fiddled with the hem of my shirt. 'I do,' I said.

'OK, I will bring you some when I have finished here.'

'I should probably ask Alessia what she has planned.'

'She wants some. I'll see you later tonight.'

I nodded and turned towards the house.

'Do you think I should wear a veil?' Helena was sitting at the outside table flicking through a bridal magazine when I got back.

Iris, who was sitting next to her, was running her fingernail through the grout between the mosaic tiles. She looked up at me, and we shared a brief moment of bored complicity. From inside, I could hear the rattle of the cocktail shaker.

'Bit patriarchal, no?' said Iris, with the hint of a smile.

'Yes,' I said, backing her up. 'There's some quite odd symbolism there. I'm not sure it's very you. Besides, it's not like you're marrying in a church.'

'I didn't think I'd want one, but I just don't think I'll feel like a proper bride without one. Won't I just look like another bridesmaid?'

Iris and I shared another look. Helena looking like a bridesmaid would be impossible, considering the dresses that we had been given.

'Martinis!' Alessia came out carrying a tray of cold glasses. 'Agatha picked up some gin from the shop this morning. Outrageous island prices, but I can't just drink wine all holiday.'

We clinked. The martini was perfect, and very cold. The vermouth tasted of pine, its creaminess undercutting the sharpness of the gin, which was faintly salty thanks to the three little olives she had used as a garnish. We made approving noises.

'Helena is wondering if she should wear a veil,' Iris said.

'No,' said Alessia, with a definitiveness that only a non-native English speaker could get away with.

Helena tried to continue the conversation, but it was obvious that we had all reached our limits. We wanted to support our friend, but the wedding planning had taken over a year, with every meticulous detail, from flower arrangements to music, discussed in the sort of agonised tones usually reserved for a personal crisis. Meanwhile, all Harry seemed to have been involved in was the choosing and purchasing of his own suit.

I thought about Rosie, and how she would probably never get married, or have a mortgage, or even a job, and then reflected, as I had once been encouraged to do by a counsellor, on why exactly I felt she needed these markers of adulthood which don't always bring happiness. Things I wasn't even sure I wanted for myself. Rosie was content as she was; she didn't need me projecting on to her.

'Ky says he's coming up here later,' I said.

Alessia and Iris looked at me, Alessia bemused, Iris frowning slightly. Helena continued scrolling.

'He's bringing some weed,' I said, by way of defence.

'You like him,' said Iris. 'Poor Greg.'

I remembered that my phone was still in the urn, filling up, I imagined, with unanswered messages.

'Since when were you so moral?' Alessia pulled an olive from the stick with her teeth. 'Aren't you in an open relationship?'

'It's the dishonesty,' said Iris.

'I haven't done anything,' I said. 'I love Greg. But come on, are you telling me that we're supposed to spend our whole lives denying our very natural attraction to other people? Surely that's a recipe for misery? At least if you acknowledge it, you have a handle on your feelings.'

'So you've told Greg about it, then?'

The martini had emboldened me. 'Iris, I don't understand why each time we speak, I come away with the feeling that your opinion of me couldn't possibly get any lower. Until the next interaction, that is.'

I got up from the table and walked into the kitchen to fix another round of drinks. Two would be the limit, I decided. Three is always a disaster.

'Are you OK?' Helena had followed me in, and was standing

next to me with a hand on my shoulder. I think she thought I might be crying.

'I'm fine. I'm just getting so tired of it. Why is she so fucking—'

'Cold? An all-girls private school, a distant mother, a fundamental insecurity that causes her to lash out against others?'

'I don't think Iris has been insecure in her life. And why is it the mother's fault? What about fathers? Hers has never seemed especially warm, either.'

'Well, I always thought mothers bear the brunt of our anger at our fathers, because we know they are strong enough to stand it, but that's beside the point. I know you two have never really clicked, and I know she can be cold and cruel and, quite honestly, cool to the point of being obnoxious, but there's a heart in there. She can also be very kind.'

Helena was mounting the defence I had made to others countless times.

'I never really understood why she didn't like me. Not even at university.'

'Well, you saw through her,' said Helena, reaching into the tub of olives and popping one in her mouth. 'You weren't impressed by her connections. And you abhor nepotism. It makes her insecure, so she tries to pre-empt it by being a bitch. It isn't that complicated.'

I laughed and gave Helena a hug. 'I'm sorry that we aren't showing enough interest in your stupid wedding,' I said. 'I know that must be hurtful. I just can't help wondering where your brain has gone.'

'I wonder too, sometimes. It's still in there, though. Under an elegant spiral of braids woven with miniature pearls and rosebuds.'

'Remember when you stormed out of anthropology because the reading list was too white and male?'

'I'd do it again,' she said. 'But while dressed in clouds of pink organza.'

Standing in front of the full-length mirror, trying to decide what to wear, I thought about John Berger. *Ways of Seeing* had been the first set text on our history of art reading list, and it had shaken me in a way reading academic theory rarely did, because it verbalised something I appeared to have known since infancy but had never seen expressed: women were bred to be looked at. I still remember the thrill that comes from seeing your inchoate feelings there in print. It made so much sense to me: men did the looking, and women internalised that gaze. To paraphrase: we saw ourselves through the eyes of men, as we walked, as we moved through the world, even, Berger says, when weeping at the deaths of our fathers, we imagined how we appeared, weeping. He expressed it much more eloquently.

Did men ever check themselves out in shop windows? What were they thinking about on the long walk home from school, when I was worrying how my stomach looked from the side?

I knew that Ky would be looking at me that night, and I wanted to be worthy of that. But I also wanted it to appear as though I had dressed as I would ordinarily, so had jettisoned the too skimpy and the too try-hard. Standing naked, I looked at my body. I didn't hate it as I was supposed to. I didn't love it, either. I knew it wasn't perfect. I remember as a teenager looking at a men's magazine at a friend's house. They had created a perfect woman from their favourite parts of female celebrities: some glamour model's tits, the legs of a Hollywood actress, and so on. She was grotesque, and for reasons I couldn't articulate, I felt sick looking at it. Much later, I was gratified to find out that it hadn't even been an original idea: the famed ancient Greek painter Zeuxis did it first.

I was no Venus, but naked, my body looked right. There was a correctness to the placement of each part. My breasts were well-proportioned, my waist narrow, my hips wide and undulating. I could be a painting. Not a Rubens – I was not that large – but a Titian, maybe.

Yet every time I got dressed, my body would suddenly look wrong. Fabric hung strangely on curves that unclothed were attractive to the eye, shrouding them and bunching up and making me appear strangely formless, thick like a column holding up the front of a building. Clothes were cut for the bodies of women like Alessia and Iris.

I settled on a loose black slip dress, cut tighter at the bust, shaped like a triangle. I pulled my hair into a messy bun on the top of my head, applied a touch of bronzer and mascara. Even my need for Ky to desire me felt unfaithful. In the urn outside, my phone's battery slowly ran itself down.

By the time dinner had ended, several strands of my hair had come loose, and the black fringing to my eyes had smudged slightly. It had been one of those meals that you remember for the rest of your days. Agatha, the housekeeper, had prepared a feast of *kleftiko* – lamb baked with local cheese – with roast lemon potatoes and *horta*, mountain greens wilted and drizzled with olive oil. Already wobbly from several glasses of cold white wine, the remains of the meal on the white cloth, lit up from the guttering candles on the table and the kitchen light through the French windows, appeared to me like a still life wrenched from the late Renaissance, edged with shadowed corners. All the scene lacked was piles of fruit on the cusp of decay. Grapes dangled instead from the vines above our heads, and the air was thick with the sickly aroma of night-scented jasmine.

As we ate, we reminisced about our student days, our living arrangements, our terrible diets, our lecturers and the men who had come into our beds (in Alessia's case, the last two were not distinct categories). The adult world had been a shock and this had bonded us. Iris reduced me to tears of laughter with a description of her second-year boyfriend, and I remembered that what I liked about her was her acerbic wit, her cynicism. Tired from laughing and gorging, our conversation had dwindled to a less frenetic pace. We were all aware, I think, that a man would soon be joining us, would cross the threshold of a world which for two days had been exclusively feminine. As Ky appeared at the edge of the garden, Iris's smile faded.

Alessia stood to kiss him, calling across the darkness in Greek. Helena stood and began to stack dishes and cutlery more noisily than was necessary. I sat where I was. Ky took the seat next to Iris, and she poured him a glass of wine from the bottle of red that had been airing, while he reached into his pocket and removed the bag of green and his papers.

'I'll try not to make it too strong,' he said. 'Or Alessia will vomit.'

Alessia told us of their teenage summers getting high down at the beach after the taverna had closed, sitting on the still-warm sand and staring out at the darkness of the ocean.

'He was usually so serious and studious,' she said now.

'Well,' he said, 'I was working hard to get out of here.' His parents never made much money, and the winters, when all the Athenians had gone home, were hard and tedious. When Alessia arrived each July with the easy nonchalance of the international rich, she showed him the possibility of a life elsewhere.

He passed the joint to Iris, who took one tight little inhale and handed it to me, making fleeting eye contact. I let my lungs fill with hot smoke, releasing it languorously, feeling my thoughts begin to swim and swirl.

As we smoked, he told us of his life in Athens, of the riots and the protests, his days at the museum. We listened to him tell us about the digs on which he had worked on countless islands, and the objects he had unearthed: ancient fragments of pottery, the fingers from statues, incomplete mosaics. I had gone very quiet. My skin felt as though it was humming. I became extremely aware of my body, placing my hand on the stem of my wine glass and then quickly removing it. All my gestures felt artificial and obvious. The others seemed to be speaking and moving with ease. I didn't know what to do with my limbs. I crossed my legs and then swiftly uncrossed them.

'The Mycenaean ruins on this island date from 200 BC,' he was saying.

I stood up quickly and walked into the kitchen to get myself a glass of water. I needed sugar, so I opened the fridge and had a dig around, found some halva, crumbled a corner between my fingers and stuffed it into my mouth before wiping my lips with a discarded tea towel.

Outside, Ky was facing the open French windows, but his head was turned towards Iris, who was asking him about where was best to visit on the island.

'We've hardly used the car,' she was saying. 'We haven't even been up to Apollonia yet.'

Rather than step back through the French windows, I walked through the dimly lit living room, opening the side door, which took me towards the west of the garden instead, near the boundary wall. Distantly, I could hear them laughing, then Helena making her excuses, saying that she was tired and needed her beauty sleep. I tuned them out and sat, listening to the waves crashing somewhere below the starlit sky, which I gawped at, astounded. I had never seen stars so bright. I was extremely high.

I had been there some time when I heard him approaching, knowing a man's footsteps without needing to turn.

'Are you OK?'

'I'm fine. Just needed a minute.'

He came and sat down next to me, leaving a polite distance between us. He turned his face towards me and looked at me for the first time that evening, smiling. 'You seem to spend a lot of time on your own.'

'The others don't like to swim in the sea as much. They prefer to stay by the pool.'

'You like the sea.'

'I love the sea. I was just thinking how I would like to swim now. But I'm too high. It would be dangerous.' I knew that I was telling him I was high so that I didn't have to take responsibility for what might happen.

'Another time.'

'I'd like that.'

We didn't say anything for a while. Then he asked to see the painting.

'It's just an outline at the moment,' I said. 'Just some faint lines in pencil, not even a sketch. There's nothing to look at.'

'Well, show me where you work, then.'

We walked through the orchard, using his phone as a torch, stumbling on the uneven earth. I was laughing, from adrenaline I think, and placed my hand on his forearm to keep myself steady.

'There isn't a lightbulb,' I said, as I opened the door. The easel stood in the centre of the room. I moved towards it. 'See?' I said. 'Nothing to see yet.'

I could feel him breathing behind me. We weren't fully touching. He was standing at a few inches distance, scanning the picture with his light, his arm grazing my side as he moved it back and forth so he could see.

'Sophie,' he said.

I was breathing hard. My arms were gooseflesh as he lightly fingered the right-hand strap of my dress, sliding it along my shoulder until it fell. As he lowered his head, he brought his lips to the space where it had sat, just above my collarbone. I tilted my head to one side and stepped back into him.

Anne W. Brigman, The West Wind, 1915

I was on a trip to New York with a man I didn't love when I almost walked past this photograph. It shows you dancing naked by the sea; your hands, raised above your head, clutch a stretch of sheer cloth. Your shadow dances in the foreground, its darkness almost matched by the looming rocks. It looks like freedom. It was taken, unbelievably, in 1915.

That day, I thought about how I hadn't been naked outside since family holidays at the seaside as a small child, and standing in the gallery in that perishing early spring, your photo made me want to run towards the shore, casting off clothes as I went. I wonder if that was the moment, actually, when I started pelting towards another kind of life, to Greece, to everything that would happen afterwards.

Even in childhood, you were aware 'of the ache in your legs for flight, of the hunger for air in your nostrils, of the wild, wonderful need to stampede'. I learned that you married a Danish sea captain as old as your father because you thought he'd show you the *world, and he took you to China and to the South Pacific. One such journey also lost you a breast, from falling on the boat during a storm. You started your career in photography at thirty-two, which accounts of your life always state is late. To me it is young.*

I admire how you made your lopsided form an allegory of female beauty. You were ahead of your time, may have been the first ever woman to photograph herself nude. Certainly you were the first to exhibit herself. You harked back to the Greek myths. Your nude figures were nymphs and dryads, merging with water, bark, earth, to become the landscape. I love how you'd trek up the Sierra Nevada in knickerbockers, looking for the most gnarled and inhospitable of settings to act as backdrops for your body.

Stieglitz may have tried to sexualise your work, to read into it the erotic and the titillating, just as he had with Georgia O'Keeffe's flowers, but she loved your photographs. It wasn't about sex with you, it was about nature's interconnectedness with the feminine form. You were a hippie before they existed.

What was it about this particular photograph that caused me to stop and look that day? Your vision of emancipation drew me in. There was something a bit pagan about it. I, too, had thought that the right man could help me find freedom. Certainly, it was his income that had taken us to New York, where I was lucky enough to see all these works by great artists. I was hardly as trapped as women were a century ago, but something wild in me was being muffled, nonetheless.

FEMALE, NUDE

In 1913, a San Francisco newspaper asked you if you were going to divorce your husband. 'Fear is the great chain which binds women and prevents their development,' you said. 'Cast fear out of the lives of women and they can and will take their place as the absolute equal of man.' (I remember underlining this part in the book I had bought about you.)

And so you left him, and came back to California to live alone, save for a dozen birds and your dog. That seems to me like a good way to live. You chose to make work on your terms, to live by the sea, and to surround yourself with other artists, bohemians and poets, dying at eighty. Georgia became great; you were largely forgotten. In a bookshop, I flicked through the index of a feminist history of art but could not find your name.

Third day, morning

Overnight, a mosquito bite had bloomed on my thigh, growing to the size of a small bread plate. I tried not to scratch too hard and wake Ky as he slept curled next to me in the hut's single bed, but as I moved my fingers gently over its surface, he was on my wrist faster than a cat, grabbing it and pinning it behind me.

'No,' he said.

I made as if to bite a chunk out of his neck, and he laughed.

'What time is it?' I asked. I was thinking guiltily of my phone, of Greg. In six years together, I had not shared a bed with another man. This perhaps felt like the biggest betrayal of all, though I had committed hundreds in the last few hours, not least in my looking at Ky. I found him beautiful in ways I never had a man before. My eyes lingered over his shoulders, his arms, the muscles of his stomach, his dick. He was like some perfect mythological creature. I couldn't believe that he was real.

'Time for our swim,' he said. Through the hut's windows, I glimpsed rosy dawn.

There was no one at the beach, so we stripped off, running into the sea until the waves started hitting us in the face. We swam further out than I had since we'd been here, past the limits of the small peninsula, past the edges of the cliffs guarding the bay. We stopped and trod water. In the distance, I could see the white buildings of the next bay over gleaming in the light of the rising sun.

'You're a very strong swimmer,' he said.

'It's because of my sister. When she was small, she almost drowned.'

'And you saved her?'

'My dad pulled her out,' I said. 'After that, they signed me up for lessons. I used to race.'

'Does your sister still swim, too?'

'My mother and father take Rosie to the swimming pool every weekend,' I said. 'She's brain damaged. I shouldn't say that. She has a brain injury, is what I mean. She's in a wheelchair because the accident she had affected her movement, and also her speech. She uses a tablet to talk.'

I started swimming back towards the beach, because I didn't want to stay there watching the pity twist across his face, but he called out, gesturing towards the rocks at the eastern side of the peninsula. 'Go there.'

We hauled ourselves out of the water on to a long, flat rock that was hidden from the view of the beach.

'Lie down,' he said.

'No way! Here? You want to do it here? Someone could see.'

He moved forwards on his knees so that his body hovered

above mine, put his lips on my lips and moved his hand downwards. 'Open your legs.'

I made a sound into his mouth. He kissed my eyelids, my cheeks, my neck, my tits, while his fingers moved against me. He dipped his head and my hands found themselves in his hair as he kissed and licked my sex. I could hear the waves against the rocks, the crickets. The air smelled of salt and dried pine. I drifted momentarily out of my body and watched myself from above, splayed on the rock naked, squirming and crying out. I was practically semiconscious with lust, and yet with some outside, spectatorial eye, I could see the whole thing was ludicrous. After he had made me come, I threw back my head and laughed.

Alessia was already there when I got back to the studio, sitting on the edge of the hastily made bed as she nursed a cup of coffee.

'That's a bad bite,' she said, looking at my thigh. 'You'll need some hydrocortisone on that. It looks like you're allergic.'

'I'm fine. The seawater is the best thing for it.'

She stood up and started taking off her clothes. Her skin, with its uniformity, smoothness and evenness of tone, had an airbrushed quality to it. She bent down to unstrap her sandals at the ankles and her breasts hung in front of her as my eye absorbed their perfect teardrop shape. Her legs didn't meet at the thigh, the knee or the ankle; there was an absence of flesh where the light shone through.

'So what happened? Did you fuck?'

'Try not to move your head,' I said. 'No, we didn't fuck.'

'Did you do anything?'

'We did other things.'

'How was it? What did you think of it?'

'Alessia, he's not a book that you have lent me. You can't demand a review.'

She laughed at this. 'He's good though, no? Ahhh – my hair is tickling me.'

'Don't move.' I walked over to her and moved some strands of hair that were brushing her waist, pushing them up over her shoulder so they fell down her back. I caught her eye and saw that she was looking at me intently, with a kind of amusement in her eyes. I went back to the canvas and continued to sketch out the lines of her torso.

'What happened between you both, anyway? Why did it end?'

'It was never serious,' Alessia said. 'We started sleeping together when I was about fourteen and he was eighteen. I was there for the summer with my family. He left for university in Athens in the autumn, but every year would come back to help his parents, and every year I would be here, so we would hook up.'

'He was your first?'

'Yes. Though that doesn't mean much to me.'

'Evidently not.'

'You look happy. It's been a long time since I have seen you like this. You seem calmer. More at peace.' She shifted her weight from one foot to the other.

I could see sweat beginning to moisten the skin between her breasts. It was getting hot. My eyes followed the curving sweep of her long legs as my pencil moved in tandem. I was concentrating intently, so I didn't reply.

'You do not seem happy with Greg,' she said.

I sighed and put the pencil down, handed her a bottle of water from next to my foot. 'I love Greg,' I said. 'But I am starting to think that he wants more from me than I am able to give.'

'While Ky asks nothing at all?'

'It's just an escape. A holiday.' I picked up the pencil again. For the next half-hour we didn't speak, but a smile played on Alessia's lips as she posed, as though she'd discovered a secret.

'Do you want to get married?'

'It's sweet of you to ask, Greg, albeit a little forward for our third date.'

'I meant, you know. Conceptually.'

'Probably not. I mean, it's a patriarchal institution used to control women and suppress dissent by atomising people into small, manageable nuclear-family units.'

'Romantic.'

'You?'

'Seems like a lot of hassle. So, you're one of those radical feminists, then?'

'Only if you think wanting to overthrow the status quo and rebuild society from the ground up is radical. My turn for a question. Who is your least favourite artist?'

'Tough one. Maybe Botticelli. Ghastly stuff. Or, actually, now I think of it, Constable.'

'*The Hay Wain.* I hear you. Just euthanise me now.'

'What about you?'

'Renoir. All those rosy cheeks. Actually feel sick looking at it.'

'He couldn't paint.'

'He couldn't paint.'

'So, do you want children?'

'Not until the powers that be pay me to look after them.'

'Pay you?'

'Yeah. Why not? It's labour. There should be wages for domestic labour.'

'Another martini? You're probably not going to let me pay for these, are you?'

'No, you can. I barely make minimum wage.'

'So you want wages for housework?'

'Absolutely. After all, I'm rearing the next generation of capitalist worker drones. And giving up everything that I find stimulating in the process. That should be worth something to the economy.'

'I like you.'

'Besides, I spent most of my childhood wiping my sister's backside. And I'll probably near the end of my life wiping some man's – maybe yours, Greg, if you're lucky! It's reasonable to want a bit of time off in between.'

'I'll drink to that.'

'To which part?'

'The you wiping my backside part.'

Years later, when Greg and I argued about children, I would remind him of that conversation. I told you from the very beginning that I didn't want to become a mother, I would say, and he would dissemble and distort and say that it had been flirtatious banter, not the sort of statement you hold a person to. In the time we had been together, Greg's career had skyrocketed. He had moved from being our small museum's designated pervert monitor to being deputy curator at the largest contemporary art museum in the country. Meanwhile, I had continued working at the shop and continued trying to paint, amassing a portfolio significant only in terms of its scale. I just couldn't settle on a style or a theme that truly resonated. Everything I produced felt passé, derivative, or simply not really reflective of the artist I felt myself to be.

About a year into our relationship, when I was twenty-five, we moved in together. Or rather, I moved into the flat Greg rented in the east of the city. I met his parents and his sisters, and he met mine. I was touched by the way he was with Rosie: kind but not patronising, and clearly only a little bit uncomfortable. I'd had boyfriends in the past who simply didn't know how to react to Rosie, and so they avoided situations where interacting with her might be required. My mum said I'd done alright for myself, and my dad liked that he and Greg supported the same teams. When I first introduced them, I was worried that Greg, who was so obviously the offspring of a pair of university lecturers, would alienate them – a full-time carer and an electrician – but he was charming and sweet, and they seemed relieved that there was someone who could look after me.

It was around this time, in our mid-to-late twenties, that the wealth divide emerged. A couple with whom we'd been friendly, and whom we had believed to be in the same financial boat – because weren't we all in the same financial boat at twenty-three? – would suddenly announce in the pub that they had purchased a house. When we enquired, in a manner that we hoped appeared nonchalant, about how this chain of events had come about, our friends would grimace awkwardly and mutter something about an inheritance, or the sale of some valuable painting or piece of furniture. And no matter how modest and open they were about it, there would be a pang.

It's just so fucking unfair, we would say to one another on the way home, through streets lined with the lighted windows of Victorian houses owned by millionaires.

And so we had watched as Iris's parents had purchased her a flat in Peckham. Helena's, who as middle-class professionals were slightly lower down the social scale, had succeeded in helping her and her betrothed to buy a shoebox flat in Walthamstow. Alessia continued to live in her father's pied-à-terre in Primrose Hill.

Now I was thirty-one and Greg was thirty-six, and we were still renting, still trying desperately to save. I applied for better-paying jobs all the time, to no avail. I had been at the museum for so long that they made me manager of the shop, but that was hardly much of a raise. Greg's parents, whose three-storey townhouse in Bristol had a stained-glass door and a tiled hallway, appeared from first impressions to have untapped reserves, but it had emerged that they had been historically terrible with money, only worked part-time and were mortgaged up to the hilt.

Greg – whose level of success as a curator did not remotely match his salary – was more disappointed at this turn of events than I was, I believe because he'd been raised to have higher expectations, whereas my own had only ever amounted to escaping my hometown. My parents survived on my dad's wages and carer's allowance from the government, a paltry sum. I knew that one day they would be gone, and I would need to go back to take care of Rosie. I was on borrowed time, trying to make the most of my freedom. I was aware that children were non-negotiable for Greg, but when I tried to picture myself as a mother, I just couldn't see it. I may as well have been imagining myself as an astronaut. It didn't seem like me.

'I don't even know who I am yet, Greg,' I would say, when we argued about it. 'I haven't even sold a single painting.'

Sometimes he would try to intellectualise it ('In a way, making a person is the greatest act of creativity there is'). He would list the visionary women artists and writers – not many, it had to be said – who had procreated and continued to make great work. At other times, he would accuse me of selfishness. I had told him about my abortion quite early in our relationship, and he had said that he didn't judge me for it. I didn't say that even choosing to frame it that way made it sound as though he did. We never talked about it, but it lingered in the air.

When we met up with friends or family who had babies and I failed to show an interest in them, opting instead to sit in the corner of the living room with a magazine, he would say that I had embarrassed him. I had limited patience with children, would enjoy, momentarily, holding them and taking in that specific milky smell as their mothers commented on how fitting a tableau we presented, before I handed the baby back with a platitude and more than a little relief. Or I would engage them in conversation and be briefly entertained before returning to what I had been doing previously. Greg liked to say that I was like a man from the 1950s, disinterested and invisible behind his newspaper. In return, I would say that he was disappointingly conventional and baby-obsessed – and how would we afford one, anyway, in a tiny damp flat on a rolling one-month contract with a box room inhabited by whichever friend or acquaintance of ours had their shit together even less than we did?

I knew that I was thirty-one, and that the time was approaching when I would have to make a decision about it. In the preceding year, people – always women – had started making dark comments about how, after the age of thirty-five, medical professionals designated you a 'geriatric mother'. When I confessed to never having had any maternal feelings, they assured me it was guaranteed that I would have some at some time in the future, and did I really want to discover that when it was already too late to conceive? At this, I would shake my head and say that even if I did experience a strong longing for a child in the future, I still believed that I could live a perfectly happy life without one. I had stuck to this party line for years because the truth – that occasionally I did feel a small and confusing burst of what could be called want – was personally infuriating, and I couldn't handle the smugness I would receive in response. What was the truth?

That I knew that I didn't really want to have a baby, but I was worried that not having had one would become my life's big regret.

Helena knew what she wanted. They were going to start trying on their honeymoon, she said.

Alessia and I emerged from the studio and walked towards the terrace to watch her boring Iris with the details.

'I came off the pill a year ago,' she was saying. 'Just to be sure. Doctors say you can conceive immediately, but the message boards say it can take months for your cycle to return to normal. I'm really hoping we have a girl, though I wouldn't be too disappointed if it was a boy. I think Harry would quite like a boy. He's going to be a really great dad.'

Iris was grimacing as she stirred the froth in her fresh orange juice. Helena paused expectantly, but instead of saying something, Iris simply sat, luxuriating in the dead air.

'That's so exciting,' said Alessia, eventually, squeezing Helena's shoulder.

'I know. I just feel ready. What about you, Sophie? Do you feel ready?'

She had betrayed me. She knew I didn't. Did she know about Ky? I couldn't tell.

'We've talked about it, as you know,' I said, pointedly. 'I'm not really where I want to be with my art.'

I walked into the kitchen and started up the coffee machine. I could hear Alessia saying that she was still in her exploration phase, and that only when she had met someone whom she could envisage as being the father to her children would this sexual dérivé come to an end.

'So you ultimately want a nuclear-family set-up?' said Iris.

'Who knows what will happen? I can also see myself in a commune.'

'Oh no,' said Helena. 'A commune is no place for a child.'

'Since when did you become so conventional?'

I walked outside just as Helena was in the process of asking Iris whether or not she wanted children. I was glad I hadn't missed it, because her expression could have turned Helena to stone. She was Caravaggio's Medusa, except her head was still attached to her body. She sat there, not saying anything, as we listened to the crickets.

'Sorry if I spoke out of turn,' said Helena.

Iris said something very quietly, which I couldn't hear because her head was turned away from us, towards the sea.

'What did you say, darling?' Alessia had always been the one who understood Iris the most, the one who wasn't intimidated by her.

'I'm not sure I can,' said Iris. 'I've been told that . . . I might not be able to.' She took a big breath. 'I have this thing with my womb.' She wasn't crying, exactly, but she wasn't not crying either. It was a look of humiliation, laced with fury. 'I'd rather not talk about it.'

'We don't have to talk about it. I'm really sorry, Iris.' Helena moved towards her, but she yanked her head up suddenly as if in warning.

In her sheer white cover-up, she could have been a piece of statuary. 'Can we just fucking drop it?'

'Yes,' said Alessia. 'Let's talk about something interesting.' She looked beyond the terrace.

The pool was a square of sparkling blue. She and Iris moved towards it. Helena stayed where she was. I didn't know what to say, and so I sat stirring my coffee, listening to the sound of the teaspoon hitting the sides of the porcelain cup.

Suzanne Valadon, Self-Portrait with Naked Breasts, 1931

When I look at this portrait, I always think I wish I'd met you. We'd have had a lot to talk about, probably over absinthe. I'd tell you that I was poor, too. Not as poor as you, but poor enough to make the work a challenge, poor enough for it to count. I have always tried to avoid self-pity. I admire how you made your way in the art world using whatever means you had to your advantage. When you don't have money, you have to think beyond the usual margins. You were canny like that.

In your late self-portrait, made when you were in your sixties, you are bare-breasted. So many male artists painted those breasts, and in the intervening century so many more men have ogled them as they have stopped before those works, aroused, or perhaps tired from a day of sightseeing, their gaze only flickering over your form before settling itself on a still life or a seascape or their phones.

The way you painted yourself was different: you are older, for a start, and almost severe. Your eyes meet ours with what could almost be disdain. Your tits are neither the focus nor an afterthought. They are simply there, a fact of nature.

Not like Renoir, whose work you said had 'no heart'. You were 'his' dancer; his eyes roamed the curves of your body underneath the dress he had made for you, and in turn you watched him work, as you must have watched so many other artists. For all the others, you were mostly nude. They said you fucked the artists after you had bared your flesh for them, and perhaps you did. You refused to feel shame.

Did you worry about how you'd feed your child, when you fell pregnant at eighteen? No man would want to trace your rounded stomach, your swollen breasts, with his charcoal. Unable to use your naked body to make money, you turned to using your hands. You became an artist. You had been watching and learning all that time.

You painted women in order to know them. Their bodies look real to me, as they engage in real tasks: bathing, fixing their hair, watching, smoking. There is no mistaking them for marble. And when you turned your gaze on the male form, well. The way you painted your lover's arse, his arms; the way the rope falls between his legs, drawing our eyes to his groin. I've felt that way when looking at a male body. Once.

A labour so difficult that they say you fell unconscious. There was no word then for what was wrong with your son, Maurice. Did you sometimes resent the way his illness dominated everything and stopped you making art for such a long time? I find it hard to admit that I'm afraid of the future and what caring might mean for my work, though I love my sister almost as fiercely as you must have loved your son. He became a successful artist, thanks to you.

Money was a struggle throughout, but eventually you made it, bought a chateau, splashed out on fur coats, fed your cats with filet mignon. When I feel downcast, I think of you.

Third day, afternoon

Ky came to pick me up after the lunch shift. It was profoundly hot. There had been a heatwave in Greece that year, across the whole of southern Europe, in fact. They were still calling them heatwaves then. Waves rise and fall, but the direction of the climate was not subsiding. The temperature had reached beyond 40°C in some parts of Greece, though the famous *meltemi* winds from the north had kept our time on the island just about bearable. Nevertheless, I put on a hat, a straw panama belonging to Alessia. It was pristine, expensive. I matched it with a silk slash of a dress in red that slid against my skin.

He was standing against the door of his father's old car, hardly showing the heat at all in a cool blue shirt, and somehow managing to look good in shorts. I liked that he was driving an old banger, the sort of decrepit ancient vehicle you hardly saw at home now that everyone bought their cars on finance. It suited him.

I gave a half-wave as I approached, and he grabbed my wrist and pulled me towards him. I could feel his teeth on my lip as he smiled into my mouth, his hand brushing the material at my hip.

'You look rich,' he said.

'I can pass, if you squint.'

He didn't apologise for the mess in the car, which I liked, and turned the radio up to blast out its Greek pop, which I didn't. The car navigated twisting roads, climbing steadily and then sharply towards the hilltop village, which I could see shining like a beacon in the distance, crouched around a summit in relief against the sky. The land itself was brown and arid, with few trees, which only made the buildings themselves seem whiter in contrast. Ky drove with one hand on the wheel and all the windows down, occasionally remarking upon something inaudible over the din of the music. His other hand was placed under my dress, midway up my thigh.

He pulled into a small car park and killed the engine. From there, we would walk, as there were no vehicles allowed in the village proper. The houses looked like sugar cubes, and most were shuttered, silent, as we made our way up little paved paths that led up the side of the hill. Occasionally the sound of a radio or the low murmur of conversation would float through a window, but apart from that our only company was from the stray cats that stalked the settlement as if it were their own. There was less wind in the narrow streets. My fringe was matted under the brim of my hat. The fabric of my dress was sticking to my breasts.

'Where is everyone?'

'Asleep. Or gone. Most people have moved to Apollonia or the mainland. For hundreds of years, this was the capital.'

'It feels like we're the only people here.'

Perhaps it was the heat, but as I stopped to catch my breath, and stood against the cool walls of a nearby house, the air began to shimmer, and for a second I felt a sense of derealisation, as though my body and the wall holding it up had become divorced from time. Reality seemed to be flickering, the past and the future coexisting within those brief few moments.

'I feel strange,' I said. Black spangles were dancing across my vision.

'Sit down for a second.' He handed me a bottle of water. Tiny pebbles dug into my bare buttocks where my dress had risen up, reminding me of where I was. 'Are you OK?'

'I'm fine. I just felt outside myself for a second. Do you ever have that?'

'Sometimes, when I've been brushing earth and dust from an object for a very long time. Maybe like you when you are painting, yes?'

He guided us to the terrace of an open bar, where he ordered a beer for him, and for me a white wine in a glass so cold it dripped with condensation. I held it against my forehead. He reached across and thumbed my cheek. He did it with such tenderness that I started to cry.

'I've been a bit lonely,' I said, when he asked what was wrong.

'This man you live with, tell me about him.'

I shook my head. 'It's not right. Fair. But I'll tell you about my sister.'

'Your sister who is sick?'

'Not sick. Rosie is disabled.'

'What's she like? What is she interested in?'

Later, I thought this might have been the moment when the idea occurred to me that I could love him. No one had ever asked me that before. Most people ask only, 'How disabled is she?'

'She smiles a lot. She loves the water, even after what happened. She can't move much, but there is a physical therapist who helps her at the pool. She likes watching nature documentaries, especially Attenborough. She loves my mother. I mean, *I* love my mother. But with Rosie, it is something else. That love, I know she only feels it for Mum. Which I understand. Mum is with her all the time; she gave up work to look after her. Rosie needs her. And I understand how much Rosie loves her, because I feel a similar way about Rosie. Like she is my child. Like I would dissolve if anything ever happened to her.'

Ky put a hand on my shoulder.

'I think maybe that's why I have never been that bothered about having children,' I said. 'I have felt that love already.'

'You don't want them?'

I shrugged and took a deep sip of wine.

'It's allowed not to want them,' he said.

'That's very modern of you. I thought you were Greek.'

He laughed at me then, his eyes wrinkling. I liked that he was older. He seemed at ease with himself.

'You don't want them?'

'With whom?' he said. 'I have family to take care of, too. My father is becoming very old.'

I pretended to pout, as if his failure to consider me a potential mother to his children was offensive.

'You're an artist, Sophie,' he said, dropping some euros into the little metal tip tray. 'I understand this, I think. You make art, not babies.'

Having walked a little longer, we rounded a corner and stood admiring, many metres below, a blue-domed little white church standing on a rocky islet. It was, Ky said, the Church of the Seven Martyrs, though he didn't know how or why they had died. There were more than three hundred churches on the island, but this one, he said, was the most beautiful. The jagged rocks on which the church stood meant that the waves around it were wilder than the weather suggested. As we made our way down towards it, I could vaguely pick out the tiny figures of swimmers in the water, which, when it reached the rocks, shifted from deep blue to that vibrant turquoise so particular to Greece.

'You're so lucky to come from here,' I said. 'My hometown is so nondescript. Nothing interesting happens there.'

'Ah, but Sophie, we must never be ungrateful to the places we are from. These places, they shape us. Anyway, you should see it here in the winter.'

'I suppose for a long time I felt ashamed of it. The other girls, they have spent their whole lives cocooned by money. They would look at the street where I grew up and feel desperately sorry for me. They'd pretend not to, but they would.'

'Why are you friends with them?'

'They're clever. And interesting. They make me laugh. I think most of all they don't think it's a waste of time that I want to make art. Everyone I know at home thinks it's a waste of time. Well, maybe not my mother, but I know she would rather I did something that made money and gave me some stability. I might have to look after Rosie one day.'

'Do you know how much money I make?'

'Tell me.'

'Five hundred euros a month.'

'That's terrible.'

'It's fucking shit.'

I reached out for his hand. 'Maybe I should pay you for the tour.'

'I can think of some ways.' He pulled me towards him and grazed his fingers across my hips, but his lips stopped short of mine. I had to focus to stop my knees from buckling.

Walking back up from the church to the village, Ky said he knew a place where we could go, if I wanted. He said this quietly, as though his proposition might travel through all the lace curtains that billowed outwards in the breeze, giving us, as we passed, a momentary glimpse of each house's dark interior. It was only as he approached a dark wooden stable door, smaller even than my own modest height, and set into a whitewashed wall, and inserted a key into the lock that I thought of Greg, of the hurt that this would cause. For a brief second, the extent of my betrayal floored me. I loved him, slept next to him, shared a home with him. He supported me in my career, emotionally and financially. He would be joining us in two days' time. What would happen then? Would Ky retreat to the taverna and keep his distance? Or would he force me into a confrontation that would destroy everything, including our life together?

There was no denying the fact that I was a bad person. I had chosen to hurt the man closest to me in the world. And I had done it almost without thinking, without any real rationale beyond my own feelings of entrapment. I had avoided Ky's questions about Greg, in part because I knew that anything I said would sound trite. It was true that Greg didn't understand me. That we had become distant from each other. That every conversation we had about a possible future together ended in an argument. It's true that, at that time in my life, I felt like a failure; that working in a shop at the age of thirty-one, even if it was a shop in an art gallery, felt humiliating in ways I couldn't articulate. After all, the most I had hoped for as an adolescent was to escape my hometown. So where had this rabid ambition come from? No one I had grown up with seemed to have it. Sometimes I wondered if I had caught it, like a disease.

I could say that I was unhappy. I could even say that I probably had something diagnosable, like Harry would say when they all picked over it afterwards, in my absence. Later, in therapy, I never used it as an explanation for the way in which events unfolded. I approached my sessions as though I were going to confession; I wanted absolution, and a feeling of relief. I suppose I got that, but none of it changed the essentials, which were that I had committed an unforgiveable offence against one of the kindest men I knew, had dismembered the love between us with an almost surgical indifference, and that I had done it because I wanted to, and because I couldn't not. It was as though this desire, which was like no other I had ever felt, consumed everything in my body that was capable of feeling, and I walked towards a tempest with scarcely any trepidation beyond rare subliminal flashes of foreboding, which I dismissed like so many mosquitos.

Perhaps it was a kind of madness, after all.

Ky held open the door for me. My arm grazed his as I passed, and all thoughts left me.

'Whose house is this?' I said. The place was scrupulously clean but clearly uninhabited. It had the feeling of a museum. The few pieces of dark wood furniture were plain but well made: a dresser topped with a delicate white lace cloth, a small table with two chairs, a single bed. On the walls were several small painted icons, a bunch of dried herbs tied with a ribbon, and a wooden crucifix. To the rear, in shadow, was a poky, rudimentary kitchen.

'It belongs to my family. My grandparents lived here before they moved to the coast to open the restaurant.'

It had been well looked after. The sheets on the bed were starched and creaseless, and fringed with delicate embroidery.

I passed my fingers back and forth over the bumps on it. They were so white I suspected they had been treated with baking soda or lemon juice and hung out to dry in the sun.

Ky bolted the bottom half of the stable door, leaving the top open but for a layer of lace curtain.

'I'm on the pill,' I said. 'So you don't have to worry about anything.'

Greg had been pestering me to come off it, but I had been insisting on both that and condoms.

Ky looked amused. I was sitting on the bed and he was standing in the centre of the room. He pulled his T-shirt over his head, unbuttoned his shorts, kicked them off. He stood there, looking at me, as I pulled the silk dress over my head.

'Come here,' I said.

By the time I was astride him, I was dimly aware that I had been making quite a lot of noise, but not in the theatrical manner of my early twenties that had hardly correlated to my own pleasure; these were delirious sounds that felt innate and, surprisingly, new. He was pressing the base of his hand against a patch just below my stomach while his fingers worked me. His other hand was on my breast, pinching my nipple; his tongue was in my mouth, and I was crying out, moving against him, seconds away. A shadow fell against the wall, and when I turned my head slightly I perceived, through the curtain, the distinct outline of a figure, as though traced. Whoever it was stood very still, slightly back from the open door, the features of their face obscured due to the thickness of the curtain. Somehow, I thought it was a woman. Perhaps

I was hallucinating the Virgin Mary, whose icon faced me from the other wall. The way the curtain obscured the face reminded me of how sculptors would compete in rendering the translucence of the marble veils that shrouded the faces of their Madonnas.

Time had taken on a syrupy quality, but the moment was too brief for me to be afraid as I scanned the shape for a hint of human features. I couldn't see the person's eyes, but somehow knew that they were locked on mine. It lasted less than a second before Ky pulled back my head so that I was facing him, and I started to come, knowing that I was being looked at as I writhed, suspended between his gaze and that of the unknown person at the window.

In the days and weeks after my abortion, I had found myself spending a lot of time in galleries. It was the summer term, there were no lectures left to attend, and I was still experiencing the voracious hunger of an expectant mother, although I was expecting nothing. The taste of salt on a fresh tomato left me dizzy with sensation. I devoured cheeses and bread and marinated anchovies, cooked pasta with chilli and lemon and garlic, then inhaled while sitting on a chair in our small paved garden. I revelled in the chocolatey hazelnut smoothness bursting through the crunch of a cannoli. I was voracious for smells, too: I would stop at flower stalls and perfume stands, and find myself on pavements outside curry houses with my nose in the air. And sex. I made screens light up all over London that summer, offering only my body and a few easy hours of wine and laughter, asking for little beyond an experience, the awareness that I was free.

Most of all, I was hungry for art. My usual gallery limit is forty-five minutes – after that, I become dreamy and restless, stop taking it all in – but that summer, I could look at art for hours, and found myself enraptured by the sorts of paintings in which I had never taken an interest before: Flemish still lifes, early Renaissance frescoes, Tudor portraits, pop art. It all had something to offer me and my appetite. My eyes were ravenous. The act of looking became fundamental. I went all over London, to large galleries and small. The commercial contemporary spaces of Mayfair held as much interest as the Hepworths in the Tate Britain. I got the train out to Hampton Court Palace and was astounded to see tourists filing hurriedly through a room replete with Caravaggios, eyes cast down. I stood and took them in, but it was Artemisia Gentileschi's self-portrait that made me gasp audibly, causing heads to turn.

The expression on her face is one of intense study; her hair is coming loose around the temples as she works. The way her face is lit emphasises the beauty of her features, but the hands clutching the brush and the palette are big and workmanlike. I stood there in awe of her boldness. I was looking at a true portrait of an artist, a woman who had made herself the personification of painting in a way a male artist never could.

That hunger was translating into my own work, too. I was finding new influences everywhere, was joyfully experimenting with different styles and colour palettes. The canvasses lined up against the wall until I had no place left for them to dry. I felt fecund with inspiration. It was the most productive phase I'd had up to that point. I could paint for hours and feel that only minutes had passed.

I could not have satiated that hunger had I had a child in my arms. Perhaps I would not have experienced it at all. And it felt like a gift to me, this knowledge that the world was full of things to offer, and that the pregnant women smiling at me everywhere from billboards and buses represented just one mode of creation. At the Tate Modern, I wandered into a room containing Mary Kelly's *Post-Partum Document*, and felt grateful that I would never have to negotiate that battlefield, that tug-of-war between the work of making and the work of caring. I didn't know what feeling or being maternal was supposed to signify. To look at my own mother, it was sacrifice, love, vulnerability and also strength. I have never felt robust enough to be someone else's protection.

Ten years after I ended my pregnancy, I would sometimes feel a pang, or a tug, from deep within, and I would think, 'Ah. There it is.' It wasn't grief, exactly; more a feeling of potential tugging at my sleeve. But it would always pass, was easily dispersible with logic and argument. Rather than hearing its siren call, I dismissed it as a fleeting hormonal inconvenience. A few days later in my cycle, and it would dissipate. I wonder now if part of the distance that had sprung up between Greg and me was due to anger. I was angry that he had been haranguing me for a child, as I saw it, but I was also angry that he had failed to capitalise on my fleeting yearning. A friend once wrote to me in an email: 'A woman who is ready and able to have a child is to be met with gratitude. She is an opportunity that should be harnessed. It is a beautiful thing.'

Greg was so focused on his own longing that he didn't see mine pass by in a blur of colour and sound like a train that wasn't stopping.

Coming home from visiting some friends and their newborn, we argued about the definition of 'work' (at times, when we discussed babies, I felt that I needed to engage a translator).

'He needs a break when he gets home,' Greg said. 'He's been at work all day.' 'But so has she,' I countered, my voice rising to a shrill pitch. 'But so has she.'

In the warm morning light of that room, holding that tiny, wrinkled creature between the two us, I had felt a complicity that we could have carried home with us and tended to. While its afterglow remained, I wanted him to say: 'I'll change nappies.' I wanted him to tell me: 'I'll feed the baby from a bottle.' I wanted him to say: 'You can still make art.' I wanted him to tell me: 'You can do both; I'll support you.'

When he said none of these things, it felt like a betrayal. He was supposed to know me better than anyone, but in his determination to argue his case, he lost sight of how to calm my fears. And then the feeling was gone.

Louise Bourgeois, Femme Maison, 1946–47

A woman's naked body topped by a house, the structure obliterating her head and shoulders and part of her torso. The house has many storeys. One of the walls is shaped like a coffin. Her arm emerges from it and appears to be dangling helplessly; the other, tiny, waves as though in distress.

I first saw your print, Femme Maison *(house woman/woman house/housewife), on the cover of a book in the university library. You painted this image, too, repeatedly, and made it from marble. We discussed it in class.*

It's not exactly a difficult metaphor to work out, a boy said in our tutorial. She's saying that domesticity obliterates your brain. Isn't that kind of offensive?

The tutor explained that you were raising your three boys when you made these self-portraits, in the 1940s. You adopted the first, having convinced yourself you were infertile, then conceived and birthed two sons in quick succession.

I thought about this picture a lot, during the years I played house with a man, the one who wanted children with me. We used to have so many dinner parties. I would cook these elaborate meals, and then I'd wash up, too. We'd often end up fighting after our friends had left. I showed it to him once, trying to explain how I felt. I wanted him to understand what I was afraid of (obliteration, sublimation, housework). He didn't get it. 'Can't you see how frustrated she must have been?' I said.

That's why I have always turned to art. He may not have understood me, but you did. You knew that caring for something more vulnerable can feel like that, sometimes: like being crushed by a house. The brainless drudge work of domesticity, the cleaning and washing and wiping and feeding, when you could be making. I wept when, years later, I saw your show, one rainy afternoon on the South Bank, my breasts tingling strangely as I stood before all these works you'd made about living in a female body, bodies shaped by pregnancy and childbirth, swollen bellies and leaking breasts. The past year has skinned me. I cry at art now.

How did you make art while raising three boys? Well, it shaped the way you worked: you chose your materials accordingly. You worked in cloth and balsa wood because it was quiet and would not wake them. They always say to sleep while the baby sleeps, but like many women artists, you had to find time where you could.

You once said that the market's indifference had been a blessing in disguise, because it meant you could focus on your work undisturbed, but it must have hurt when, after a few initial shows, the interest dried up and the art world turned its back on you. You kept on, building up an incredible body of work that, for a long time, went unseen and unappreciated. Quietly, you had become one of the greatest, most disruptive, disturbing, radical artists of the century.

Whenever I stood at the sink in that flat, I thought about how, when your husband died, the first thing you did was tear out the kitchen. You were done with the cooking, the washing-up, and looking after other people. It became the space of a working artist.

Your artistic career lasted seventy years and used sculpture, printmaking, painting, textiles, drawing and installation, spanning the surreal, the abstract, the conceptual and the figurative.

When, in 1982, MoMA finally gave you a show, you were seventy years old.

Fourth day, morning

I woke in the studio, my body naked under tangled sheets, which, bathed in cold pre-dawn light, looked pale blue. Ky had finally left an hour or two before, though I'd told him that he needn't, that the others all knew. When we had returned from Kastro, we had skipped dinner and gone straight to the little bed in the outbuilding, and no one had disturbed us. I had never thought that I could be so brazen, but the need I felt for his body overrode any shame about what Helena and Iris would think. There were two days left until the men arrived.

We spent the in-between hours talking in low voices as we stood, naked or wrapped in sheets, smoking on the patio in front of the building, not caring if the insects came to feast on us. When we stood like that, I couldn't stop looking at his face: the strong nose, the jutting angle of his jaw, his dark eyes. In bed, it was his body: the muscles of his arms, the strong shoulders against which I grazed my teeth as his large hands clutched my behind and lower back, pushing me hard against him, him into me, as we fucked. I'd never felt so visually stirred by the way a man looked before.

'I almost forgot,' he said, at some point in the small hours. 'I promised that we would go night swimming.'

And he took my hand and led me down to the sea. As we swam, I felt the cool, dark water stroke every facet of my naked body. There were so many stars that I couldn't stop swearing. He laughed and said I was vulgar, and kissed me in the shallows, and I thought, this memory will come to me on my deathbed.

The sky was turning pink as I got out of bed and made my way over to the urn containing my phone. Miraculously, five per cent of the battery power remained, enough for me to stand, shivering in my T-shirt, while I went through all the unanswered messages: my mother, telling me that they all missed me, sending me a photo of Rosie smiling from her chair; my friend Tess, asking after my 'posh villa holiday'; Greg, whom I had expected to be irritated by my lack of response, but who instead only assumed that I was having too good a time. *Can't wait to see you, Soph. Thinking about you in your bikini. I love you. Not long now.*

I was too exhausted to swim this morning. Instead, I returned to my bedroom, knowing that Alessia would come and wake me when the time came to continue our painting.

'You look tired. Long night?' She smiled as she pulled the shirt over her head.

'Maybe we shouldn't talk,' I said.

'Don't be prudish.'

'I'm not. It just feels . . .'

'Private?'

'I always thought that when you sleep with someone, it's like you sign an unwritten contract not to tell people what they're like in bed.'

'But I know what he's like,' said Alessia, waving her finger. 'Did you try putting your finger up his arse yet? He loves that.'

'Oh my god, stop,' I said. I was laughing, but I also felt a lurching jealousy at the thought of them in bed, and the shared hinterland, begun in youth, that their bodies had constructed together over the course of many intimate hours. 'You're outrageous.'

'I don't understand why people get so embarrassed about sex. It's not some sacred rite.'

'It can feel sacred, sometimes.'

'You should see your face. You mustn't fall in love with him if you can help it.'

'Don't worry. I never fall in love with people. Why do you say that, though?'

'You're wondering if he is married? If he has some secret family in Athens?'

'He told me that he lived alone.'

'Then you should believe him.'

The conversation lulled after she got into position. After making a couple of sketches, I had decided to paint her turned slightly away, one leg bent in contrapposto, her arms above her head, both breasts pulled back a little from the way the pose stretched her torso. I had given her a difficult stance to hold, but she never complained, just occasionally asked to stop and shake herself out, at which point I would usually avert my eyes. Now, though, I found myself pilfering glances at her form as one might size up a rival. I had always been attracted to Alessia's sense of ease; it was a confidence that came from being told, from a young age, that she was beautiful. That beauty had beguiled me from our first meeting. Everyone wanted to be near to Alessia, as though her looks were somehow transmissible. That they could pose a threat was a novel feeling, and it was interfering with my concentration.

Our friendship had begun on superficial terms, as they are wont to do in your early twenties. We had little in common when it came to background or life experience: simply a shared taste for vodka, a love of dancing, a generosity with cigarettes. We didn't know then that these trivial things can end up binding you to a person for life as, little by little, you become enmeshed – each time you follow her into the toilets to cry, each conspiratorial shaking-off of a group of tiresome men, each phone call in a crisis (her father's heart attack, my abortion) – until you realise you're in a friendship that has lasted over a decade.

I did not know what kind of life I wanted or how to go about getting it, only that I wanted it to be bigger, and nothing like my mother's, which was so mired in the labour of caring that she said she had ceased to recognise her younger self. Not that she complained; she was saintly in her acceptance, which in many ways made it even more frightening. Alessia, meanwhile, seemed to care only for herself. I did not aspire to Alessia's lifestyle; did not even envy the safety net underpinning her every move. I think I was drawn to her defiant autonomy, and her quiet certitude, her belief in the rightness of all life had to offer her. Greg was always telling me to have more confidence in my art and my abilities, but confidence comes from a lifetime of being reassured of your validity. In our house, surviving day to day was the most any of us could hope for.

Most of all, Alessia understood art. Even before asking me to paint her, she had been a kind of patron; she had believed in my work, and in me, in a way I hadn't known I needed, and which I couldn't risk losing. I'll never forget my parents at my degree show, trying to make polite chitchat with the wealthy families of my contemporaries, who threw around phrases such as 'subjectivity' and 'semi-figurative' and 'representation'. My mum nodding, smiling slightly, my dad uncomfortable in the suit he'd last worn to Uncle Iwan's funeral, his too-loud accent booming out as though each sentence was the first uttered after a day spent in solitude. Oh, to have breasts like that again, my mum said, as she stood in front of my best life drawing. My dad beaming, saying, You'll be in the Manchester Art Gallery before too long, Soph. I loved them best in these moments, for coming to see my art and saying that they were proud, even though it was a bit lost on them. Rosie was in respite care, an opportunity that hardly ever arose, thanks to government cuts to social services. I couldn't remember the last time they had been out together, let alone had come to the city.

'You know you frown when you paint,' said Alessia.

'Lift your head a little,' I said. 'You're wilting.'

We passed another hour in silence, the only sound the buzz of a fly against the windowpane, the breeze through the open door, the occasional splash from the direction of the swimming pool. I could see rivulets of sweat making their way down between Alessia's breasts, but she held still. When I finally told her we were finished for the day, she grasped her hair together in one large bunch and lifted it from the back of her neck. Then she made her way towards the door.

'Your clothes,' I said. She waved her hand.

I stood in the doorway as I watched her sprint through the trees, pausing only for a fraction of a second before her sprint segued into an elegant dive. As I approached the pool, I could hear Helena laughing. Iris was feigning indifference behind her novel, but I saw her looking as Alessia spun over on to her back and floated in a starfish position.

Our eyes made contact and Iris said:

'A stranger walks among us.'

I didn't say anything or try to explain my absence from their company, though it was unsettling that she had noticed it. I felt that edge in her voice, which suggested she was in one of her gorgon moods, primed to wound, but she didn't say anything further, just watched me as I arranged a towel on a lounger and prepared to take a long nap.

At the taverna, it was Ky's father who came to take our order, the sort of portly, smiling man whose idea of humour was to tease you by withholding the bread basket while demanding a thousand euros, making me feel a pang for my own dad. We ordered widely, and far too much. For the past few days, I had found myself ravenous, and when the appetisers arrived – balls of courgette, cheese and mint encased in the lightest of batters, anchovies butterflied and dressed with lemon and black pepper – I fell on them as if I had been starving. I sipped my wine and tried to listen to Iris talking about her housing arrangements, but I could see Ky darting between tables from the corner of my vision, and my awareness of his presence at all times was making concentration difficult.

'We want to find someone to sublet my flat for a year so I can go and be with Edwin in New York,' Iris was saying. 'But we don't want a stranger; we want it to be someone we know and trust. I'm particularly worried about the floors.'

'What about you, Soph?' Sweet Helena, how could she not understand, after all this time, that I would rather give up painting, or die, than have Iris as my landlady? She always thought so kindly of people. 'After all, you're the only ones still renting.'

'Do you take DSS?'

'Rude,' said Iris.

Alessia was laughing and topping us all up, and did not appear to notice the blotches appearing on Iris's cheek.

I realised, too late, that I was a little bit drunk. I adopted a tone of fake lightness. 'I've yet to meet a decent landlord,' I said. 'What makes you think you would be the exception?'

'You could at least pretend not to be so bitter,' said Iris.

Alessia was still smiling as she traced her finger over the rim of her glass.

Helena's mouth had formed a pursed, anxious little hole, and she was tying her fingers in knots. 'I don't think it's fair to call Sophie bitter,' she said. 'She just has socialist principles. Harry and I could never have afforded our place if we hadn't had help from our parents, and that really isn't fair. It's not like we *deserve* it. I feel a bit embarrassed about it, really . . .'

'You don't need to feel embarrassed,' I said, 'because you don't see home ownership as some sort of achievement.'

'And you think I do?' Iris's voice had risen slightly.

'I didn't say that. But you're invested in a certain kind of life, aren't you? You've never left north London, except to go to your parents' house in Italy in July. After university, they just bought you a flat. I'm not saying that you're not clever and that you haven't worked hard, but you know you wouldn't have that job if it weren't for your family, and we're all supposed to pretend that isn't the case. You just seem to have a blind spot when it comes to your advantages . . .'

I paused to fill my wine glass, and take a large gulp. Iris was possibly going to murder me, and I at least wanted to be drunk while she did it.

'Do go on.'

'. . . which I get. I truly do get it, because admitting anything else would mean admitting that the position you are in has not come entirely from merit, and whether you are consciously aware of it or not, you are invested in that structure of meritocracy. Admitting that it's all lies would cause it to come crumbling down, leaving you with . . .'

'With what?'

'Your own mediocrity.' I knew I had gone too far, that what I had said was cruel, but I hadn't been able to stop.

For a moment, I thought Iris was going to retaliate. I knew what was in her mind. There were any number of things that she could throw at me: that I was the mediocre one, who was filled with anger because I hadn't made it as an artist, and possibly never would. That it wasn't her fault that she didn't grow up poor in some shithole town. That at least she didn't hate herself to the point that she went around hurting people, including the man who loved her and wanted to start a family with her. But she didn't say anything. I watched her engage in the almost physical act of regaining her icy composure. The blinds went down, as did her fork. The feeling of relief from the other two was palpable.

'I do hope that has made you feel better,' she said.

Greg always said I hated rich people. I disputed this and pointed to my friendship with Alessia as evidence to the contrary, but it's true that I spent a lot of time thinking about wealth back then; not so much about how to acquire it as what it did to people. It seemed to me that in Iris, it had created a sort of suspicion, a defensiveness that was impossible for someone of my background to transcend.

When we had first met, she had asked me a series of questions that, to a casual observer, might have seemed offhand – where had I grown up, etc. – but were obviously attempts to place me within a context she could understand. Once she had surmised that, her enthusiasm for me dimmed as if by the flick of a switch. Back then, I assumed the reason for her cold shoulder was a simple one: I was from the wrong social class. As I got to know her better, though, I came to realise that in fact she was threatened by how I had gained access to our prestigious college based on nothing more than my abilities. She could never, and would never, know for certain the measure of her own talent, or lack thereof, because the networks around her made it impossible for it to be viewed in isolation from all the helping hands that elevated her towards success.

Our shared friendship with the other two meant that we were required to remain in one another's company, but she treated me as one might a ghostly presence. I was a spectre holding a pint glass at the edge of these interactions, but rarely if ever directly addressed or responded to. The most I usually got was a smile, and that was only if I succeeded in saying something cruel or amusing. I had never met a person like this before, who could be so nakedly impolite. It made me, against all my better judgement, want her approval, especially once I was floundering in a post-university job market.

Part of it was that she could be incredibly charming. In our second year, towards the end of the summer term, she'd held a party at her parents' house (they had already departed for their Italian villa). The kitchen, at the extended rear of the property, had one wall entirely comprised of folding panels of glass.

These had been moved back, opening the room to a large garden strewn with lanterns and fairy lights. Plates of prosciutto and cheese were laid out on the sides. On the kitchen island, rows of champagne flutes were lined up, being filled by a girl from a catering company who looked about my age.

I stood there, wondering what she was thinking, while Helena fetched us drinks. We clinked our glasses and moved into a corner of the garden to smoke near a rose bush. Inoffensive electro floated from indoors into the jasmine-scented air. Guests were speaking in loud, confident voices, the girls in mid-length dresses in chiffon or lace that were obviously vintage designer but the right side of unfashionable, while the boys wore art-student T-shirts and had similar crew cuts to the lads I had gone to school with, though their voices betrayed them. It was clear that Iris moved with a creative crowd whose parents, like her own, fancied themselves as similarly bohemian. I had already spotted a small Lucian Freud in the hall.

'You're quiet,' said Helena, from behind the black gauze veil attached to her pillbox hat. In the last few minutes, it had dawned on me that she had dressed carefully for the occasion. In contrast, I was wearing the same pair of black jeans that I would have worn to a party back home, where we'd all crowd into a paved yard out the back of someone's pebble-dashed council house, spliffs and cans in hand.

'I feel a bit uncomfortable,' I said. 'I'm not sure I fit in here.'
'Why? They're just students, like us.'
'They're all really posh, though,' I said.

'Well, maybe. But you're just as good as them.'

'I know. It's not just that. I can't explain. They feel kind of . . . old before their time, if that makes sense?' I waved my hand towards a platter of ham. 'There's something middle-aged about a party like this.'

She laughed at that, and tapped her glass against mine. 'Look, it's Iris.'

Iris was wearing a ruffled polka-dot cocktail dress that made her look like a 1980s *Vogue* cover star, and seemed to be moving from group to group with perfect ease. We stood there, watching, as she laughed at someone's joke, urging them to help themselves to more drinks, leaning in to listen closer to their friend's earnest opinion. I hardly recognised her as the arctic, spiky acquaintance I had come to know. Helena had begun speaking about her plans for the summer, an invitation to go away with an older man she had been seeing, a relationship in its early stages or a fling, it wasn't yet clear. I half listened to what she was saying as my eyes followed Iris around the garden, watching the way her hair, almost opalescent, moved when she laughed, the angular, rigid lines of her model-thin limbs. She evidently had the capacity to illuminate conversations. Male eyes followed her as she withdrew.

Eventually Iris made her way towards us, her warm smile, directed towards Helena, fading only momentarily when she caught sight of me, standing at her side. She kissed Helena, then me, on both cheeks in greeting.

'Alessia's through there with some Italian architect,' she

said. 'She has some coke, if you're keen.' This was directed at Helena alone.

'Your parents' house is lovely,' I said. I wanted to ask her how you came to own a house like this, what evil deeds you needed to have committed to achieve such an existence. This was before we were regularly exposed to the gilded lives of others mediated through screens. I had walked out of my life and into another through a wisteria-framed front door, and it had felt seamless. Back then, I was still under the impression that proximity to such people rendered such a life achievable. As I said, I thought a lot about money in those days.

I said nothing more, and she gave me a nod and turned away towards someone more interesting.

An hour or so later, and I was drunk. I had lost Helena somewhere between looking for another drink and getting into a lengthy argument with a Courtauld student about Joshua Reynolds, a painter whom he loved and I despised. When it became clear that I had won the argument, he decided to remind me that I was a woman by lurching towards my mouth with his. I walked away with drunken abandon, and, weaving myself through the packed ground-floor entrance hall, made my way up the stairs, past the smokers and the entwined lovers and the queue for the toilet. The first-floor rooms – a library and sitting room – were full too. In the library, a raucous dramatic reading was in progress, snippets of which could be heard over the Donna Summer blasting from the dancefloor in the sitting room next door. The huge arched windows had been thrown open, filling the room with the smell of honeysuckle and weed as people draped themselves over the balconies.

'For fuck's sake, Cecily,' someone drawled, as a row of glasses smashed to the floor and a girl twirled into the fireplace.

I took the next flight of stairs up to another landing darkened by four closed doors, opening two to be greeted with empty bedrooms. The third was also empty, but unlike the others it was lit. Discarded on the carpet were various pairs of shoes, including Helena's ballet pumps. I heard a laugh through the door of what I had assumed was a cupboard, and turned the handle gently, revealing an enormous bathroom.

Helena was kneeling next to the toilet, with Alessia and Iris standing around her, and for a moment I assumed she was vomiting. What she was actually doing was snorting a line through a rolled-up note. They hadn't seen me, so I stood there watching them for a minute. Then Iris turned and her eyes met mine, before, smiling faintly, she leaned towards Alessia and spoke quietly into her ear, her hair a shining barrier preventing me from deciphering the mocking words that I knew played upon her lips.

Amrita Sher-Gil, Self-Portrait as a Tahitian, 1934

I was in my early fifties when I finally got to India to see your painting in New Delhi. Standing in front of it, your work seemed more radical than ever. The unashamed nudity, yes (you were expelled from art school in Florence for such crimes), but also the composition. In the painting, you look away from us, your expression stern and a little sad. You are topless. I studied your youthful, taut body, your pert breasts. 'I will enjoy my beauty because it is given for a short time and joy is a short-lived thing,' you once wrote. How I wish I had been more like you! I look at photographs of myself in my gorgeous youth, especially from that summer on the island when I was overflowing with feeling, and wonder what all my neurosis was about.

I was in India because it was one of my 'summers of freedom'. I hadn't much money but was otherwise at liberty, and would always try to travel a little, and produce at least the bones of a painting by the autumn, when my life would return to its usual cycles of work and care. I had long come to terms with the fact that I would never be a known, or a successful artist, and I no longer sought meaning in the endorsement of the art world. The work was good and I knew it was good, and that was enough.

How I used to envy you and your precocity. Your Grand Salon gold medal, the access that you had to the very best tutors and materials. Your bohemian, wealthy background and your privileged, cultured parents' commitment to your talent, which took you from Hungary to Florence to India to Paris and beyond. You moved in artistic circles, had affairs with both men and women, and were unapologetic about it. Perhaps I envied that, too.

You knew you could be one of the greats, and that a child would get in the way of that. You were single-minded in your wish to paint. That day in the gallery, I thought about how you were just twenty-one when you made your self-portrait, but you wouldn't make it to thirty because of the botched abortion – your second – that would kill you at twenty-eight. All because your husband couldn't take the shame, and so performed it himself.

Your self-portrait was a knowing nod at Gaugin and the way he devoured brown women's bodies. The dark shadow that surrounds your figure could be him, or it could be a generic male viewer. Either way, he looms, sinister, his face out of sight. I had barely noticed it when I saw the painting in books, but standing in the gallery that day I saw so clearly how his spectre dominates. It's black, almost like an omen. I shuddered.

That painting of mine, I made it years ago, during a time when I was brimming with desire, long before I consciously noticed what you had done. Yet in it there is also a shadow, and like yours, he is watching.

Fourth day, evening

Ky was sleeping, and I was looking at him. The way his chest moved as he breathed, the dark fronds of hair that curled at the back of his neck and around his ears, the long, dormant eyelashes against his cheeks. I gazed at him because I knew that soon I would be unable to; we hadn't discussed it, but we both knew that from tomorrow, when Greg and the others flew in, we could no longer be together in this way.

After lunch, I had stayed behind at the taverna on the premise of waiting for the change. Iris had jumped up the moment the meal had finished, and Helena had given me a reproachful look and followed. I knew that I had been cruel to Iris, but I didn't care, just as I seemed unable to summon any guilt about what I was doing to Greg. Once or twice, as a sort of test, I had tried to picture what his face would look like when he found out what I had done, but still I felt nothing.

Alessia stayed behind only for long enough to tell me that it was probably best if I didn't ruin Helena's special dinner that evening, the last chance for 'us girls' to all be together and celebrate for her.

When the last tourists had gone, Ky came over to sit next to me. His hand immediately went to my inner thigh under the table, and he stroked the skin there as we negotiated how we would spend our last eighteen or so hours together. Helena's big celebratory dinner was to take place at a restaurant in Apollonia that evening, which left us only snatches of time.

'Let's go up to the studio now,' he said.

'From the way you behave, you'd think you only wanted me for my body,' I said, and he laughed and asked what it was I wanted him for.

'It is not as though you are trying to run away with me to Athens.'

'Do you want me to?'

The truth was, I had thought about it, if only in an abstract sense. In this vision, I was painting him as I stood at an easel in a poky apartment, my feet bare on slightly warm terracotta tiles, the balcony doors opening on to a jungle of pot plants. I was older and wearing an oversized man's shirt. He was wearing nothing. There was something farcical about the picture, if not about the situation itself, then about the vision of domestic bliss I had attempted to conjure with a man who had only been inside me a handful of times and who didn't even live in the same country. The possibility of a shared life together seemed outlandish.

'I could get you a job in my museum,' he said. 'Then we could fuck behind the statues in the storeroom at lunchtime.'

'You're an exhibitionist. You like the idea of them watching you.'

'You are.'

'Maybe. I don't think I'd get much painting done if I came to live with you.'

'Oh, I'd let you paint. Sometimes.'

'It's that sentence. That's the reason it would never work. All this talk of letting me.'

We didn't mention Greg; there was no need. He followed me up to the studio in the afternoon heat, and he had me in front of the full-length mirror, then again on my hands and knees on the bed. I couldn't help but imagine Greg watching us as we fucked, and, fleetingly, the thought of it got me off. Perhaps it was all Ky's talk of the statues, but I imagined him standing there in the doorway and then, as though reanimated, touching himself. I was crying out again, and Ky had to tell me to be quiet.

It was late afternoon when we got into the car. The others would meet me at the restaurant, but first Ky wanted to give me a tour of Artemonas, a settlement in the interior of the island that stood above the capital, Apollonia. He drove us north along the quiet roads, past the turning we had taken before that led up the hill to Kastro, with its mass of white buildings cloudlike above us. I felt dazed. Since arriving on the island, time had expanded, and the shimmering heat made me feel receptive and dreamy.

'You're breathing very hard,' Ky said, as he parked the car in the shade of a tree next to a large, pale yellow church. It looked deserted, the car park empty.

'I feel nervous. I don't know why.'

He slipped his hand into the front of my dress, and I felt his finger graze my nipple as he exposed first one breast, then the other. Then he reached down and tugged on my underwear. 'Lift.'

I lifted my body for a moment, allowing him to pull down my underwear. As he did so, he hiked up my skirt.

'Open your legs.'

I was breathing harder now, and instinctively reached downwards to pull the cloth over to hide my body.

'Put your hands behind the seat and do not move them,' he said. 'Keep your legs open.'

His fingers were there now, moving against my skin as I gasped. His other hand was on my breast, occasionally moving up, grazing my mouth for wetness. The cautious part of my mind had fogged over.

'I want you to imagine how you look right now,' he said. 'I want you to feel as though you were watching yourself. As though you were standing over there.' He pointed. 'You can see everything I'm doing to you.'

I came quickly, my breath sharp and rapid. As the sensations subsided, I felt a wave of sudden awareness. It wasn't embarrassment, exactly; it was more a slightly abashed reacquaintance with my surroundings. The sunlight was turning faintly pink through the trees.

'You're going to touch yourself thinking about that for the rest of your life,' he said.

'Don't spoil it with your arrogance,' I said, pulling up my underwear.

'It's not arrogance. I will, too.'

The mansions of Artemonas were crumbling. The houses, unlike those elsewhere on the island, reminded me of some of the more upscale neighbourhoods of Athens. They were neoclassical in design, all swirls and columns like a mafia bride's wedding cake, but painted in pastel pinks, oranges and greens. Giant cracks and chips appeared in their facades. Most were clearly uninhabited, their wrought-iron gates locked with large padlocks and thick chains, the gardens overgrown, the surrounding vegetation in some cases having made its way inside the buildings before regretting the decision and attempting to escape, forcing walls to collapse or breaking windowpanes.

'It's like a journey to the past,' I said.

Ky reached for my hand and was quick enough to take hold of it.

'I can see why an archaeologist would like it. Who owns the houses?'

'Mostly wealthy Athenians. Men in shipping who got rich long ago.'

'They're beautiful. There's something so sad about them being abandoned.'

'When I was a child playing in the street with my cousin, we used to stand and watch the families through the railings. It was like looking into a different world. We would talk about what it would be like to have money, how one day we would be rich.'

'I thought you were a communist.'

'I am,' he said. 'I want everyone to have money. You too, I think.'

'I'm not sure I like what money does to people. It makes them harder.'

'Alessia isn't hard.'

'She isn't, no. She's the only one.'

'There is a warmth to Alessia.'

'Yes. People want to be close to her. Though perhaps not as close as you.'

'You like the thought of me painting her.'

He didn't say anything to this. He was still holding my hand as we rounded the corner. In front of us was a large house, perhaps the largest we had seen. The windows on all three floors were framed with shutters, and above the front door was a large balcony entwined with vines.

'Anyway, this is her family's other house.'

'You're fucking kidding me.'

'And guess who has the spare key.' He unlocked the gate. 'Come.'

'I'm not having sex with you in another abandoned house.'

He tutted and shook his head. 'No, I want to show you something.'

The house was in better condition than its neighbours, though it had obviously been closed for a long time. Most of the furniture was covered with dust sheets, giving the eerie feeling that we were wandering among an army of shrouded statues. The shutters had been tightly closed, and light came from the open front door, though there must have been an opening somewhere on the upper floors; a single dust-freckled beam made its way down the grand staircase to our feet.

'Come.'

We made our way up the stairs, his hand still in mine as he led the way. I watched the way his broad shoulders moved under his T-shirt, the flash of olive skin where the material rode up at the lower back. At the top of the stairs, he paused in the shadow of the next flight and pulled me towards him. I could just about make out his face as he raised his hand to cup my cheek.

'I know you don't want to talk about him,' he said. 'And I am not going to ask you to, but I want you to know that I won't tell him anything. OK?'

'I didn't think—'

'I will keep away. When you come to the taverna, I will not serve your table. If Alessia asks me to bring drugs to the house, or to have a drink with you, I will make an excuse. I don't want you to feel bad.'

'I don't want you to feel bad, either,' I said. To my surprise, I was crying. 'It scares me how much I don't want you to feel bad. If that makes sense. I didn't expect this to happen.'

'I think he is a good man, this man?'

'He wants to have a baby with me.'

'And you?'

'Sometimes. Sometimes I want to run away. The idea of being alone doesn't scare me. I could live in one of those abandoned houses, and just paint.'

'You don't think you would be lonely?'

I shook my head. 'Looking after other people can be lonely, too.'

'Your sister.'

'I guess I fear the loss of identity.'

'When I first met you, you seemed very unhappy.'

'You think?'

'I could see it. I see you very clearly.'

'I'm supposed to decide about having a baby.'

'Well, if you decide that you want one, you must pray to the goddess Artemis. She is the goddess of childbirth. The locals say that is where the name for the village comes from, though I am not sure if it is true.'

'Didn't she ask Zeus that she be allowed to remain a virgin forever?'

'This is also true.'

'No wonder she turned that guy into a deer when he tried to rape her, then.'

'Best not to fuck with her. She killed Adonis for saying he was a better hunter.'

'She's a man-hater. I like her.'

He walked across the darkened hall and pushed a door, which opened with a creak. I heard him rustling inside the room for a moment, and then the building was flooded with light. As we made our way through, I saw that I had entered the chamber with the balcony. Ky had thrown open the glass doors and was standing looking out towards the sea.

'You can see all the way across to the *kastro*,' he said. 'Look. Look how the buildings look pink in the light.'

'A sunset, really? You're trying all the tricks.'

'I want you to remember.'

'Just don't say anything romantic.'

'I won't.'

We stood there, looking down the hill towards the blue-domed churches of the capital.

'You're so beautiful,' I said. 'You're the most beautiful man I ever saw.'

'This is a word you use for men?'

'Sappho uses it for men.'

'You know Sappho?'

'A lot of what you tell me, I already know.'

He laughed, then.

'I will be sad when I can't look at you anymore. I like looking at you,' I said.

'And I'm not allowed to say anything romantic to you in return?'

'Better not.'

'I can't even ask for your phone number?'

'A bad idea, I think.'

'This might be the most beautiful dinner I have ever eaten,' Helena said. 'A private rooftop, just for me.' She raised a glass to Alessia. 'Thanks so much for organising it.'

We had started with octopus, sliced so thinly that it melted in the mouth alongside tingles of citrus marinade. I interspersed each bite with small sips of cold wine, and tried not to think about how I was eating a being capable of feeling love.

'There isn't really anything I can say that won't sound mawkish,' Alessia said, as she raised a glass in return. 'So all I'll say is this. Thanks for volunteering to be marriage cannon fodder. You're the best of us, and this act of bravery moves us all. Harry does not deserve you, because no man deserves you, but I think I speak for all of us when I say that I hope you make each other very happy for the rest of your lives.'

'Hear, hear!' Iris and I banged our palms against the sides of the table as we all drank.

Helena was the first among us who would become a wife, and though we teased her about it and how remote it felt from her firebrand university persona, we felt the significance of that transformation. Though we each hated the ritualistic 'sending off' that came with most hen parties, it was impossible to escape the reality of the transaction entirely: she would now belong to Harry. He would refer to her in conversation as 'my wife'; her Christian name would evaporate quicker than the specially formulated perfume that she would spray on her neck as she dressed in the ivory gown on the morning of her wedding, and though she kicked against it with all her intellect and obstinacy, she soon would come to embody some elements of that role. Certain things would be expected of her, especially once she had children – she would go on to have three – and her feminist politics would prove quite futile in the face of those expectations, at least while the babies were young.

Since leaving university, there had been points where I would find myself wondering whether it was all a shabby racket. All those hours of teaching and reading, enabling us to forensically deconstruct the multiple inequalities we would face without being able to do anything about them. In my more cynical moments, I would look at my mother and at Tess, and wonder if I would be happier had I not been encouraged to expect more. Maybe I had become greedy.

We didn't speak of any of this, then. It was one of those perfect evenings, where any tension that had existed between us seemed to have dissipated in the knowledge that tomorrow the men would arrive and the atmosphere would change. Iris was all smiles, while I was in one of those expansive moods where I felt lucky for everything life had thrown at me – and that included Ky ('No tears, then,' Alessia had said drily, when he dropped me off). After the octopus, we ate platters of pearlescent fresh white fish with lemon potatoes baked in the oven and scattered with thyme and feta, and raised glasses of rosé to our past and Helena's future, until we became tipsy with sentimentality and impassioned in our declarations of love for one another.

Though I cared deeply for Helena and Alessia, and for Iris not at all, what observers such as Greg had never understood was that the threads that bound us were stronger than love. With Iris especially, there was something that drew me to her even as she did her utmost to repel.

It was something to do with pain, I thought foggily, and the witnessing of it. They may not have privately approved of what I was doing to Greg, but I knew none of them would judge me for it or ever mention it, even Iris, just as I had never judged them for their abortions or their exes or the conflicts in their families. There was a tacit understanding between us that, had I reflected on it, I might have called solidarity. Yet when I look back on the events of that holiday, I find myself wondering whether it was something more like cowardice.

Ana Mendieta, Flowers on Body, Silueta Series, 1973–78

Two years after the trip, I finally got myself into therapy. I sat in a shabby, municipal office while a clinical psychologist darted her fingers back and forth in front of my eyes, and often your Siluetas would come to me, unbidden. I was supposed to be picturing difficult memories: that night on the island; then, later, the hospital, the blue light of the ward with the beeping of its machines, and the lonely days that followed, after returning home to a place that felt transfigured.

We went back further, as well, to Rosie's almost-drowning, the times my mother almost cracked. These were important events that needed processing. So it was confusing to me why your images kept appearing in between them. There was one in particular. Your nude form in the ground, with flowers sprouting out of it, some might say like a corpse. You called it 'earth-body' art, and it was elemental, magic, almost, the way you used flowers and feathers and blood and sticks and mud, like a kind of witchcraft from your native Cuba, an attempt to return to the earth in a way that you, sent away as a child to America, could never fully return to your homeland. Siluetas, *or* silhouettes, *you called them. I thought of you in Greece, all those times I lay on the shore or on the ground, sometimes with him, sometimes without.*

Like so many women artists, you have come to be defined by your death: you were killed, possibly, by a man who was supposed to love you. During drunken rows, you used to taunt Carl Andre that minimalism was over. Your career was taking off, while he wasn't selling as much. The night you died, it was alleged you drank four bottles of champagne between you. He said he couldn't remember, that you'd somehow gone out of the window. You were found on the roof of the all-night deli thirty-three floors below.

¿Dónde está Ana Mendieta? Where is Ana Mendieta? the signs outside the museum said, as the biggest names in the New York art world passed a picket line of protestors.

Yet to me, your Siluetas *have always been about life, not death. Maybe I kept seeing them because I never felt so much like a body as I did in those early days. That year, we would lie in the grass and, though I would be too watchful to fall asleep, I would enter what felt like a fugue state. What my body had just done felt like a voodoo magic, pagan, arcane. There was a lot of blood, enough to paint with. But that strange, wonderful time wasn't just about abjection. The fluids that flowed from me flowed into the earth. It was as close as I have felt to the holy feminine. I was filled with an urge to create (and no time in which to do so). And once again,* Flowers on Body *would surface in my mind. Lush, white*

FEMALE, NUDE

wildflowers seem to sprout from all over your naked form: between your legs, obscuring your chest, your face, a cloud around your head. I give life, you seem to be saying. My body gives life, even after I am gone.

Fifth day, morning

In the night I dreamed I became an island. I fell asleep to the sound of Ky whispering to me tales of myth and metamorphosis, and like Perimele, I was thrown from a cliff into the sea and transformed. For much of the dream, I struggled for breath as the swirling seas pulled me under and salt water breached my mouth and nasal passages, filling me like a bloated balloon. As I drowned, I was me but I was also Rosie, looking up when breaching the surface to see her sister, me, at six, screaming from the shore in one, long, piercing ululation and thinking that I would die.

It was just as the fight was beginning to leave me that the transformation began, and in heaves and creaks and splinterings, my body hardened and expanded and I became land. Achelous had prayed to Poseidon to grant space to an innocent drowned, or to 'let her become space herself'. In the dream, I found refuge in my new terrestrial solidity. I-Rosie was saved.

I woke sobbing, Ky holding me until I stopped. He kissed my face and then my shoulders and my breasts before he entered me, and we had one last sleep-tinged screw, sinking back into slumber afterwards, twisted together in that single bed. When I woke for the second time, the mid-morning sunlight streaming through a large gulf between the shutters, he had gone.

Next to the bed was a note.

'Someone will remember us
                      I say
                                      even in another time'

I once read the fragments of Sappho described as being like 'beautiful, isolated limbs'. An ugly thing to imagine when reading words of such tenderness.

Ever since I was a child, I have thought a lot about death. After all, my sister almost died before my eyes, and trauma can confer a certain fascination. The subject of my final-year thesis was artistic portrayals of drowned women. They were quite the fashion for a time. Drowning is a truly feminine death. Passive, less violent: female suicides merely surrender to the current. The Victorians loved depictions of drowned women in both literature and visual art. Ophelia, with her 'muddy death', was their waterlogged muse.

These drowning women reinforced everything that they thought about us: that we are weak and prone to madness; that our sexual transgressions must be punished. A watery death will purify us. Usually, the drowned woman had been seduced and then abandoned. 'The passion of love makes girls mad,' wrote one doctor.

Our bodies, too, are wet. We secrete fluids; we cry. Like water, we give life.

In Ovid, Arethusa prays to Diana to save her from the pursuit of Alpheus, who, as Ky pointed out to me, is yet another voyeur – and is determined to take her against her will. She is transformed into a spring that flows deep under the ground – becomes, essentially, water – but still she is not free: the river-god changes back into his watery form and rapes her.

She eventually emerges at Ortygia, transformed into a freshwater fountain.

Though the Victorians loved a drowned woman, hardly any drownings in ancient Greek literature and mythology were female. We were water nymphs, like Arethusa, or sirens, luring men to their deaths.

I stuffed the note into my wallet and put my shirt back on. Greg would arrive in an hour or two. Walking out on to the terrace, I nodded *kalimera* to Agatha, who was clearing the remains of brunch from the table. I went into the kitchen and poured myself a coffee. The light outside when I emerged was so bright that I had to squint through my puffed-up eyes. The loungers by the pool were empty. I walked over to the urn and retrieved my phone. Two messages from Greg, one from the airport and another, about an hour ago, from the ferry terminal, a photo in which he was doing a thumbs-up like a teenager on a school trip. I realised, somewhat perversely, that I would be happy to see him.

I walked over to the wall and sat on it, my back to the blue horizon. I wanted to see what the others had been posting. Helena had been the most prolific, though images of herself were noticeably absent. Instead she had focused on still lifes: a bowl of oranges in the kitchen, a tin of black cherries in syrup, a jug. The table after dinner was over, the candles still burning, the napkins in disarray, the bougainvillea that ensnared the house, purple in the fading light. Alessia had opted for a different aesthetic: her focus was on people. Iris lay on a lounger in a black one-piece and Ray-Bans, smoking and reading another one of those novels about young women having depressing sex. Helena up to her waist in the ocean, her back to us, the outline of her figure dissolving into squiggles as your eye approached her arse, a deliberate disruption, the beer in her hand proclaiming: *This photograph is different.* There I was, tucking into a plate of mussels placed on a table with a blue checked tablecloth, freckled and damp and a tad pink, but not unpretty. And finally Ky, that night at the villa, flicking his joint into the ashtray and looking intently into the lens, a smile that presented as shy, but that he knew made his eyes crinkle in a way that was attractive and sort of sleepy. It was a look of complicity from one person who understood the other: a look of friendship and knowledge, of a fondness that had extended to sex.

As for Iris: just one photograph, of a set of blue-and-white steps, which, because of the whiteness of the building to which they were attached and the contrast with the sky beyond it, had been flattened to the point of abstraction. Only the presence of a lamp attached to the wall caught the eye and grounded it in familiar reality. It was pure Iris.

I stopped scrolling and went back to the studio. I had just finished making the bed when Alessia tapped on the door with the back of her knuckles.

'You're going to have to stop living in here,' she said.

'I know.'

Alessia took off her dress and assumed the pose. I was reaching the halfway point, and today would be moving on to paint. My tutor at college had hated the pencil and was always encouraging me to break free of its tyranny and apply paint directly to the canvas with no preliminary sketches. But I liked the pencil, enjoyed the process of working and reworking, how its movements interacted with the act of looking. Sometimes I had wondered if my fidelity to the pencil meant that I would never be a great artist, but I was beyond such anxieties now. I started to mix the paint.

Seeing that I had not yet started work, Alessia shifted on the balls of her feet and then pinched a piece of flesh from her navel and said, 'This holiday is making me fat.'

'There's barely a scrap of flesh on you,' I said, putting down the fruit container I was using as a palette.

We were quiet for a while as I started to blend the tones of her skin.

'You must have painted some very beautiful women,' Alessia said after a while. 'Who was the most?'

'Are you fishing?'

'No!' She laughed. 'Just interested.'

'To be honest, you don't really think about beauty or otherwise when you are drawing someone. I've painted women who I guess would be called beautiful, and men who align with that ideal too. Muscular men who are toned in all the right places, with big cocks.'

'And it doesn't turn you on to look at them?'

'You look in a different way. There are bodies I've painted that have stayed with me afterwards. One woman just had the most amazing tits. Just incredible, like something from a magazine, and no cellulite anywhere. I remember thinking, "To have a body like that . . ." But then something else switches on and the figure breaks down into a series of shapes. Dissolves, you could say. And you're just thinking about the line and the way it travels across the page and whether that conforms to what you are seeing in front of you – not in, like, a hyper-realistic way because that's boring, but in a way that belies some version of the truth as you feel it.'

'So you don't see flaws when you look at me?'

'It depends what you mean by flaws. Do I see the crease in your flesh when you twist at the hip? Yes, I do. Because that crease exists. And we have grown so used to seeing depictions of these hard, shiny bodies that the crease feels unsightly – but it isn't. It's natural and it's animal and it's you. Everyone's skin creases like that.'

'I hate that crease. I hate it when I spot it in those changing room mirrors that let you see yourself from behind.'

'Because you are looking at yourself in an objectifying way.'

'Doesn't everyone?'

'Yes. I mean, I'm a woman. I've painted myself naked a handful of times, mostly in college. I did it from the mirror and then from photographs, and at first it felt almost painful how much I disliked my body. But drawing it over and over made me see it as just that: a body. A bag of bones and fat and blood, which, were it assembled in a certain way, would make me seem conventionally attractive – but it isn't, and that's OK. It's still worthy of being painted. And of more besides.'

'I wish you knew how good you look,' Alessia said.

'It's sort of beside the point,' I said. 'When you paint, it doesn't matter. Look at Egon Schiele. All those skinny bodies, shrivelled. Those jutting bones. You know all this.'

'I never liked his work much.'

'I know.'

Alessia shook out her hands.

'Did I ever tell you about the first naked man I painted?' I said, as she resumed her pose. 'At uni.'

'I think so, but I can't remember.'

'It was our first life-drawing class, and I was expecting some voluptuous female model, and instead we had this bloke in his seventies who was friends with the tutor. He was almost painfully thin and his skin was all wrinkled. His knob was just hanging there. I didn't know where to look. Anyway, we were doing this exercise that involved him shifting pose every ten minutes, and when I sat down, he was sort of at a three-quarter angle, hadn't adopted a pose yet. Then the tutor said for him to get into position, and he turned around and *bent over*.'

'Oh my god . . .'

'So his arsehole and dangling balls were literally right in

front of my face. Directly in my line of sight. I nearly died. No one else in the class could look at me.'

Alessia was laughing. 'So what did you do?'

'I drew his nutsack like I was supposed to. It actually ended up being a pretty good drawing. Greg sometimes jokes that we should have it framed.'

'OK, I feel better now.'

'You know, it's an act of humility to pose for someone like that, to be prepared to seem vulnerable. You have to respect that.'

We passed the rest of the session in silence, with occasional bursts of laughter.

'I'm still picturing it,' Alessia said, when we finished.

In the second kitchen, Iris was assembling a salad. Despite having no wish to be involved, I offered assistance.

'That would really help, actually,' she said. She was slicing onions with a precision I found intimidating – or maybe it was just seeing her with a knife. 'It needs to be about three times bigger than when it's just us.'

I didn't mention that I had been finding the portions agonisingly small.

I set to work chopping and salting the tomatoes that Agatha had harvested that morning from the garden. 'After that, there are some walnuts that need chopping and some goat's cheese that needs crumbling over the top.'

'It looks nice,' I said. I had never imagined Iris would be like this in the kitchen. She didn't really eat. Every woman has a friend who doesn't eat, seemingly subsisting on espresso and the occasional piece of fruit, and after years of observing such behaviour, you forget that it's at all abnormal. According to my Greek mythology book, even the gods and goddesses ate, though I was struggling not to picture custard each time ambrosia was mentioned. Another marked difference between the two of us: not only would Iris never have heard of that particular brand of tinned custard, but she would rather ingest crack cocaine.

We were quiet for a few minutes, the chop-chop knocks of metal against wood filling the room. I knew she was waiting for me to say something about Ky, so I tried to keep a deliberately tight focus on the task in front of me, occasionally moving over to the bin to scrape away the goo from the tomato seeds.

Eventually, she cracked. 'Are you nervous about seeing Greg?'

'Nervous how?'

'About how you are going to be?'

I avoided her eyes, instead gazing at her clavicle, its bow-like elegance casting a stark shadow on her pale skin. The kitchen, which was usually Agatha's domain, was dark and, unlike the rest of the villa, old and disordered, as though it were owned by a French grandparent. Dried herbs hung from the ceiling; the table was covered with a piece of checked oilcloth. Illuminated by the dusty window light, Iris looked pure, and clean.

'Guilty, you mean?'

'Sophie. You know I'm not making a moral judgement.'

A few years ago, while interning, Iris had had an affair with her boss, a friend of her father's with a wife and a teenage daughter not much younger. It had had all the potential to become an unholy mess. The man had fallen for her hard, had once made a drunken scene. But Iris had managed to extricate herself with a cool grace, and seemed not to have suffered any lasting effects.

'I feel like a cunt,' I said.

'You're not a cunt.' Her expression hardly changed.

I raised an eyebrow.

'I know we are not exactly friends . . .'

'Not for want of me trying.'

'Sophie.'

I put the knife down and started breaking up the feta with my hands. My nose had begun to tingle. It had never taken much to make me cry. Or, rather, it had never been something I was able to control. When other children made fun of Rosie, mocked the strange noises she made, I knew that controlling my reaction would make it stop. And yet I never could.

'I've just been so unhappy for so long.' I was at very real risk of sobbing now, so I raised my eyes to the ceiling and pulled tight on the skin under my eyes. 'I know it's not an excuse. Sorry. I didn't mean to cry. I'm just tired. I don't know what I'm doing. It's all such a mess. Greg wants to have a baby, and I . . .'

'You're scared of what you'll be giving up?'

'It isn't just that. But still. How do you know?'

'I notice things.'

And then Iris did a thing I had not expected. She stood, walked over, and put her arms around me. Their hold was loose – even in an embrace, she held herself at a distance – but I felt comforted by this gesture, which had not come easily to her. It may well have been the first time that we had ever properly touched, in all our years of knowing each other.

'Go and wash your face.'

We could hear the crunch of tyres on gravel. There wasn't time. Instead, I splashed some water from the tap on to my cheeks and put my sunglasses back on. Then I picked up the salad and walked out on to the terrace, leaving Iris, inscrutable, in the dark room behind me.

'There were a few plebs on the plane. Some real troglodytes, boozing it up nonstop from the departure lounge onwards, spaffing their benefits . . .' Harry was saying.

Greg made eye contact with me across the table. Though he had sat separately from Harry on the plane and had, he told me as we put his suitcase in the room, succeeded in avoiding more than a brief conversation with him until baggage reclaim, Harry had informed him that he had ordered and consumed a bottle of champagne alone during the flight.

'. . . covered in shit tattoos, hollering the whole time. Thankfully those types had dropped off by the time we got to the ferry terminal. They can never be bothered. Want everything laid on for them. A coach to an all-inclusive, where they just stay all week expanding themselves with chips and all-you-can-drink piña colada.'

'The sort of people who look as though they belong in a Martin Parr photograph,' Iris contributed.

'Who's that?' said Harry.

'He does people smoking fags at the seaside,' I said. I was gripping the side of the table with some force.

'We have that in the States when people go to, like, Mexico,' Edwin said. His voice had the dog-tired quality of a man who had taken a transatlantic flight to Athens the day before and a connecting flight shortly afterwards, followed by a taxi, a ferry and a hire car.

'Spring break? That sort of thing?' Helena wrinkled her nose, and I reflected that the middle classes often seemed as capable of snobbery as the truly posh.

'We used to go to all-inclusives,' I said. 'My parents love them. They're really great if you have a disability, because you don't have to go far, and they're pretty forward thinking on accessibility. They're able to provide wheelchairs, even.'

Everyone looked horrified, except Greg, who reached for my hand across the table, and Iris, who strangely seemed to be enjoying herself.

'Sophie's sister is disabled,' Alessia said.

'I hope you have not been offended,' said Harry. I noted his use of the passive voice, and knew that later, when alone with Helena, he would call me precious. I took a moment to hate him, privately.

I had never liked Harry. In his presence, Helena folded

herself up like a deckchair, muffling her intelligence to make herself more pleasing to him. It was depressing to watch, but too intangible to raise with her, especially once they had announced they were getting married.

There was an awkward lull in the conversation, which I spent observing the men who sat around the table. Two spots of pink had appeared on Harry's pale white cheeks, as they often did when he was hot or tipsy or irritated. He had the sort of wavy blond hair that, in a man's twenties, looked as though it belonged on a yacht in the Mediterranean, and in his thirties began an irrevocable thinning process that would end in baldness. He was wearing a striped linen shirt, chino shorts and deck shoes. There was a thick smudge of sunblock on his face where he hadn't fully rubbed it in.

Edwin, meanwhile, had one of the most interesting faces I had ever seen. I traced his cheekbones with my eyes. Unlike Harry, who had a rather static countenance, Edwin's face was expressive, changeable like a mackerel sky. He was quick to laugh, but his eyes could sometimes show a seriousness that made his conversation compelling. He was, he told Alessia, half Dominican and half Japanese, genetically – and he drew on both in his work. Culturally, he was a New Yorker. As was her way, Iris had told us hardly anything about him, even though their transatlantic relationship had been going on for almost a year. She was her usual restrained self around him, but when he spoke, her gaze flickered towards him in a way that made clearer how she felt than her verbalising it would have.

'What sort of art do you make, Edwin?'

Edwin said he made installations, though he had made mixed-media pieces in the past. He had just had his first big show. Greg responded to his words with an eager, open face. He was always fascinated when anyone talked about art, never snobby or patronising. Anyone's practice was interesting to him, even if it produced the sort of work that he personally disliked. He was more generous than other artists, in that respect, and also more so than the public, my parents included – on one gallery visit, my dad had stood in a room of Rothkos and declared that he hated it all, that any child could do it, that there was no skill in art-making anymore, and what a shame that was. I was curt with him, interpreting his displeasure as a judgement on my own work after art school, where the figurative drawings he had once so praised had tended more towards abstraction. But Greg was patient and kind, despite having specialised in abstract expressionism, despite the point being that any child *didn't* do it, despite coming from the sort of house where people debated and challenged each other, including their elders, and told them that what they thought was bullshit, and here was why.

But I couldn't forget what he had said to me afterwards: 'They don't know any better.'

I turned my eyes to Greg as he and Edwin talked. His dark brown curls, with their slightly-too-long cut that was almost teenage. His handsome face, made more so by his slightly crooked nose. His freckles, which would soon be underscored by a layer of tan; his eyes, blue, which had met mine when he emerged from the hire car and walked through to the terrace. For a moment, I had thought: He knows everything that I have done.

Maybe, I thought, I am the one who does not know any better. It was a tempting line of reasoning, to conclude that I was the victim of forces that I didn't understand. That all these people, their motivations and desires, were somehow beyond me, as mysterious in their caprices as the Greek gods in the myths that they had learned about at school. My grandmother spoke that way sometimes, of the upper echelons – politicians and royalty. They always had their reasons, as far as she was concerned, and who were we to question them? We were just corks bobbing in their wine-dark seas.

Gwen John, Self-Portrait, Sketching, c.1909

The day I moved in, I put a copy of your self-portrait in my studio. It's curling at the edges now, but there you are. Reminding me.

In the midst of a mad affair, you painted yourself nude in the wardrobe mirror of your room. You are standing, drawing, a thatch of brown pubes between your legs. It plays on your multiple identities, artist and model, object and subject of desire. We forget how daring it would have been for you to paint yourself like this. Your hellfire-preacher father would have thought you brazen.

This nude is unfinished. I wonder what made you stop. Were you too delirious with passion? You struggled to be your own muse. To be his was easy; you loved him, with that annihilating love that can make you unable to recognise yourself. I have felt that love, too – take it from me, you should have put countries between you. 'I'm not an artist, I'm your model,' you wrote to him. Rodin was thirty-six years older than you, a horny old man with a string of mistresses. Yet he, a great artist, could see the great artist in you. He was always encouraging you to paint.

I first came across you when I was only ten: a small, shy little girl much like you were. (Who would have thought you, a slip of a Welsh child, would make it to the Slade, and then to Paris? You followed your brother, who in life always overshadowed you, yet insisted you were the better artist.)

Quiet, shy, reticent, self-contained: these are the words used about you. A still life. I don't agree. You were on a courageous quest for a room of your own. And you found one, or many: usually basements and attics. You lived modestly, focusing on your work. A need for creative solitude in a male artist is treated as a mark of his genius. In a woman, it made you a source of pity.

There's no denying that Rodin opened something up in you. And you liked to be watched. Once, he ambushed you with a threesome. When you arrived at the studio, having been sent for, Rodin wanted to fuck you while the other model watched. Then he made you pose together for him (the resulting drawing is highly erotic; you're the skinny one on top, I think, straddling her beneath, your curved stomachs touching).

He watched you, but you watched him, too. Filled with pain and longing, peering through the window of his studio, trying to make out his figure in the dim light. It was only when he died that you felt free. You said it was as though you had been unwell for a long time and were now getting better. I felt those words. Haven't we all been there?

FEMALE, NUDE

I prefer your picture to Rodin's. You were good at women's interior lives. In fact, you once said: 'It seems to me that I am not myself except in my room.' And isn't it only in our rooms that women are entirely liberated from the gaze? Freedom comes in many forms. It can be a quiet space, in which to work and think.

Those who pitied you didn't know that, some nights, you would break out from the walls that contained and sheltered you, to sleep among the stars.

Fifth day, evening

After lunch, Greg and I slept. I said I was too tired for sex. When we awoke, the crickets were in resounding chorus, and the heat of the day was beginning to lift.

'Let's go swimming,' I said.

'In the pool?'

'No, silly. In the sea. There are loads of bays around the headland. Let's get away from here.'

'Are you climbing the walls already?'

'Not really,' I said. 'Iris hasn't been too awful, and we're all pretty good at giving each other space. But now that Harry's here, I wouldn't mind getting away for a bit.'

'You wouldn't mind. I sat on a ferry and then in a car with him blathering the entire time. He seems to think the government *knows what it's doing.*'

'I know. I know. I mean, I'm glad she's happy, but I'll never pretend that I understand it.' I got up and put on a plain black swimsuit with a low back, then a cotton shirt, frowning in the mirror as I pulled up my hair.

'You look good,' Greg said. He walked up behind me and

kissed my neck, pretending not to glance at our reflection. I felt a flicker of something. 'I missed you.'

'I missed you too,' I said.

'Remember the first time we came to Greece?' he said, as I packed the bag (I always packed the bag). We had been maybe three times, the first shortly after we first met, always staying in cheap, Spartan apartments on the outskirts of mainstream resorts, hardly leaving except to swim, subsisting on bread and feta and tomatoes.

'Of course.'

We had spent the holiday fucking, though Greg was too polite, even with me, to ever state this outright.

'Not quite the same luxury,' he said, grinning. 'I always thought Alessia's dad was loaded, but this is next level. Still, the bed is better. Maybe it'll be here that we make a baby.'

'Maybe,' I said, walking into the bathroom.

Or maybe, I thought, but didn't say, you could lay off and let me enjoy my holiday.

We followed a scrubby path that gradually climbed the cliffs to the right-hand side of the bay, and found ourselves walking alongside olive groves. The air had the dry, dusty smell of grass and leaves about to combust. There had been wildfires on the mainland, though not here, not yet. The saw-cry of the crickets almost drowned out the sea; it crashed against the rocks below, and I felt that sudden urge to launch myself forward towards the blue like a starling in flight.

After about twenty minutes of walking, by which time

we were both dripping sweat, we chanced upon a narrow path that was almost obscured by heavy undergrowth. It lay opposite the entrance to a villa that my grandmother would have described as *clarty* – a northern word that she used for anything gaudy or distasteful. The castle-thick exterior walls were broken up at little intervals with alcoves containing poorly made cherubs in an Italianate flourish that jarred with the surroundings. High above us was a terrace into which I presumed a swimming pool had been carved; I could just make out the pristine cream-coloured parasols that lined it. There were no signs of life.

'Sophie, I'm hot,' Greg said, when I suggested we explore the path.

'It probably leads to a beach.'

I was proved right, because after a short, steep climb, we found ourselves in a hidden rocky cove bordered by deep, aquamarine water that was even clearer than at our local beach. It was deserted, apart from two expensive-looking sun-loungers and another cream-coloured parasol, marked with a sign stating: 'Property of Villa Kamelia. Do not occupy.'

'Bliss,' I said, once I had arranged myself on one of them.

'These aren't ours,' Greg said. I had forgotten his facility for stating the obvious.

'All property is theft,' I said. 'Besides, there is no such thing as a private beach in Greece.'

'Who told you that?'

'Alessia, probably.' I stood up and ran into the sea, stumbling a little on the rocks. The water, not even cold, hit my legs and crotch. I stood there for a moment, peeing, before propelling myself forward into the lapping waves, which, every time they touched the shore, provoked the rumbling sound of pebbles shifting beneath the surface. I felt the water wash away the traces of Ky on my skin. It was only as I had lain there next to Greg after lunch that it had struck me that I hadn't showered; could he smell this other man on me? Ky's mark was not only superficial. There were traces of him swimming inside me, that could be leaking out of me, even, as my boyfriend's arms encircled the body that had betrayed him. I reflected that, were Greg and I to fuck, his sperm would annihilate the competition. Or perhaps it was the reverse. I had read about this once in a magazine.

'Don't go out too far,' he called. He wasn't swimming. He would get in occasionally, but he was never one to go out of his depth.

Were you never taught to swim? I had asked him on our first trip, and he insisted that he had been. He was far from confident, though.

Having swum out to a distance that I knew he would consider too far, until he was an annoying, gesticulating speck on the shore, I let myself fantasise for a moment about never swimming back in, never having to tell Greg that I didn't have to have his baby, and never having to spend another minute of my life with Iris or Harry. In this fantasy, I wasn't dead, exactly; I had just dispensed with my own consciousness and dissolved into the ocean.

'For fuck's sake, Sophie.' Greg's pale, angry face greeted

me when I returned to shore. 'I don't understand why you take risks like that.'

'You don't need to say it.' I flopped on to a sunlounger.

It's like he wants me to be traumatised, I thought, not for the first time. What to say to him? That my mother got me back in the water almost as soon as it happened, signed me up for swimming lessons, unwittingly giving me a sort of exposure therapy? He knew all this. He knew, too, that while I didn't fear the sea, I did respect it, familiarising myself with tides and currents, acquiring local knowledge, never swimming out so far that I wasn't confident I could reach the shore. Greg lived in a world of worst-case scenarios. I wanted to say: The worst has already happened. I already live in the worst. I have made my home here.

'I'm sorry,' I said, instead. He liked apologies.

The baby conversation hovered above us like a malevolent deity, waiting.

'It's like you hate the fact that I want to have a baby with you,' he had said, during our last row before I left for Greece. 'Aren't you flattered? Can't you see it's a nice thing?'

'I know it's supposed to be a nice thing,' I had shouted. 'Believe me, I'm fucking honoured.'

Sometimes, during these arguments, I would leave my body and watch us from above as though we were the wooden actors in some awful play, the gestures familiar to the point of cliché: his head in his hands as he cried; my cold refusal, arms crossed, to embrace him (it was supposed to be the other way round). For days afterwards, I would feel as though I was reeling, would find myself clutching walls and furniture as though I had staggered away from a disaster zone.

'I don't know how we got here,' I had said, as I packed my suitcase. 'I don't know how we became two people who understand each other so poorly. Who show one another so little empathy.'

We wanted radically different things from life. It was so utterly unoriginal, and also horrifyingly true. And yet we each thought that we could bend the other's will.

I stood and walked back to the water's edge, then turned to look at this man who had given me so much of his love.

'Come here,' I said. 'At least dip your toes in. It's the sea!' I mimicked a frolic, smiling, then held my arms open to him.

'Later, maybe,' he said, and rolled over on to his front.

For dinner, I put on a trapeze-cut linen dress that hid my body's outline. This mode of dressing went against my instincts. Knowing that Ky would be there across the terrace, serving us, probably, made me want to wear the same dress that he had lifted up so gently in the car the day before. I liked the idea of him watching me and reliving it. I confess I also liked the idea of him wondering what I had been doing with Greg that day, imagining my body and feeling sick about it. I remember reading once, in my younger years, that romantic love couldn't exist without jealousy. The writer had been a man who had famously had many affairs, and it had seemed to me at the time like an excuse.

'You really do look so beautiful at the moment,' Greg said. 'Greece is really working for you.'

I took the compliment, burying the feminine urge to ask whether I looked terrible normally. When we walked out to join the others, I noticed him noticing Alessia, Iris and Helena in that tactful way of well-brought-up men.

'The three graces,' Harry said, in lascivious tones, ignoring me.

At the tavern, we were seated at the largest table, under a small iron-framed canopy entwined with vines and bougainvillea. Candles in small jars hung from a nearby olive tree. I could see the other diners look up as we entered, led procession-style by Alessia in her short black dress, a band of delicate gold leaves in her hair.

'Shall I order for the table?' Harry said. 'A giant plate of lobster spaghetti, I think.'

'I'm vegan,' said Edwin. 'In fact, I'm struggling to find anything at all that I can eat.'

'Stuffed tomatoes,' I said.

'Well, there goes that idea,' Harry said.

'I'm in for lobster.' Iris raised her hand and Alessia followed. 'Me too.'

'Did you know lobsters mate for life?' Helena said, reciting a fact we had all learned from a popular nineties sitcom. Harry cut her off.

'Everyone knows that. Can I have the wine list?'

'I didn't know that,' I said, although of course I did know.

'She certainly won't be mating with someone else when she's Mrs Capell.' Harry commanded Ky over with a wave of his hands. I watched him flinch, then use his eyes to give me a voiceless apology for breaking our agreement, before painting on a pleasantly blank expression.

'You're changing your name?' I said to Helena.

She squirmed.

'I have to say, I did not see that coming,' said Iris.

Alessia said nothing, but her face said it all.

'Of course she's changing her name,' said Harry.

I could feel Ky standing behind me, as though every atom in my body was humming at his presence. He leaned forward, bending slightly to fill my glass.

'Don't drink too much', Greg said, under his breath.

I took a too-large gulp, and said, 'You always said that you would never take a man's name.'

Helena was looking at me.

'I already have a man's name,' she said, affecting nonchalance, sipping. 'My cheating father's. And I'm not so bothered about jettisoning that.'

Undercurrents of understanding passed between us. Of course she thinks badly of me, I thought. I drained my wine, which was weak, or at least tasted that way, and reached across the table for the bottle.

'Allow me,' said Harry.

Iris was saying something about property and ownership, but I had tuned her out. I was thinking about how Helena's mother had struggled with suicidal thoughts after the divorce;

about how, once, Helena had had to talk her down. The word 'chattel' floated in my direction several times.

'Even if her father wasn't a cheating bastard – sorry, darling, but you know how angry it makes me – she'd still be changing her name. As any wife of mine would. It's tradition.'

'It's patriarchy,' said Iris, with unexpected vehemence.

Alessia looked up from the menu. 'She can do what she wants,' she said, 'though I have to say it doesn't seem especially modern to me. Can we order?'

'Lobster?'

'I'm vegan, I told you.'

Laughter.

'The question that you have to ask,' said Iris, who simply would not let it go, 'is this: would he change his name for you?'

'Absolutely not,' said Harry.

'I'd change my name for Sophie,' said Greg, kissing me on the cheek. 'I don't care.'

I felt a creeping horror at how little I deserved his love, and stood up to go to the toilet, apologising.

Inside, Ky was waiting next to the kitchen pass, behind which I could just glimpse his mother and another woman stirring and clanging. I had to pass close to him in order to reach the corridor leading to the bathrooms, and as I did so, I turned to speak.

'He looks kind,' Ky said, before I could say anything. 'He looks like he will be a good husband to you.'

'Aren't you jealous?'

'Of course. I want to tear his limbs off and then fuck you right here while he lies dead on the floor.'

'Don't talk like that.'

'Because you like it?'

Ky's mother shouted something in Greek. He shouted back, smiling, and turned towards the plates.

After peeing, I continued sitting on the toilet. If I stayed in here long enough, perhaps they would forget all about me. They would eat their lobster and have their political arguments, and I would only come out when everyone had gone home and the restaurant and the beach were in darkness. Then, free, I would walk across the terrace and slip invisibly into the night.

Carolee Schneemann, Interior Scroll, 1975

It's 1975 in East Hampton, New York, and you're in a gallery, standing on a table in nothing but an apron. You take it off, and draw thick, dark brushstrokes across your naked form, before adopting a series of life-model poses for the assembled audience while you read from your work, Cézanne, She Was a Great Painter. *After putting down the book, you squat slightly, which widens your legs so that from your vagina you are able to slowly pull a scroll of paper. It's long and stringy, reminiscent of an enormous tampon string, or an umbilical cord. You unroll it. On it, you have written some criticisms that have been made of your work (criticisms like 'personal clutter', 'diaristic indulgence' and 'painterly mess'). You read them out.*

In this performance, you're saying this body is a site of liberation, my vulva is a sacred, creative space. You didn't want to pull a scroll out of your vagina and read it in public, you said. That made me laugh, because, really, who would? You did it, though, to make overt what the culture wanted to suppress.

FEMALE, NUDE

They said it was porn, of course, but your body was simply your material. You asked the question: 'Could a nude woman artist be both image and image maker?' and in response, the art world said: 'If you want to paint, put your clothes back on.' But you refused to bury your body. You made it central, instead.

I have tried to do the same, except on canvas. I'm not sure if I've succeeded, but it stands testament to the lifelong argument I have been having with you. For all your talk of sacred, creative spaces, you didn't think that motherhood could be either of those things. You dispensed with that aspect of femininity. Before I had my abortion, I read what you had said about yours: 'You are not invited into my body. I did not invite an alien being, a "child", into my future. I had a mountainside to climb, my back pushing against a heavy rucksack filled with paints, turpentine, oils, brushes, the roll of canvas.'

That is not how I thought of the child inside me. I could never separate the cluster of cells from its potentiality, knowing scientifically that the being in my womb was not a baby, while also knowing that it would be, if I let it. Some women are like you, Carolee – they can throw a party after every abortion – but not me.

On what would have been my due date, I painted my not-child. I imagined a toddler: pure and nude, a cherub. An archetype. Yet he felt real to me. I felt no guilt. It had been my choice. I could not have given him a life he deserved or the care he needed. It was, though, a heavy choice. That's my inconvenient truth.

I still talk to you in my head, sometimes, now that I am approaching the age I was when you died, having finally made it as one of the twentieth century's most important artists. On my bad days, I think you'd be disappointed in me, but growing life was, for me, a creative act. Perhaps not the greatest or most remarkable there has been. It certainly brought me no acclaim. But that life I made is also a kind of interior scroll, one that will keep on unfurling and writing itself long after my body is gone.

Sixth day, morning

I left the man who wanted me to bear his children sleeping and walked yet again down to the sea. I swam out as far as the monastery and then around the rocky outcrop, making sure to surveil all the little inlets as I went. But there was no sign of the person for whom I was searching, and if he was there, watching me, he did not make himself known, though I felt his gaze on my hips and arse as I walked back across the beach, felt the telltale tingle between my legs, the hardening of my nipples. I had thought that I could somehow put myself through a process of re-education, that I could emerge from it after a mere day and a night cured of my desire for him, but instead I felt it more than ever. As a feeling, it seemed to eclipse everything, even the guilt. The previous night, before going to sleep, I had treated myself to a replay, watched our writhing bodies dance across my closed eyelids until I drifted off, Greg's heavy hand placed protectively on my thigh, the man attached to it oblivious to my treacherous fantasy.

I woke needing more.

* * *

Alessia hardly spoke during our session; I had asked her not to, claiming a hangover and a need to concentrate. I had told Greg what I was doing in the studio, and he had agreed not to mention it in front of Harry, who was, he said, an ignoramus whose prurience we could do without. I could just imagine his lecherous face.

The rest of the evening had passed tensely, with Harry alternately pushing everyone's buttons and attempting to gain control with acts of largesse such as paying the bill. I had not risen to any of it, simply choosing to observe, and becoming wildly drunk as I did so. The others were not much better: when we returned to the house, we sat under the lighted olive tree and argued about the government, drinking Metaxa until someone suggested that we all get in the pool. Alessia was the first to disrobe, and as she did so I saw her body not as an artist but as a man might, with admiration, awe, even. It was an impulse I knew well, from adolescent trips to the beach. The presence of a beautiful woman had a magnetism to it that was powerful even to straight women. I would notice some girl or other who so perfectly encapsulated ideas of female beauty that I could barely look away, as though the looking would somehow reveal the secret. It was not lust, unless you count an urge to inhabit another's beauty as a form of lust, but more a symptom of the hypnotic power of a female body that conforms exactly. These girls, women, were just as they should be.

This is how you find yourself gazing at a woman from behind, admiring her figure for its perfect thinness, only to have her turn around and for you to realise she is a child.

I watched Alessia walk to the edge of the pool wearing nothing but a pair of silk briefs, and dive in. The others all followed, all stripped down to their underwear, even Greg, who was beginning to slur. I remained at the table, not wanting to walk the length of the pool observed by them, feeling pink and fat and wobbly, listening to them splashing and laughing. Besides, I wasn't wearing any underwear. Two days previously, I had lain spread-eagled on a rock while a man I scarcely knew pleasured me in broad daylight; now I felt only inhibition. I did not want Harry to see the curve of my stomach. I didn't care about the others; it was Harry. For some reason, his ruthless eye, his harsh, male judgement, made me nervous. And yet an uncomfortable realisation threw me: I wanted him to find me attractive, and by keeping my clothes on, I was increasing that chance.

In the studio, Alessia's body once again organised itself into a series of shapes. The circles of her breasts – how did they stay up so high? – the small shadows that they cast against her skin, were to be rendered in paint. The breasts alone would take one session.

In the silent, unspoken competition between women, breasts are held up for judgement. As a teenager, it was all about size. The girls who developed theirs earliest became automatically the most popular. The boys coveted them, ceased to stare their female classmates in the face, sent wolf whistles down the corridors as rudimentary mating calls. It was these girls who got boyfriends, who spoke with authority about fingering and orgasms while they sat smoking at the back of the bus. How we envied them, with our washboard chests and our bralettes from the children's section, stuffed with toilet tissue. Until their bellies and their breasts swelled, that is. Then they had got themselves in trouble. Most snuck off to the nearest city with an older sister or cousin for a quiet, anonymous procedure, but some sat their exams with their bumps rubbing up against the desks.

In my early twenties I had pitied these women, all mothers of four or five, their beautiful breasts, I imagined, drooping and depleted, their bodies marked irreversibly by birth. They had peaked too soon, had been too tempting to the male gaze, and it had trapped them. We were all so keen to avoid pregnancy then, were terrified of it. It wasn't until my late twenties that I truly understood that I could conceivably be someone's mother. Do you have children? people asked, people thought it was normal to ask, and it occurred to me that I was of that age now, the age where it was not just possible but supposed to be desirable. Surely you want it. It's what all women want.

It was at around this time that I had started seeing women who were mothers who were thinner and younger, and the rules of the competition seemed to shift imperceptibly. At twenty-three, to be a mother was to lose: it made a woman fat, and dull. She ceased to be a sexual entity. Men saw right through her. But now these women seemed to be winning: they got their bodies back, or never lost them. Suddenly, they had it all.

They are hard to stomach, these thoughts. You are not supposed to verbalise them.

'I invited Ky to join us for dinner tonight. I hope you don't mind.' I looked at Alessia's kindly expression. 'I know you're not bothered about him, but I didn't want to put you on edge.'

'Of course, it's fine.' I squinted at the canvas and put down my brush.

My eyes flickered down to Alessia's hips. So narrow were they that she would surely never succeed in producing a baby from between them. But what did I know?

We all sat by the pool with our books, which we placed next to our loungers optimistically before ignoring them to squint at our phones. I scrolled through an art-world spat about whether curators should be credited in reviews of their shows (obviously), then segued on to a more image-based platform to peruse photographs that women had uploaded of their bodies, all glossy, hard surfaces and taut muscles, the curves of their backsides angled towards the camera as their backs arched. They all wore the same, blank facial expression that had come to signify beauty: a sort of vacant, open-mouthed, wide-eyed look, borrowed, I thought, from porn. A prelude to a blowjob.

I looked for a while, feeling a mix of amusement and envy, then moved on to property sites, flicking through photographs of the small, bare rooms in poky houses in commuter towns we could just about afford, trying to muster some enthusiasm. They all had low ceilings and galley kitchens, small scraps of concrete yard out the back that looked as though they had been filled in to hide a body. These were houses far smaller than my parents' house, and they were poor by anyone's standards.

I tried to picture myself there, somewhere on a train line out: a crib in the box room, padding down sleepily to the galley kitchen to sterilise a bottle while Greg commuted into the city to work. There was no space to paint in any of these houses, no art scene to speak of in these humdrum towns. But that was life, wasn't it? This was how millions of people lived, and they were happy, or near enough to it. Why did I so struggle to picture myself there, and why did leaving the city take on a tinge of failure? Where had I got such grand ideas, that I could be someone in the world?

I used a finger to banish a two-bed terrace 'in need of updating' for two hundred and seventy thousand into the ether, and checked my email. The name of an admissions tutor hovered teasingly at the top of my inbox, and I felt a surge of anxiety in my chest, the palpitations that accompany a potential life-changing moment.

We regret to inform you . . . many hundreds of applications . . . hugely competitive . . . wish you all the very best in your future endeavours.

My eyes filled with tears behind my sunglasses and, embarrassed, I tried to wipe them away without anyone noticing. Greg had put his phone back down and was absorbed in *The Magus*. I had not told him, or indeed anyone, about applying for a master's in fine art. So convinced was I of the inevitability of emails like the one that I had just received, I had barely acknowledged it to myself.

I took several small, shallow breaths and closed my eyes tight. It wasn't the one I had desperately wanted, anyway. I allowed several minutes to pass, until I could be convinced there would be no wobble in my voice, and stood up.

'I might get myself a wine, if anyone else wants one?'

'It's only eleven.' Greg was wearing that annoying, concerned look, which I hated. It made me want to drink more.

'I've been up since six,' I said, bending down to put my phone back in the urn.

'It's so bloating,' said Iris. She sat impassively behind her large sunglasses, but I could sense her looking at my stomach.

I ignored her, addressing the others.

'Besides. We are on holiday.'

'Still, I really think . . .' Greg's voice was tight with the effort of trying to make it sound casual. There was nothing he hated more than a scene.

'I'll join you,' said Alessia. I looked up at her in surprise, knowing that, in an oblique way, she was trying to defend me. 'I'll call Agatha.'

'No, I'll get them,' I said. Greg was still looking at me, and I raised my eyebrows as if to say, 'What?'

Let him treat me as an incubator. It made the thrill of rebellion feel even better.

Artemisia Gentileschi, Susanna and the Elders, 1610

For a long time, no one cared about your work. Most was attributed to your father, Orazio, who taught you to paint. Your training probably started not long after your mother died in childbirth in 1605, leaving you, from the age of twelve, a mother to five younger siblings. Academics even claimed that your Susanna and the Elders, *painted when you were seventeen, was done by him.*

This, despite the fact that it bears your signature.

This old tale of sexual harassment and blackmail was an interesting choice of subject for a young woman who would be brutally raped a year later, and whose reputed beauty was already making you the subject of rabid male curiosity and innuendo.

When I saw it, on loan to the National Gallery, I thought that what makes it so obviously a work by your hand is your intimate understanding of the female form, as well as the psychology of how it feels to be a young woman under siege. Your nude Susanna looks so alive that she could stand up from where she cowers and wander from the canvas. For how long did you study your own figure reflected to be able to paint a nude like that? This is not a painting that exists for male titillation, but one that tells the story of life in a woman's body.

It was the year of the pandemic. Desperate for culture after weeks of confinement, I bought a ticket for your first major retrospective in this country. I walked around, masked, in that hallucinatory haze that comes from weeks of sleep deprivation. I had a feeling at that time of almost splitting open. The strain of keeping us both alive with so little contact with others was getting to me. I was not used to being around people, and my new status and the paraphernalia that came with it made me a source of annoyance to them, even though the baby slept throughout, her breaths a constant, reassuring snuffle against the warmth of my chest.

I was still negotiating this new, tender self. When I read that most of your children died in infancy and how, after you lost your four-year-old, Cristofano, only a daughter survived, I felt a visceral nausea.

I hadn't expected to laugh in the gallery, either, but the realisation was so delightful that I couldn't help it. There you were, unmissable, in almost every painting of a woman. Either your face or your body or your hair, or all three. Seeing these works side by side, in full size, made it unmistakable. You had put yourself everywhere. There you were as Cleopatra and Mary Magdalene and Danae and Saint Catherine of Alexandria, and, of course, Judith. Judith brutally beheading Holofernes as your maidservant holds him down, a painting full of blood and rage, a revenge fantasy in which you hold the sword, your brow knitted in calm concentration. When I was taught about you, my tutors were still very much of the mindset that our appraisal of art should be separate from the artists' biography (funny how that school of thought came in just as feminists were bringing stories like yours out into the light). They said your rape was irrelevant, but you only have to look at that painting to feel your fury with men.

But it was in front of your Susanna that I stood the longest. Here I am, you're saying. Let me show you what a woman can do. Because only a woman could have made this.

Sixth day, afternoon

By 2 p.m. I was drunk: that lovely wine-drunk high that feels giddy and whimsical. The art-school rejection had ceased to mean anything; nothing could touch me. Alessia and I had moved our sunloungers into the shade of the jojoba tree. She had stopped after two and fallen into a sleep, occasionally emitting elegant little snores from the back of her throat, but I had carried on, polishing off one terracotta jug and then going in search of another. Now, I desperately wanted a cigarette, but glancing over at Greg I knew this would be beyond the pale, and so I was trying to work out how to smoke one without him noticing. In the end, I didn't need one of my many rehearsed excuses, because he fell asleep, and didn't even stir when *The Magus* fell with a thud from his stomach on to the stones of the terrace.

I went to the bedroom to fetch my cigarettes, and was surprised to hear raised voices from another part of the house: the outraged plummy tones of a well-bred Englishman and the high, slightly desperate insistences of a woman attempting to defend herself. Harry and Helena. I couldn't make out what they were saying.

It was the hottest part of the day, and outside even the crickets had stilled. The ground beneath the olive trees had that parched quality that warned of its potential to catch alight. Not wanting to be the cause of the loss of thousands of acres of ancient trees in a forest fire spanning miles, I had brought a large glass of water with me for the purposes of catching any sparks and extinguishing my cigarette. The path was steep and, I knew, at some point would lead me to the wall marking the far periphery of the property. Sweat clung to my upper lip and I was grateful for the shade of the silvery leaves. I felt that I had been walking for a while, but it could really only have been a matter of minutes. Perhaps it was the groves that gave me a disjointed feeling of having travelled back in time. Ky had told me that some of the trees dated back to Roman times. The colonised inhabitants of the island had been guaranteed a certain sum for each tree they planted, and so they had planted millions.

The sea appeared and I found a pleasing groove in the surface of the wall in which to park myself. I lit up and exhaled, closing my eyes and thinking of nothing in particular, until I heard a *miaow* from the direction of the trees. I had had cats growing up and understood their language. This particular sound was a sort of plaintive greeting, a way of saying, *I'm here, human.*

The cat was extraordinarily beautiful, as Greek cats – often semi-feral and accustomed to the rough and tumble of outdoor life – rarely are. A long-haired tabby and so, probably, a boy. He had large, yellow, enquiring eyes and a milk-white bib.

Long whiskers. He stood for a moment where the tree line began, sizing me up, before stalking over with that feline false nonchalance. Then, purring, he hopped up on to the wall, nudging me with his cheeks. I hovered my left hand tentatively just above the fur on his back, and when he made clear that he would be amenable, I began to offer him strokes. This went on for a little while, long after I had smoked my cigarette. At a certain point, I realised I was crying. Cats do that to me. My cats growing up, Luna especially, were always the keepers of my secrets, their fur moistened with teenage tears, their faces impassive as they tolerated my need for comfort in the form of hugs.

I need to leave Greg.

The thought arrived with cold clarity. It was going to have to be me that did it. I may even have said it out loud.

'There's a secret for you,' I said to the cat.

It wasn't about Ky. Anyone could see that the infidelity was a symptom, a trying out of how it felt to be with a man who made no demands upon me. No, I needed to do it because it wasn't fair. Greg wanted children, and I couldn't, wouldn't, give them to him. I had tried to tell him, but in this I had been cowardly, and so, easier though it would be, he was never going to be the one to leave. I had left room for hope, yet my feelings were definitive.

The craven part of me knew that leaving meant that my MA, if I got in anywhere, would be a lot harder. I would probably never get on the property ladder. Greg brought financial stability and support to the relationship, and I knew what leaving would mean: less stability for me, and possibly, in the future, for Rosie. Admitting this made me feel like an awful person. I wondered if this was how the others saw me, as a grifter. Iris almost certainly did. The fact was that the marriage market was alive and well. At times, I felt like a heroine from an Austen novel, a woman of reduced circumstances who had luckily met a decent man of relative means who also loved and cared for her. What more could anyone want? My parents would be so disappointed. Disentangling myself was going to be an unpleasant business.

Poor, sweet Greg. He would not take it well. I could easily picture it, the way his face would crumple like a little boy's. He didn't cry much, but when he did, he did it without the usual masculine shame, and with the abandon of someone who, as a child, had been held, and comforted, and understood. He had been so kind to me, had always loved me, often too quietly and patiently for my own liking, but he had not wavered. Perhaps I didn't know how to be happy. That's what my mother would say. A good man who wanted a family with me, and who was happy to support my artistic endeavours despite the fact that they seemed doomed to amount to nothing.

I knew how it would play out. I would paint, happily, throughout the pregnancy. I might even feel content. It was not as though I found the notion of being pregnant abhorrent – far from it. I liked the idea of my body doing what it had been built to do, the cascade of hormones, a new, liberating plumpness. I would prop a full-length mirror against the wall next to my easel and I would paint my naked body, feeling beautiful and natural, a vessel for creation.

It would be after the baby came that the problems would arise. Greg would go back to work, and I would stay at home with the baby. The frustration and resentment would set in. I had once read an interview with Barbara Hepworth in which she'd said a mother-artist only needed half an hour a day for the images to grow in her mind, and she'd had triplets. Couldn't I be like Barbara Hepworth? Half an hour a day couldn't be too difficult to achieve, could it? Yet somehow I knew instinctively that even thirty minutes would be unattainable, and that I probably needed more time than that. I would fail both as an artist and as a mother. In a different life, a different time, a different society, maybe it would work. But in the here and now, I knew I was dreaming of the sort of creative freedom that only women of connections and means could realistically achieve.

The cat had stretched out next to me on the warm stone and was basking in the heat of the day. It occurred to me that I would soon burn. Far below, the beach was dotted with discarded towels. Everyone would be lunching in the shade of the taverna. I thought about Ky darting between the tables, his body moving quickly and gracefully, and I felt a jolt of lust. Then I thought about him coming for dinner, and panicked. It wasn't that I thought he would say anything; I knew that he wouldn't. It was that our mutual attraction was so intense that it seemed inconceivable that Greg wouldn't notice. What really concerned me was that Harry would see it, too, and would use it as an opportunity to exercise his penchant for fucking with people.

What did Helena see in him? He was intelligent enough, and she insisted that when they were alone, he really made her laugh, which we know is a powerful aphrodisiac. But he struck me as one of those men who was frightened of women. Having been educated separately, we would always be strange, unfathomable creatures to these eternal schoolboys: objects of undoubted beauty, worthy of gifts and compliments and entertaining jokes, even worship; deserving of education, certainly (one must be able to hold a conversation, after all). But beyond that, our needs and our concerns were arcane mysteries, our feelings irrational impulses not worth the fuss of solving. Helena was so fiercely clever, even if we weren't seeing much of that cleverness while she planned this wedding. If only she had met someone who shared her passions: an academic, or a writer. Instead she had gone for a corporate lawyer who could give her the financial stability her own father couldn't.

She'd get a bigger house but would have years of dinner parties ahead of her, where the men talked endlessly about their school days and never seemed to ask the women questions, and while they wouldn't exactly retire after eating for brandy and cigars, the respective genders would take it in turns to smoke fags in the garden. I'd be seeing a preview this evening, no doubt, though robbed of his dormitory chums Harry would have to seek solidarity in other male experiences. What exactly he would find in common with Greg and Edwin, both extreme art nerds, would remain to be seen. Meanwhile, Helena would watch him, her eyes glowing, laughing at all his jokes.

The thought made me want to stab my eyes out with a fork.

'You look nice.'

I was standing in front of the mirror in our room, trying on some earrings Greg had bought me. He was always good with gifts, another thing that made me feel terrible. These were baroque in that uniquely Sicilian way: large and gold and festooned with small white flowers and little clay lemons. I thought they might contrast nicely with the pale, minimalist silk of my dress, but they looked affected, so I tossed them aside.

'You're getting brown.' Greg walked over and put his arms around me. He was definitely studying our reflection.

'What are you thinking about?' I said.

He hesitated for a minute and then, breaking eye contact, said: 'I was thinking that in that dress, you look a bit like a bride.'

Instead of feeling irritated, I felt only tenderness. I couldn't begrudge him for wanting the things that he wanted. I could only blame myself for not being able to give them to him. I held him close to disguise the tears in my eyes until I collected myself, and then wandered into the bathroom to pee.

'Helena's the bride,' I called through.

I couldn't hear if he replied over the sound of the flushing toilet.

We walked out on to the terrace together, where Agatha

had laid out aperitifs. The others were all already there, Ky included. That afternoon I had worried about how I would act, and had decided on a polite distance. I was afraid of the story my face would tell if I looked at him, but knew that if I avoided looking at him entirely that might also seem suspicious. My eyes darted towards him, and I took in a blue shirt against the tan of his arms before I looked away.

'Sophie, you look like a statue of a goddess,' said Alessia. 'Very Grecian.'

I smiled, embarrassed, and helped myself to a limoncello spritz. I nodded along to the music that was playing, and then stopped when I realised it was 'You Know I'm No Good'. I didn't know how to be in my body. Greg slipped his hand into mine and gave me a gentle kiss on the forehead while I carefully studied a tree in the middle distance.

I was saved, unexpectedly, by Harry, who was already merry and telling a story at top volume, something farcical about a wedding he'd been to. There was something almost relaxing in being able to stand there and allow it to wash over me, making sure to laugh in the right places despite not processing the words that were being said. By the time he had finished talking, I had drained my first drink and was feeling calmer. I went to get another one and sidled up to Iris, who was looking bored.

'That was a bit much last night, about the name stuff,' I said.

'I know it was. I was a real harpy. But I just can't . . .'

'Stand him?'

We both laughed. A moment of complicity.

'God, he's a prick,' she said. 'I sort of thought she would realise, but she seems totally blind to his faults. I just can't work out if he's a standard, workaday prick, or the dangerous sort that will make her miserable and potentially ruin her life.'

'I've been wondering that, too.'

'The thing is, you can't say, "Don't marry him." People say it in films. In novels, even. Never in real life. It's too much of a social hand grenade.'

'All we can do is be there when it falls apart. Hard to watch, though.'

She nodded.

We were over by the drinks table, out of earshot. I watched Ky lean in to something Alessia was saying, his cheek almost brushing her ear. She smiled up at him. They looked so right together, bronzed and gorgeous, eyes locking. I looked around for Greg. He was talking to Edwin, who, by the way he was moving his hands, seemed to be going into great detail about the structure of one of his installations, miming its construction in stages.

Iris smiled at him with an emotion that could almost be fondness. 'You'd be throwing away a good one, you know,' she said. 'And what for?' She looked at me.

'Oh, I know he's a good one. I know, I know. It's what makes it so bad.'

'I never thought you'd get into a mess like this.'

I shrugged and bit into a stuffed vine leaf, which disintegrated slimily in my mouth. 'I didn't, either. Still, three days to go. I'll tell him it's over when we get home.' I took a big gulp.

Iris put a hand on my arm and then awkwardly removed it. 'Just stop touching your mouth so much when he talks to you,' she said. 'You were doing it the other day. It's so obvious.'

I gave her a quick nod, indicating that the others were motioning us over, and then said, 'Thanks.'

At dinner, I was seated between Edwin and Alessia, so I didn't have to worry about how often I put my finger to my lips. Instead, we all enjoyed a good-natured argument about an exhibition we had all seen, followed by a nostalgic discussion of London nightclubs past whose doors had long since closed. Though I was aware of Ky's presence, I had also relaxed enough to be able to follow and conduct a conversation. He was on the other end of the table, speaking mostly with Helena and Harry, and then he and Greg had a long, involved tête-à-tête, which, from what I could glean, was mostly about museum administration.

As it had been for all the dinners at Alessia's villa, the table was simply but beautifully decorated, this time with deep blue Murano glassware and taper candles in small, hand-painted holders that were abstract in that way that still made it obvious they were human figures with tits. I was surprised that Alessia could be so humdrum. Perhaps her father had bought them.

To start, Agatha had laid out platters of octopus carpaccio, in the Italian style, sliced to a cloudy transparency, like tissue paper, and glazed with oil, lemon and freshly cracked black pepper. Greg gave me a look, and I returned it in silent apology. You don't have to eat it, my eyes said to him, but now is not the time for your highly intelligent invertebrate rant. I wouldn't be embarrassed for class reasons – Greg was better acquainted with the rules of behaviour than I was – but for cultural ones. I didn't want Ky to feel judged. The octopus had come from his family's fishing boat.

'Best octopus I've ever had, mate.' Harry had become slurry. 'Let's all raise a glass.'

'*Yamas*!' said Alessia, while Ky smiled and held up his hands in sheepish mime.

'Do you ever take people out on the boat?' asked Harry. 'Quite fancy a boat trip myself. Maybe tomorrow?'

'Harry! You don't just invite yourself on to people's boats.'

'You can invite yourself to people's summer houses, so why not people's boats?' he shot back at Helena.

Greg mimed chewing and got away without eating the rest of his octopus by feeding it to me in a way that felt awkward and uncharacteristic. He had never fed me in my life, but I took the mouthful. I caught Ky's glance and turned my attention back to Harry, whose cheeks were now very red.

'We could,' said Ky. 'We're not using it in the afternoon, and the weather is supposed to be OK. However, it is not . . . how do I explain? It is not a pleasure boat.'

'He means it smells like fish,' Alessia said. 'It's a shame my father's boat is in the yard. But there's enough space on Ky's family boat to sunbathe, and we can swim off the side.'

'Sounds great!' said Iris. Her tone sounded jarringly exuberant. Was she drunk?

Greg gave me another pleading look, and I almost felt worse about the octopus and the boat trip than I did about the cheating.

Later, when the main course was a stripped carcass that had been picked to the bones, and traces of the halva mousse with chocolate sauce could be found only on the fine cloth napkins, Alessia racked up the lines and we all danced by the pool. I wasn't going to have any, I told myself. I was wary of the potential for verbose self-exposure. That lasted an hour, and then I relented, as I always do. I avoided conversing, however, and focused on the music.

One of the things I had always loved about Greg was what a great dancer he was. Much like his penchant for a well-cut suit, such skill was unusual in an Englishman, especially one as modest and self-effacing as he usually was. He had that natural rhythm and looseness in his body, coupled with a complete lack of self-consciousness, that I suspected came from the fact he had done so much acting in college. It wasn't something I had ever seen in lads growing up, though the thing about working-class lads is that at least they do dance, even if it's after ten pints and there's quite a lot of fist pumping involved. It's the awkward public schoolboys who don't know what to do with their neglected bodies.

Which is a longwinded way of saying that Harry was doing the sort of comedy wedding-dance moves that only people who can't relax enough to let themselves go opt for. I could see a pained look on Helena's face as she tried to join in with him; she'd told us that they were taking ballroom classes for the big day.

Meanwhile, it was as though Greg seemed determined to suddenly show me all the reasons I had fallen in love with him. He was spinning me and occasionally even dipping me, but in such a charming way that it didn't seem cheesy. And I was enjoying it.

Maybe I'm wrong, I thought, hazily. Maybe we're good together.

On the side of the terrace, Ky sat and smoked a cigarette and pretended not to watch us.

'I'm going to smoke,' I said to Greg. And though he looked disappointed, he was enjoying 'Never Too Much' so much that he wasn't about to break character to argue. Another thing I loved about him: abandoned on the floor, he always just carried on dancing.

I sat down next to Ky, but didn't look at him. I couldn't.

'He's a good dancer,' he said, also not looking at me.

'Yes.'

'You want one?'

I nodded and he put the cigarette between my lips and lit it.

'What?' I said. I was looking at him now.

'You know what.'

I felt what he wasn't saying between my legs. 'How can we?'

'The studio . . .'

'It's too close. We can't.'

'The . . . the boat?'

'The boat?'

'There's a small cabin.'

'Greg is coming. It's too risky.'

'After that.'

'No. The other day was the last time.'

'It can't be.' He smiled, then. 'How am I supposed to live?' He put his hand to his chest with a flourish.

'You're being dramatic,' I said, flirting. I felt the same way. I ashed on the ground and took a deep inhale, looking up at the sky, back towards the dance floor, anywhere but at his face. I heard him take that small intake of breath you need before saying something, but I held up my hand.

'What the *fuck*?' Helena flopped down next to me, clearly drunk. 'Why are you wearing *white*?'

'I don't understand,' I said, as Ky stood up, gave me one long last look, and made his way to the kitchen.

'It's my hen party,' she hissed. 'And you're wearing *white*.'

I looked at her for a moment, stunned. She made a face and a gesture that meant, explain yourself.

'I didn't realise there was a moratorium on wearing white for the entire duration of this holiday just because you are getting married,' I said. 'It's Greece. In July.'

'You're supposed to be my best friend, but I just don't feel as though you care about my wedding.'

I wanted to say that it wasn't chic for anyone to care this much about a wedding, but I was worried she would cry, or slap me, and so instead I shrugged in a way that could be construed as apologetic, stood up, kissed her on the head, and walked over to the table to get more cocaine.

After my line, I put the note to one side and lifted my face from the table. Through the French windows, in the dim light of the kitchen, Ky and Alessia were leaning towards each other, talking. Her face was tilted up towards his and his head was bent as he scratched the back of his neck in a gesture I had come to recognise as perplexed. She caught my eye, and for a fleeting second, the look she gave me was that of a guilty child caught in a forbidden room.

Emma Amos, Work Suit, 1994

I love this self-portrait. It's the pissed-off expression on your face. And yes, it's a nude, in a way. You've appropriated Lucian Freud's pallid ageing naked body, from his self-portrait Painter Working, Reflection, and are wearing it like a jumpsuit, his flaccid penis hanging between your legs, making it ridiculous. In your left hand, you confidently brandish a paintbrush. Beneath your feet is sprawled a nude white woman – is she a person or merely an image? She is cartoonish, her mouth opened in shock. You're asking, 'Is this what you have to embody, to make it in the art world? This maleness?' It's a scathing critique.

I think about you, as a little girl in segregated Georgia, sneaking into the museum at night. Everyone said from the start that you were an artist. It was a shock when you encountered white people who refused to accept that. I imagine you in 1960s New York, traipsing from gallery to gallery, only to be met with rejection after rejection. It was crushing, you said, and you stopped being able to paint. Then you had a child, then got pregnant with another. That's when they offered you a show, but to make all the work they *wanted didn't feel possible. 'Now, young women have assistants, have babies, and continue to work. They want it all,' you told your friend bell hooks, thirty years later.*

Now I am old, too. It felt more possible for my generation than it did for yours, at least if you had money. Does it feel more possible for our daughters? The culture isn't changing fast enough for artist mothers. I couldn't afford an assistant, but I still wanted it all, especially at first. In those early months, I cried and cried. I felt like I would never work again, would never come to anything of significance. Then I decided the weight of abandoned dreams is too much for any child to carry.

Now I look back on all I have made and I am proud, even though I never sold a painting. (Well, once, but that hardly counts.)

What is admirable to me is how you kept on working. You made amazing mixed-media pieces about the civil rights movement and the whiteness of the art world. And you refused to offer up Black female bodies: there was always something in the way, preventing us from being able to ogle a full nude, or they were halfway off the canvas, as though making for the exit. Instead, you made use of art historical nudes. I like how disrespectful you were, how cheeky. You drew attention to Western art's racist, colonial roots. To Gaugin, especially, for how he fetishised Teha'amana — the thirteen-year-old Tahitian girl he took as a wife — in paint.

White male artists in Paris and elsewhere had historically used Black women as models, because they were cheaper, and would turn them into white women on canvas. You said you could spot which ones, if you knew how to look. That a Black woman artist walking into the studio would always be a political act.

You were a trailblazer, yet you said: 'I really thought that I would have done better.' My heart broke to read that. And this: 'Here I am at seventy-three, and I wake up in the morning and say, "I have one piece at the Museum of Modern Art. I wonder, is it still there?"'

You got your first major retrospective in 2021, a year after your death. I wish you could have known.

Seventh day, morning

That night I dreamed again that I was a mother. In the dream I woke, tossing, in damp sheets to feel an empty space next to me, searching for my child. As I stood, I heard her cry, muffled and indistinct, and, gripped with terror, I groped the bedding, feeling for her tiny body and finding nothing. Standing, it came to me that I was in the darkened rooms of the villa in Artemonas where Ky had taken me: the peeling plaster, that damp old church smell, it was the same. I wandered the dark corridors, following the cry, until I came to the room I had been in with Ky. A woman stood with her back to me, silhouetted against the dawn light on the balcony, making little comforting *shhh shhh* noises as the baby rooted and snuffled. The child was safe, because she was in my own mother's arms. I would know her outline anywhere. Or so I thought – but then she turned and handed me the baby, and it was Alessia's cold, appraising eyes that looked back at me, and I felt afraid.

But then the tone shifted, and I basked in the elation of having my baby in my arms, kissing every inch of her face as she cooed and looked at me, inhaling her slightly stale milky smell, running the pads of my fingers across the softness of her cheek. A serene acceptance had come over me, but beyond that, a love that had, in the moment she was back with me, ceased to be the terrifying fear I had felt when I awoke. Instead, sublime delight.

Then I woke, for real this time, and ran to the toilet to vomit.

At some point, while I emptied my stomach for what felt like hours, I sensed the touch of his fingertips at my back, and I realised that Greg was gently stroking me, holding my hair with his other hand. 'Shhh, shhh,' he said, making the same noises as in my dream. He would be a good father to someone, and that knowledge felt painful in that moment.

'A good morning to be taking a boat trip,' he said, and I groaned.

I wanted to get out of it, but also wanted to see Ky, could not envisage not being near him. What a nasty, duplicitous creature I was. I had not understood my capacity for cruelty until now. The hangover made the self-loathing worse.

As Ky had predicted, the sea was calm and there was hardly a breeze when we headed down to the bay mid-morning. Everyone was worse for wear, but Harry was really making a meal of his suffering, and so we were already on edge as we made our way down the path. No one felt like taking a boat trip. Hardly a word had been exchanged by the time we were greeted by Ky, who, in a white linen shirt and knee-length denim cut-offs, looked as good as I had ever seen him. It pained me not to be near him and so I pilfered short, darting little glances, which he caught and returned while Greg rested his face in his arms at the side of the boat. I wore my black bikini and a sheer, pale blue cover-up that looked more expensive than it was.

Ky handed me a bottle of water and his fingers lingered on mine for a second. I noticed Harry noticing.

'So, where are we heading?' Greg was speaking in the trepidatious tone he always used when about to enter a body of water.

'I think we will go to some hidden bays for swimming,' said Ky. 'Then stop at a fishing village for lunch. I was going to take you to the uninhabited island of Polyaigos, but it's the season of the *meltemi* wind and so I'm not sure it's a good idea. The currents can change very quickly, and the sea can get quite rough.'

'Yeah, doesn't sound like a good idea', said Greg.

'Oh, come on!' said Harry. 'Where's your sense of adventure?'

'I like the idea of visiting an uninhabited island,' said Helena, in her it's-my-party voice. 'Can we?'

'Is it very dangerous?' I asked, seeking reassurance for Greg's benefit.

'No, not very,' said Ky. 'You might get seasick on the way home, is all.'

'We can cope,' said Harry.

'Can we?' Greg gave me a desperate look.

Alessia looked at me with laughter in her eyes. 'Yes!'

Ky relented. 'OK,' he said, 'but I'll need to pack some lunch.'

After Ky's mother had given us half of the cold mezze in the taverna's kitchen, as well as an ice box containing several large plastic bottles of table wine and something clear and smelling of petrol fluid that he said she made herself, we all made ourselves comfortable on the deck of the boat. Harry and Helena took the shaded platform in the centre upon which you could lie relatively comfortably, topped as it was with two padded, gym-style mats, and Edwin and Iris, too, grabbed a small square out of direct sunlight. Ky and Alessia, having been raised on sailing boats from infancy, took charge, while I made an effort not to look at his tanned, wiry body. This left the bench running around the edge to me and Greg, who was already beginning to look green at the gills though we hadn't even left the shallows yet.

I tried to position myself in a way that showed off the angles of my body to their best advantage. I have always hated sitting in a bikini, the way your paunch juts forward over the seam of your bottoms unless you spend the whole time breathing in and leaning back. It's simply impossible for me to appear nonchalant in swimwear. Even then, when my body was young and lithe and unscarred by events, I could not escape the feeling that I was seeing myself through the eyes of men, and that the sight was an affront. Ky didn't seem to notice. In fact, he seemed to be busying himself with looking anywhere but at me. It was only when I moved my eyes away from him that

I saw Harry had fixed me with an insolent stare. He saw me catch him looking and, instead of looking away, embarrassed, he moved his eyes very obviously down towards my breasts and ... did he lick his lips? If so, the flick of his tongue was so rapid and subtle, like that of a lizard's, that only I could have noticed. I pretended to scratch the side of my face as a way of giving him the finger.

The astonishing clearness of the sea was a much more pleasing sight, and as we changed direction, I moved over to the sunny side of the boat to get a better look. I had never seen sea like this before coming to Greece. The sea that we swam in every summer holiday as children, the sea that had almost claimed Rosie, was far murkier. It seemed to have absorbed the greyness of the British sky even on beautiful, clear days, when it would shimmer almost silver. Of course, I loved the Atlantic's salty roughness, the way its waves slapped any tiredness or bad feelings out of you as they crested, how you could catch glimpses of all the debris that had been wrenched from the seabed. Here, shells and seaweed sat undisturbed to the point where I could pick out their individual features as I leaned over.

'It's incredible,' I said to Greg, who only nodded.

Iris came over to look, and to my surprise she linked her arm with mine in a schoolgirlish gesture of affection. She leaned her head towards my ear. 'I saw Ky coming out of the studio this morning,' she said, in a low voice.

'I don't know what that's supposed to mean,' I said. 'Maybe he was drunk and couldn't make it down the hill.'

'Or maybe he was in there with Alessia,' she said.

It had crossed my mind the night before that they might sleep together; it wasn't like she had anyone with her. I shrugged. I wondered what Ky had made of my painting of her. It wasn't quite finished, but you could now see what it was going to become.

'It's not like I own him,' I said, affecting carelessness. In fact, my whole body seemed to be vibrating with envy. 'I went to bed with Greg, after all. It's over. It has to be over.'

We both paused to look over at them. Alessia had her hand on his forearm in a way that managed to be both relaxed and proprietary. Why hadn't she been threatened by me? Why, in fact, had she encouraged our liaison? I had assumed it was because her ardor had waned into feelings of affectionate friendship, but I found myself wondering then if she still loved him. The destructive, petulant part of me wanted to claim my territory, to walk over to him and grab him and put my lips to his in front of everyone. There was something almost violent in my need for his body that seemed to make me immune to the fear of consequences. If I could have pushed Greg overboard in that moment and got away with it, I would have.

Iris said nothing. We stood like that for a while in silence, and I found myself wondering about her and Edwin. They were one of those couples who made sense, aesthetically, with their angular cheekbones, their art-world hair and directional ways of dressing. They had an essence that I could envisage working well at gallery openings, but which didn't make as much sense on holiday. Iris looked the part with her oyster pearl earrings and her minimalist linen cover-up, but there was a tightness to her jaw that betrayed her chronic inability to relax. Perhaps she had Mediterranean boat-trip fatigue. Edwin, in contrast, seemed to be loving his time on the island, and was stretched out on the deck, his stomach taut under his open shirt, a sleepy smile on his face. He could afford to relax after the rapturous response to his show. He planned to return to New York in the fall to make new work, and Iris, she said, would follow. Perhaps there he would get to see more of her fun side.

Halfway to the island, we stopped in a secluded bay for a swim. The cliffs were pockmarked with caves, the surface of the rock flickering with the reflected blue of the ocean. It was long before midday, but when we stopped, Ky brought out the plastic bottle and poured shots into plastic cups, handing one to each of us despite protestations that it was too early. The raki burned the back of my throat. I held out my cup and he poured me another, his eye contact lingering for just a little too long. Feeling my cheeks flushing, I turned my face away and pulled off my shirt as Alessia performed a perfect swan dive from the side of the boat.

There's a special shade of aquamarine that the Greek sea takes on when it collides with the pale rock of an island cliff face. When I think back to that summer, which shaped me in so many ways, it is that sparkling sea that comes to mind. I have never been able to capture it in paint, and I don't mean photorealistically. I am not a landscape painter, though I am classically trained. I can render a tree that looks like a tree if it is demanded of me. Yet when I have tried to incorporate that sea into my self-portraits, something of its spirit has eluded me.

I think I was happy that day. Perversely, you might say, as the implosion of my personal life and relationship was looming, and I was well aware of it. Is that what you would call being in love? A daft, beatific feeling of peace that flies in the face of hostile circumstances? If so, then I would say that I was in love.

Greg wouldn't swim, and his priggishness made me feel better about it all. The rest of us spent a glorious half-hour in that place, before drying off and setting sail again for the islet, our stomachs rumbling. More raki was consumed, and someone opened the wine, which made for a wobbly wade on to shore. By the time we had put the rugs down and set out the feast, we were all drunk and starving. I sat there, sea- and weather-beaten, relishing the saltiness of the feta and the taramasalata between my lips, how it contrasted with the acidity of large, plump tomatoes, their flesh rough against my tongue and washed down with gulps of more wine. When we had finished we had more raki, and Helena wept to be in a place so beautiful, and to be a bride, and we all forgot our boredom with her wedding and enveloped her in a shared embrace, slurring well wishes.

People fell asleep in the shade one by one, until it was only Ky and Greg and me who were still awake, and Greg wasn't going to come into the water, even though Ky made a show of urging him to join us. And so, as we swam out together to a safe distance, I felt that fizzing thrill of being alone with him, despite the fact that Greg was watching. I could still make out his pale, pensive, frowning face from so far out.

Neither Ky nor I spoke until we were certain we could not be overheard, and even then, when he finally turned to me, his voice was low.

'I know I can't touch you.'

'I wish you would. It's all I can think about.'

'Don't say that to me. You don't know how difficult this is. I just want to pull you to me. I can't stop looking at your body, your face. I try to look at the horizon or at the boat's controls, but all I can think about is your skin and your body and how it feels.'

'I do know how difficult it is. I feel it, too. But I also feel really fucking guilty. He's right there, Ky. It's cruel. He's kind and sweet and, OK, we want different things, but he doesn't deserve to have the person he loves fucking someone else under his nose.'

'You said it wouldn't happen again, but you are talking as though it will.'

'How can it?'

We were both treading water, side by side, our faces both turned towards the shore, a picture of conversing innocence.

'What if I told you it was going to happen and that you can't stop it?' he said.

'That doesn't sound . . . consensual,' I said.

'Except you know that you want me to take you. You just don't want the responsibility. Well I'm telling you, you want it too much to stop yourself, so stop fighting it and just yield.'

'I can hardly yield here, can I?'

At that point, he turned to face me and said: 'Lower your bikini for me.'

I paused, gave a short laugh. 'Top or bottom?'

'Go on. He won't see.'

'He can see. He's looking.'

'I promise, I will hardly move.' He shifted slightly so that he was about half a foot closer, but he was staring forwards again. To Greg, it would have just looked as though we were chatting amicably.

I took one breast, and then the other, out of the small triangles of fabric that contained them.

'I'm going to touch you now.'

'Be careful. I think . . .' I was on the verge of hyperventilating.

He reached sideways, fixing his eyes on the cove, and pinched a nipple between his fingers. He rolled it, quite forcefully, between the tips, then pinched again. 'Do you like that?'

'You know I do.'

'Say you like that.'

'I like that.'

He did the same with the other. I thought I might actually sink.

'I want them to stay hard for me. Can you do that?'

'I mean, it's quite warm out of the water.' I was incapable

of talking like that with a straight face, and snorted a little as I said it.

'Then if you feel them getting soft again, I want you to go somewhere private and pinch them yourself. You can touch between your legs, too. I want you to be ready for me.'

'For when?'

'For tonight. When we fuck.'

'Ky, we can't.'

He shook his head, his eyes creasing at the corners. 'We can't not.'

I was laughing then, and so was he. I felt the imminent insanity of what we would do later, and it was freeing, like that moment between someone handing you a dodgy pill and you placing it on to your tongue.

'Fuck it.'

'As you say: fuck it.'

Jenny Saville, Propped, 1992

You sit, staring down at us from narrowed eyes, surveilling us from a great height. Your mouth is a parted Cupid's bow; your expression pained and vulnerable; your head tilted to one side. And then: your breasts, smushed together between your fleshy upper arms, huge, but not as big as the hands that clutch the bulging fat of your gigantic thighs, your fingers digging into the flesh as it spills over the side of the stool on which you sit. You wanted to make a painting of a nude in your own voice, and you more than succeeded.

You are looking down as though at your reflection in a clouded mirror. Gouged into the mirror is an inverted quote by Luce Irigaray. 'If we continue to speak in this sameness – speak as men have spoken for centuries, we will fail each other. Again, words will pass through our bodies, above our heads – disappear, make us disappear.'

Propped *made you famous overnight; Charles Saatchi bought most of your work and became a patron. By 1997, you were in the Royal Academy. By the late 2010s,* Propped *had broken the record for the most expensive painting by a living woman artist.*

'I think in paint,' you said, and flesh is one of the most beautiful things to paint. I believe that artists are half made before they even pick up a brush. It's in the way we look. You watched the way your piano teacher's thighs smushed together, how her fat moved, fascinated. You weren't interested in conventional beauty.

Your art historian uncle meant you were well versed in the Old Masters. It was at Glasgow School of Art that the epiphany came: the great artists of the past were not women. You didn't want to be the one just looking, or just looked at. You wanted both roles. You established your signature style, huge canvasses using thick oil paints, which are smeared, scraped, stroked in impasto brush strokes. How I love the way you channel the poetry of paint into figurative art. Your command of paint is that of an abstract expressionist, your preoccupation with the figure that of a Renaissance Old Master. You are not afraid to reference the greats, to compare how you build a painting from abstraction to figuration in the same way Michelangelo built forms from marble.

Your talent is awe- and envy-inspiring. It is inspiring. You showed it was possible. Then you became a mother. When you said, 'I spent my life painting flesh, and then I was making flesh in my body,' I felt that – how a body moves from one to two. You didn't want to make work about it, thought they'd take you less seriously, but something happens, doesn't it, afterwards? Your soul shifts.

All those Madonnas, they start to hit differently. I wept, like a madwoman, at a Raphael, cringing, but unable to stop.

No wonder you wanted to redraw, scrawl over, almost, those images by Leonardo and Michelangelo, their pentimenti Marys hovering metaphorically like charcoal ghosts behind your body as you manhandle writhing babies, pregnant and knackered. No wonder they put The Mothers *in Florence, alongside its inspiration. On the same footing as the greats. How did that feel?*

You did it, Jenny. You did it painting after drop-off and then again post-bedtime, late into the night. You mastered the art of looking and being looked at in a way that only you could. You said to hell with your visions of perfect female beauty. You are a disruptor: of history, of tradition, of convention, of aesthetics. You refused to disappear. I like to think you did it for all of us.

Seventh day, evening

That night, we screwed against the cool wall of the only building on the islet, a church slightly set back from the bay. It was stupid and risky and, most of all, unkind, especially considering the events of earlier that evening. For the entire swim back to shore, Ky had told me what he intended to do to me, and I feared the expression on my face when I staggered out of the sea may have told Greg something. Either way, he was tetchy and restless for the rest of the day, and when the others were awake and the time came to leave, as predicted, the wind had changed. It wouldn't be as rough as all that, Ky said, 'Just a little, how would you say it, bouncy?', but that was enough for Greg. He had a sort of panic attack, and walked away into the olive trees, hyperventilating. I followed, itching with a girlfriendish compassion that he interpreted more accurately as pity, so he told me to fuck off, and when he came back he announced that he wouldn't be getting back on to the boat until the sea was calm the next morning.

'There is no need,' Ky tried to tell him. 'We would be sleeping on a cold beach for no reason.'

Yet Greg would not be moved, and the others, wine-drunk and seduced by the prospect of a campfire and a night spent under the stars, went with it. There were blankets on the boat and enough food and drink to see us through, so why not?

Around the fire, we spoke of ghosts and demons. Helena, who had been raised Catholic, told of an exorcism in the upstairs bedroom of her cousin's house. Harry's offering was less haunting, the sort of urban legend that has been trotted out around campfires for generations: a curse whispered in a mirror, or a murderer banging a cheerleader's decapitated head against the roof of a car, that sort of thing. Iris was, somewhat surprisingly, also game. Her tale of being shipped off to her grandmother's every childhood summer, and the footsteps that circled her bed at night as she lay alone in the darkness of the nursery, left us all shuddering. She made light of it all in that blasé manner posh people use when they talk about ghosts, as if they are just part of the antique furniture. She had a flair for storytelling, yet as she spoke, I found myself imagining how abandoned she must have felt.

And then came Ky's turn. He told a story from ancient Greece of a woman who returned from the dead to consort with a young male guest in her mother's house. 'Her name was Philinnion. She had died unmarried and been entombed many months before,' he said, 'only for her to return one night to make love to this young, handsome guest.'

'How can a ghost make love to anyone?' asked Helena.

Harry made a snorting noise.

'Ancient Greeks saw ghosts differently. She was more

like . . . an animated corpse, I suppose,' said Ky. 'A bit like a vampire. Anyway, a servant went to the door of the bedchamber and was distressed to find there her old mistress, risen from the dead. She ran to Philinnion's mother, who had been suspicious of this mysterious guest, to tell her that her daughter was alive, but the mother thought the servant had gone mad. Eventually, she was convinced to go and look, but seeing only in the darkness the couple's sleeping forms, she decided not to disturb them and to wait until morning. But by dawn, the girl had already left. When confronted, the young man recounted how the girl had come to him every night, presenting her ring and breast plate as evidence. These were the items with which Philinnion had been buried. At the sight of these treasures, her mother screamed and wailed as she had upon her daughter's burial.

'That night the girl came again, and ate and drank with the young man as normal. As he had promised to alert the parents if she returned, he secretly sent his slaves away to tell them. They arrived quickly and, overjoyed, embraced their daughter, only for her to return to her deceased state as punishment for their having initially begrudged her presence as a guest in her father's house – hospitality is important to us Greeks, as you know. And so they lost and were forced to grieve their daughter anew.'

'How sad,' said Iris.

'How *creepy*,' said Harry.

'What happened to the young man? It must have been very shocking to learn that he had slept with a dead girl.' Of course Greg would think of that.

'He killed himself. And the townspeople, who were understandably spooked – I think that is the right word – burned Philinnion's body outside the city to ensure that she never again returned from the dead.'

As Ky spoke, I watched the movement of his mouth, the way he gestured with his hands when he talked, his dark, dark eyes, the faint muscular outlines visible through his T-shirt. I could look at him for the rest of my days, I thought.

Later, against the wall of the church, my skirt hitched up, his hands in my hair.

'Were you trying to tell me something with that ghost story?' I grazed my teeth against his earlobe.

His breath was hot on my neck when he laughed. 'That you were entombed but I raised you from the dead?'

'I'd come back from the dead for you.' I too, was laughing when I said it, but it was true. Ky made me do things that I had not thought possible. An hour earlier, I had stood up from my position next to Greg's sleeping but restless form, and had walked off into the darkness of the olive grove without looking back, and without a care for who saw me.

Let him see, I thought. Let them all see.

Yoko Ono, Cut Piece, 1965

1965, New York. A woman sits silently on a stage before an audience, her legs off to one side. She is wearing her best clothes. In front of her, she places a pair of scissors. As a woman takes to the stage, picks them up and starts to snip, it becomes clear what is happening: the artist is inviting members of the audience to remove her clothing. This is your performance, Cut Piece.

In the darkness of the lecture theatre, I watched the video of them stripping you. While they snip away at you, you stare ahead, expressionless. You have said that when you perform this piece, you have to go into a trance in order to not feel too frightened. My heart is in my mouth as I watch, listening to the incongruous laughter and applause of the people in the audience. The tension is palpable: here is a woman who has surrendered her power and submitted to the whims of others. You have become the object of their gaze, and some of the people looking and cutting will be aroused by you as you grow more exposed. How far will they go? How far will you let them go? Who holds the power?

Some are tentative, respectful. They snip a small fragment. Others are aggressive and lascivious. It is uncomfortable viewing, watching a man laughingly cut away your vest down to your bra. It feels predatory, horrible. It is the only moment where your stillness almost breaks: there's a flicker in your expression, the shine of tears; perhaps he hears your breath speed up. We are witnessing the visceral understanding that you can't control what happens next. Yet you've consented to this act of intimacy and complicity.

You performed Cut Piece *a total of six times, and twice in London, they cut away at your clothes until you were fully nude.*

Some men do not see us as people. I always think about that when I watch the footage. It is a fact that we know in our bones, a fact that terrifies if we think about it too much. Like every woman, my romantic life has included a series of red flags and near misses. I have been lucky to have mostly loved good men. The women I have loved have not always been so lucky. They have had men that have cut away at the parts of them they didn't like until little remained. That's what happened to Helena, over the years.

So much of your work has been overshadowed by your marriage to one of the most famous men in the world. How did it feel, when people mocked your art? When they dismissed it as avant-garde bullshit? I don't think I'd have coped, but despite the sexism and racism, you persisted. So much of your work, and how it pays tribute to women, especially mothers, has moved me.

FEMALE, NUDE

When my daughter was still small, I went to your retrospective and performed Bag Piece. I know that in the original conception, the participant was supposed to be fully nude. I wondered what would have happened had I tried that, sixty years later, as a woman approaching middle age. Would I have been arrested for public indecency? Despite much doom-mongering, I did not feel ashamed of my new body: my sagging breasts, emptied of milk, my nipples now large and wrinkled, my newly rounded stomach and hips. My stretch marks and my beautiful scar that marked the moment my child was freed from me and quickly whisked away because she was blue.

This body felt right. If anything, it felt more natural to me than it ever had. I felt liberated by my invisibility to men. At the changing rooms after swimming, I no longer tried to conceal myself as I had before. The fact of my body, what it had achieved and endured, made me feel proud and shameless.

I did not strip before donning the bag, as you had, but being inside it made me feel free. As in Cut Piece, a female body stands before an audience, but in Bag Piece, she is completely free of their gaze. I felt the pure joy of dancing as a shape, and not a woman, for the first time. It was euphoric. Thank you for giving me that moment, at a time when things felt very hard.

Not that I danced for very long, or at least not that day. I lay down on the floor for a while. I was very tired in those days. Still am.

Eighth day, morning

In the cold dawn on a remote beach, a realisation. How I reached it, I still don't know. Had it emerged from my subconscious during a forgotten dream, or had there been some sign of her presence as he pinned me against the wall? Some gasp, some rustle in the foliage? Or was it simply the human being's atavistic instinct that they are being watched?

I woke for the second time that day to feel Greg's fingers lightly dappling my inner thigh. Cold and stiff from the night, we had sailed back at sunrise, falling into bed and out cold by mid-morning. Greg had been quiet but affectionate on the boat, his fingers entwining with mine as if to silently apologise for his tantrum of the previous afternoon. Now, I could feel his growing penis against my backside, and made a muffled, wary groan.

'I'm not feeling it,' I said, but he knew what to do and did it.

Despite our problems, there was a familiarity to Greg that felt comforting, and we had always worked – sexually, I mean. It wasn't the passionate, abandoned sex I had with Ky, but it was good, defined by mutual fondness. Perhaps that sounds unromantic, but I have always thought that fondness was underrated, erotically. I knew and cared for every inch of him, and though he didn't send me into a frenzy of desire, the familiar pattern of his actions and the positions he chose, the beats of his strokes and nibbles, created a rhythm that was sort of exciting, because I knew what was next and I liked it, always had, right from the very start.

Greg was usually silent during sex. By the time we met, I had had men who told me breathlessly how beautiful I was, how they would die without me (these men were usually French, or Italian). And I had had men like Ky, who whispered a constant stream of talk into my ear, some of it filth, and some of it funny. Greg was the only one who said scarcely a thing, but he did look. His gaze was fixed and intense and full of meaning, and it had the ability to make me feel desired, loved and, conversely, respected (not an arousing quality, always). He could usually give me an orgasm within half an hour. We knew what the other one wanted, and fulfilled it almost automatically.

This time, though, many minutes passed, and I understood that I would not come. I had known it almost from the start, because I was chasing it in a way that felt conscious and a bit desperate. I could feel him losing it, too, though I tried to keep things going by doing the things he liked: letting my teeth graze his neck, putting his finger in my mouth, using my feet to push him further into me. I shut my eyes and tried to think of Ky, then felt horrible and stopped. Instead,

I imagined faceless couples fucking, but as they writhed and gasped, I caught a glimpse of their faces and recognised not only my forbidden lover – what a word, 'lover'! But there could be no other – but also Alessia with him, her figure reconstructed entirely from the hours that I had spent looking at it and painting it. Then I was on the bed with Ky and she was watching, and this is when I came close, only for the building wave to dissipate dully with the flapping noise of Greg withdrawing.

'I don't think it's going to happen,' he said.

How sad that I felt affronted, as though his orgasm were a challenge I needed to complete. I had never been successful at separating male desire from female responsibility. It was work, and I was failing.

'Let me get on top of you,' I said, taking off my bra, which I had still been wearing, but which had been pushed down below my breasts.

He adjusted the condom I had asked him to use, which had become slack over his softening penis, pulling it back, and I straddled him.

'I know you like it when I go down slow,' I said, and he nodded in agreement, but said nothing.

Soon, he was grunting in time with my bounces, getting louder before he closed his eyes tightly and a deeper, throatier noise left his mouth. I was out of breath and shining with sweat. As I climbed off him, he didn't ask me if I'd come, and I was grateful that he didn't, though I knew he knew I hadn't.

We went back to sleep, him holding me, me turned slightly

away from him so that I was almost face down on the mattress. The moment we got home, I would end it. I had to. I wouldn't tell him about Ky, nor would I tell Greg that I didn't love him the way that he wanted me to, or the way I knew I should. I would just say that I didn't want to be a mother and wouldn't be changing my mind. It wasn't fair to string him along with the belief that one day maternal instinct might suddenly strike, I would say. He had plenty of time to find a woman to do it with. It would hurt him less to put it that way, even if it sounded far more definitive than I think I felt.

Of course, I had thought about what sort of father Greg might be, and had concluded that he would probably be the best kind. He would be calm and quietly loving, a father who knows to offer comfort to his frightened child, who would wrap his arms around them and say soft words and make them smile. He would be part of a new generation of men who took time away from their careers to be there in the early days, and I knew – I was sure – that he would at least try to give me time for my art, even if in practice it would fall by the wayside as soon as he returned to his job. He would not be one of those partners, like some of my friends' husbands, whose unsubtle belief in the primacy of domestic work for mothers suddenly came to the fore after they had given birth.

'That is all he thinks I'm good for,' Helena would say to me, sitting at my kitchen table with a glass of wine years hence, when she was finally getting divorced. 'Babies. And laundry.'

A few months after I came back from that trip to Greece,

I was standing in line at the pharmacy to get something for my terrible heartburn. In front of me was a small boy, no more than five, and his young father. The boy was wittering away about the lollipops on the counter and then, apropos of nothing said, 'I love you, Daddy.'

'I love you too, son,' the father said, in the sort of natural, straightforward way that was loving without being mawkish.

It felt like a different language to my ears; I had never heard a father speak publicly to his son like this. It looks like advertising copy written down, but I promise, it was in the delivery. It was just the sort of thing I could imagine Greg saying to his child, and in that moment I was filled with the most spectacular wave of revulsion for what I had done. I wanted to walk out of the chemist and call Greg and ask him to come back, to say that I couldn't do it, this, without him.

I didn't, of course. I got my antacid and trudged back to the rented studio flat I'd secured three weeks after I left him, with what remained of my savings.

As for Ky, had I thought about what he would be like, as a father? Not consciously. We were not committed, had never discussed the likelihood of becoming so. Yet I have come to believe that my body marked him out from the moment that we met. It was temporary insanity, like being on drugs. I have never wanted a man like that since, have never hurt people so cavalierly in pursuit of an as-yet-unacknowledged goal.

Of course, he and Alessia hurt me, too.

* * *

It is impossible to paint a female nude without feeling, as your eye scans the model's figure and your wrist moves the brush over the canvas, that you're in dialogue with all the other female nudes throughout history, especially those painted by men. It's not that you're imagining them, exactly; they are simply so encoded in your subconscious that even as you sketch the outline of the female form in preparation for the layers of paint that will become her flesh, there's a sense that you are working for an audience. All those Venuses, it's like they're peering over your shoulder, waiting for justice. I used to think that a woman artist could never break free of the male gaze, that it's so pervasive that, as women, we can only define our practice in opposition to it. As I spent all those painstaking hours making that first nude in the small stone outhouse on an island in Greece, I came to understand that the answer lies in our bodies. Only a woman artist can tell the truth of what it means to live in a female body; only we can transpose how it feels on to the canvas in front of us. A male can only ever be an observer. It's no coincidence that I felt, at that time, perhaps for the first time, entirely present in my own body. It is in embracing, rather than rejecting, the corporeal, that we are able to get to the heart of meaning.

This act of rebellion has been going on quietly, on the sidelines, for as long as humans have been making images of themselves, exploding only at the dawn of modernism. It had been a long time coming. I understand why a suffragette slashed the smooth, cream back of the *Rokeby Venus*.

Greg and I used to argue about the destruction of art for political causes – especially after the environmental protestors started following her example. There will be no art when the world ends, I used to say. Throughout my career, in moments when I have felt especially envious or disillusioned or thwarted, I picture my life's work floating in a rising sea, and feel almost relieved.

We had two days left on the island, and my portrait of Alessia was not good. That is not to say that it wasn't technically accomplished – it was one of the finest figure paintings that I had ever made – but there was something inauthentic about it. It's no wonder: the rationale for its creation was based on a lie. I believed that Alessia intended to add it to her collection, but as yet her collection did not have its own home. By hanging it in her father's gallery, it would exist for male eyes. I had done my best to disrupt that gaze, but the work of detachment takes a lifetime.

These were the thoughts that clouded my mind as I stood in front of the canvas and watched Alessia take off her clothes. There is no denying that I felt a flicker of desire. I was all desire that summer; it had overtaken me. Perhaps it had suffused the painting and made it a failure. I was looking at her as a man would, as he did.

Though I had not fully comprehended Alessia's game, I understood enough to make a conscious decision that morning in the studio to take the painting in a different direction, and as she held her pose like a sculpture, I mixed up a new colour palette. Paint dried so quickly in the heat that you had to be fast, but if Alessia caught a sense of my urgency, then she didn't show it. She was one of the best models I had ever used, in her stillness and her understanding of posture and form. It helped that she had an almost ventriloquist-like ability to hardly move her lips when she talked to me. When she finally spoke, the tumbling hairs on her head hardly shifted.

'Is Greg alright? The whole thing with the boat?'

'He's fine. He's just afraid of water.' I wasn't going to be embarrassed for him. Now that I had decided to leave, all the dormant compassion I had for him welled up in me.

'Apart from that, has he had a good time?'

'No, I don't think so,' I said.

And we both laughed, because her question had been so anodyne and my response was the truth.

We didn't speak after that. I worked furiously, and as I did so that lovely blankness overcame me, almost like being stoned. I hadn't felt this before while working on this painting, which should have been a clue that it had not been going well. Now, as I built up layer upon layer of paint, I felt a surge of quiet excitement.

When I returned to the room, Greg was still asleep, and I stood for a moment, watching the way his chest rose and fell while he breathed, the sheets all bunched up around his waist. I have always thought that the way people sleep tells us much about their character. Greg slept curled tightly in a ball, like a child. His mother always said that he was afraid of the dark, and for many years in his childhood he had suffered from night terrors. Though he had been free of them for years, I wondered if somehow his body had retained the memory of the fear and horror he had felt.

Now that I knew the number of times I'd share a bed with Greg was limited, I felt a compulsion to draw him as he slept. I grabbed a pencil and my sketchbook, and quickly captured him.

Ky, in contrast, slept on his back with his arms outstretched, like Christ on the cross, even in a single bed, and that, too, was an assertion of who he was: serene and unafraid.

I put down my sketchbook and got a bag together. I had decided to head down to the beach for a swim, knowing he would be there, setting up for lunch. I threw on a baggy striped linen shirt dress, the sort Frenchwomen wear when spending August in the south. I shook my hair down from its messy bun and put some oil through the ends.

I walked through to the kitchen to fill up my water bottle. The remains of a hastily assembled breakfast lay on the countertop, and an egg-encrusted pan sat on the stovetop. No one had bothered to soak it. It was Agatha's day off.

I went over to the sink to get the dish soap, squeezing it into the pan before filling it with hot water. What a thing, to have grown up with help. My mother would be mortified to think I'd left anything to be cleared away by anyone else. A picture came to me of her up to her elbows in dish soap, joking sarcastically that you just can't get the staff these days. Her mother had gone into service, and had worked as a cook in the big house, only leaving when she became pregnant out of wedlock. It was her skill that I called upon every time I made a béchamel, passed down from mother to daughter for who knows how long, and I felt proud of it. Alessia couldn't boil an egg.

As I loaded the dishwasher, I thought about Agatha, quietly observing everyone in the house as she waited on us hand and foot. What did she make of us? Alessia said she'd been with the family since she was born, had essentially brought her up. 'My summer mother,' she had called her, nestling into her arms as she introduced us upon our arrival. 'Well, my year-round mother, really.'

Exiting the villa, I walked past the others, all of whom were lying practically comatose by the pool. Iris had moved herself into the shade and was wrapped around Edwin, and Helena had pulled a sarong up to her chin, but Harry was in direct sunlight and would surely burn. I considered waking him, or putting up his umbrella in order to protect him, but then I turned and took the path towards the sea.

He was exactly where I'd known he would be. I stood at the edge of the taverna's terrace and watched him as he unfolded the tablecloths, clipping them with their silver clamps. I liked how his body moved as he did it, and he smiled as if to himself while he worked. He had held up a hand to me when I arrived and shook his head, a silent warning against distraction. After standing there a moment, I unfurled my towel under the trees and removed my shirt, knowing he was looking, paying his gaze no mind.

The sea was exquisite, as usual, but I was too tired to push myself, and just wanted to cool off. So I swam out and spent a while floating on my back before coming into shore. Ky was sitting on my towel when I walked up, had taken off his shirt and was daubing his face with a napkin.

'Let's go somewhere,' I said, as I dried myself off.

'Where?' he said. His pupils were already dilating as they flicked between my own eyes and my lips. I slipped off my towel and grinned as I pulled my dress over my head, feeling the moistness of my swimsuit saturating the thin gauze of the cotton.

'I don't know,' I said. 'Around the back?'

'Are you insane? My mother's in the kitchen.'

'I want you inside me,' I said.

'Sophie, that's not fair. And we should probably talk.' Now I wonder if he sensed my awareness, and wanted to pre-emptively explain himself. Yet I wasn't ready to hear anything that might make me have to examine the trust I'd placed in him. There was a conversation I needed to have first, some questions that needed answering. Besides, he would see the painting soon enough.

'What about? Time is of the essence. So, where shall we go? Up in the trees? Your car?' I looked around. There were a few people milling about. 'Your room?'

He shook his head, smiling.

'The bathroom?'

We were both laughing, then.

'I don't want last night to be the last time, either,' he said.

'Well, it looks like it has to be,' I said. 'Whether it happens or not, this all has the same outcome.'

'Which is?'

'The end, obviously.'

'Is it? The end?'

'We live in different countries.'

'You sound so cold about it,' he said. 'This has meant something to me.'

'Just being realistic.' I turned away, acting harder than I felt. I don't know what he wanted me to say. That in a different life, I could love him? That much was plain to us both; naming it wouldn't make things easier.

He put a hand on my jaw and tilted my face upwards towards his own. 'Tell me it didn't mean something to you.'

I opened my mouth, which was inches from his, then realised where we were and swiftly looked around. 'Greg could see us.'

'Who gives a fuck? He's not a total fool. He knows you're not his anymore.'

I wanted to say that I wasn't anyone's, but I didn't want more of an argument. Instead, I said: 'Of course it meant something. No one has made me feel like this.'

Ky sat there, looking. One hand was still on the side of my face. The other picked at the hem of my dress. Though it wasn't a declaration, it seemed to be enough to satisfy him.

'The way I seem to respond to you – it's not normal,' I said.

He was circling the inside of my leg with his thumb. I shifted and moved his hand towards my bikini bottoms. He tutted and grabbed my wrist, moving it behind me.

'Can we really not go somewhere?'

Ky shook his head.

'You'll just have to help me imagine it,' I said. 'The last time, I mean.'

'Do you think you could come without me touching you?'

I told him that that had only ever happened in my sleep, but that he should try.

'I can do that. But first I have to make some distance between us, or else we will both get arrested.'

He shifted down to the edge of the towel and told me to put my hands where he could see them.

'Take off the shirt. No, actually – leave it on. Open that button. Yes, like that.'

He told me he was taking a photograph with his mind, then took out his phone and took an actual one, before putting it back in his pocket. My eyes followed.

'No, you look here,' he said, pointing at his face. 'All of the time. And you don't move.'

He began to talk. He started by describing what we had done the night before, against the wall, how I had felt, how he had felt, what had been going through his mind before, and after. How I had sounded, how I had looked. Then he talked about the other times, which had been his favourites, and why. Despite his slightly halting English and how explicit he was being, he made it sound quite poetic. He did all this without breaking my gaze, and it was this that made it almost unbearable. I shifted slightly, and he ordered me to stay still.

Then he started telling me what he was going to do to me later. I said there couldn't be a later, because of Greg, and he told me that wouldn't be a problem. 'We'll wait until he's asleep, and then I'll take you to the hut.'

There, he would ask me to take off my nightdress and get on my knees and – well, you can imagine. Then, after that, he would lie me on the bed. As he described in great detail each part of my body that he would touch, first with his hands, and then with his mouth, I told him I actually thought that I was getting close, and that's when he leaned forwards again and kissed me, softly, just for a second, the tip of his tongue the only point of contact between our two bodies. That's when I came.

Lisa Brice, Untitled, 2019

A woman stands, smoking, contrapposto in thigh-high stockings, her hand on her hip. It's that classic artist's model pose, like a statue, except for the full bush and the hair sprouting from her armpits, and the paintbrushes she clutches in one hand. Her face is turned away from us towards the mirror, which reflects her narrowed eyes. There's a palette on the floor. She is blue.

I was halfway through and already waddling when I went to see your show at a Mayfair gallery.

I walked around smiling, my hand on my stomach, my heart soaring, for once, with excitement instead of fear (my blood pressure was high; I was terrified of what was to come). Your paintings made me feel elated. These are women enjoying life. They're nude, or half-dressed, chatting, smoking or drinking beer, posing, but not for men. They're defiant, often painting themselves or looking at their own reflections. They are, overwhelmingly, blue.

Why? Blue has baggage, most of it male. Matisse, Picasso, Klein, who used women covered with his own patented shade – close to the colour you have chosen, a big fuck you – as human paintbrushes. There's a racial aspect, too, with echoes of the Trinidadian 'Blue Devil', of the Reckitt's blue people throughout the colonies used to lighten skin. Your blue is protective: the viewer cannot tell the race of the woman whose body they are looking at. The blue erodes their preconceptions.

(I have always loved that particular cobalt blue. I think of it as the blue of the shutters that concealed us as we lay in that outbuilding, and the blue of the church dome that cast us in shade as we kissed on the rocks.)

Seeing that show at that time in life set off something within me. Some of it was regret at not being a part of the onward march of artistic progress, as you so clearly were. I also felt thrilled by your act of repainting. You take these women whose images were created by white men for white men, and release them into new, independent lives. You dragged Ophelia from the water and gave her a fag and a beer. Courbet's cunt in a frame became an artist painting her own vulva.

Just as you were putting them back in the picture, I was walking out of it. Would I ever stand like that again, exuberantly nude in front of the mirror, paintbrushes in hand, perhaps a cigarette dangling from my lips? Or would this pregnancy crush my spirit, my agency, my engagement with art? That day, I would have traded places with the stocking-clad woman in a heartbeat. She looked so free, in a way I no longer would be. As I walked out of the gallery into the winter sunlight, I vowed to keep her spirit with me.

Eighth day, afternoon

I woke when I sensed Ky standing above me.

'What time is it?' The sun had moved. I put my hand to my face to shade my eyes.

'It's three. Come and have a drink; it's quiet now.'

'Hold on, let me put some more cream on.'

I shook out and rolled up my towel, gathering my things. The taverna had cleared out – on the way, we had passed a dozen snoring punters lying sprawled on the beach – and only a couple of tables were still seated. Ky put his hand on my back and steered me towards the table closest to the sea, then pulled out my chair.

'Are you hungry?'

'Not hugely. Perhaps something small.'

'That doesn't exist in Greece.'

He came back with a plate of dip, made from capers and caramelised onions, and a basket of pillowy, fresh toasted pita. The saltiness stung my lips where he had bitten them the night before, so I took quick little gulps of the cold wine he had brought. He returned to the kitchen and came back with a small dish of prawn saganaki, a speciality of his mother's. He pulled up a chair and sat down, pouring himself a glass of wine.

'So, tell me about yourself.'

He laughed. I suppose it felt like a funny question, while at the same time it acknowledged that we hardly knew each other at all.

'Tell me what it was like, growing up here. I can't believe I've never asked you this, but do you have any siblings?'

'No brothers or sisters. Lots of cousins. What is there to say? I went to school, I played with my friends, I worked in the restaurant when I was old enough.'

'What made you want to become an archaeologist?'

'I was always digging for things, even when I was very small. I found an arrowhead, when I was four. Right over there. One of my aunties used to clean the archaeological museum up at the *kastro*, so she took me up there to meet the director and show it to him. I loved it there so much I started going with her in the mornings before school.'

'That's so sweet.'

'You can ask my mother about it, if you like.' He nodded towards a woman in spectacles, who had just come out of the kitchen and was standing at the edge of the terrace.

'I wear them, too,' he said, as though reading my mind. 'When I'm at work.'

'Mama,' he called to her, beckoning her over. As she came closer, I could see that they had the same good genes. I felt a rush of nerves suddenly. 'This is Sophie.'

I stood, unsure how to greet her, and she pulled me towards her into a warm hug. Then she held me at arm's length and looked me over, saying something rapidly in Greek.

'What did she say?'

'She says you're very beautiful.'

'Liar.'

'No, it's true! She says she can see what I see in you.' He replied to her then, also in Greek.

'You told her about us?'

'No – she says she can read me like a book.'

'Will you translate for me? Will you ask her to tell me what you were like as a little boy?'

Ky affected to look embarrassed, but asked the question, at which point his mother became animated, and started gesturing wildly.

'She says I was very affectionate. A real mummy's boy, as I think you say. She says I wouldn't sleep in my cot at all and had to be on her all the time. She says that I was always attached to her, always clutching her skirt and playing with her hair. This isn't making me look cool. She was always encouraging me to go and play with the other children, but when I wasn't showing her things that I had dug up, I wanted to sit in the kitchen or watch her cook.'

His mother pulled out her purse from the pocket of her apron and showed me a faded photograph of a small boy, the most notable thing about him the large, brown eyes that dominated his face.

'He looks like quite a serious little man.'

Her voice started rising then, and I saw that there were tears in her eyes. Looking concerned, Ky turned his body towards his mother, perceptibly, but not in a way that excluded me from the conversation. He put a hand on her shoulder.

'She's saying something that I haven't heard before. She's saying that before having me, she dreamed of me. She says that she had – I don't know how you say it in English. When you are pregnant but the baby dies?'

'A miscarriage.'

'Three. The way she actually said it is that Gello had come to curse her. That's a demon in Greek folklore that takes babies. People on the island still hang garlic in their houses when they are pregnant to protect against her.'

His mother was smiling now, and saying far more than he was able to translate.

'She's being embarrassing now. She's saying that I am a miracle to her, that she could not hope for a better son.'

At this, she reached up and ruffled his hair. 'What you want to eat?' she said to me then, in English.

'Oh ... this is fine,' I said. 'I'm not really that hungry.'

'Sophie. You can't say that to a Greek mother,' said Ky.

'Well, Greg will be wondering where I am, and will probably come and find me soon. I should really be getting back.'

'It won't be long. She'll think you're rude if you don't.'

I relented, but told him to choose what we had. Ky and his mother had a passionate and surprisingly long discussion, before she evidently won out and returned to the kitchen, motioning to my glass before she went. He filled it before filling his own.

'She seems like an incredible woman,' I said.

'She is. She was born very poor, and she is very proud of this business. She is known as a gifted cook throughout the island. Really, she is a chef, not a cook. People come from Athens to eat here.'

We fell silent, both staring out towards the horizon. His arm was grazing mine on one side, and I liked just sitting, feeling the hairs softly brushing against my skin.

'She must think badly of me,' I said, eventually. 'I bet she loves Alessia.' It came out sounding more bitter than I had intended it to.

'No.' He shook his head. 'She has always said Alessia was spoiled. She used to say, she's too beautiful. She doesn't know how to suffer.'

'Beautiful women suffer,' I said. 'They suffer more than the rest of us, in some ways.'

He had reached over and was using a finger to lift my chin when his mother came out, brandishing a large fish surrounded by roast potatoes, glistening with oil and salt. We made the required exclamations and she batted us away.

'Thank god,' I said, smoothing my napkin on my knees. 'I know whatever you were about to say would have been nauseating.'

He made a hurt expression and used his cutlery to expertly lift out the fish spine, moving it to the side of the plate. 'Now you will never know.'

But I knew. Or, at least, I had an idea of what he had been going to say. Some of me wanted him to say all those things, even if they were going to make everything a lot more complicated. It can be like that, sleeping with a man.

When, years later, I tried to explain it, all I could say was that I hardly knew what I wanted; my body had taken over.

'So why are you telling me about it, if it didn't mean anything? What's the point?' she said. My daughter was at an age where she spoke to me like that. I don't miss those years.

I said it was an interesting question. 'I think I'm telling you because I want you to know that I was happy. In fact, sitting there, sharing that fish with him, might have been the happiest I've ever felt. Not in my life – you gave me that – but with a man. I felt like I could sit there eating lunch with him and making jokes at his expense for the rest of both our lives.'

'So why didn't you?'

I didn't know how to answer her, except to say that she would understand one day. Young girls hate it when you say that to them.

As predicted, Greg was making his way down the path to the beach. I could see his dark curls bobbing as he navigated the steep side of the hill. I stood up quickly, thanking Ky's mother at the door of the kitchen, and kissing him gently on the cheek, then walked to meet Greg. The path ended in the groves at the centre of the bay, and I stood in the shade and waited.

'I'm so sorry,' I said, as he approached.

He had a resigned look about him. 'What for?'

Everything, I almost said.

'Disappearing.'

'It's cool. I was sleeping, and then I was reading. I knew you'd be swimming. I'm used to you needing your alone time,' he said, with false lightness.

'Fancy a walk to the next bay? Alessia says there's a path.'

'It's so hot.'

'It isn't far.' I waved my water bottle at him, and he sighed. 'There'll be a bit of a breeze up there.'

We trudged to the end of the beach, where a paved path slowly wound its way up the cliffs until it curled out of sight.

'So, how's *The Magus*?'

'It's good. I mean, it's dense. I'm not sure I'm in the right headspace for it.'

'From what I recall, isn't it about someone who is suicidally depressed on a Greek island?'

'Well, yeah.'

'Probably that, then. I don't know how you could be depressed here. I don't think I've ever been anywhere more beautiful.'

'I bet it's brutal in winter.'

I thought of Ky's parents, the taverna all shuttered up against the howling winds.

We were quiet for a while as the path rose. By the time it levelled out, we were both panting and dripping sweat.

'It'll be worth it for the swim afterwards,' I said, knowing he wouldn't go in beyond his waist.

We paused to look at the view, Greg reaching around me with his clammy arms, pulling me close. His body made me feel safe; it always had. It suddenly seemed bizarre that I should choose to throw that away after a fling with a man I would never see again. Perhaps staying with Greg was the mature choice, and I needed to grow up and accept that the kind of frisson I had with Ky is never sustainable. Yet once you've felt it, even once, its absence becomes impossible to ignore. Knowing there was at least one person out in the world who could make me feel that way had exposed the paucity of my own relationship, and, like a curse, had made the settled life I had been sleepwalking into impossible.

Greg said something indistinct into my hair that I nonetheless understood to be 'I love you'. I pretended not to hear, and he didn't say anything else. It was quite windy up there, on the cliffs.

The next bay over was as beautiful as we had been promised: smooth and sandy, yet not in a way that seemed to affect the clarity of the water. A few holidaymakers were gathered under the shade of the pines, but the beach had a sleepy feel. Next to it was a small hamlet of white oblong houses with pale blue shutters.

The path declined steeply as we approached. On the right-hand side was a row of old fisherman's huts, their wide doors and window frames painted in bright colours. The tide came almost up to their thresholds, and we were ankle-deep in water as we navigated our way past. There didn't seem to be any fishermen using them these days: beach towels and swimwear hung drying from balconies.

I stopped for a moment to watch a young couple sitting on the stone jetty. The man's legs were hanging over the side and he seemed to be reaching for something in the waves, but as I approached, I saw that he was rinsing a sea urchin. The woman had in her arms a small, wriggling child wearing a bucket hat and a frilly swimsuit. She was obviously holding her daughter back while her dad set upon the urchin with his knife, splitting it expertly and prising the flesh from its interior before he passed it to the woman. I watched her put the little slither to the girl's lips. She ate it, squealing with delight.

'They must be Greek,' Greg said. 'No one British would give a toddler raw seafood. And *she* shouldn't be eating it, either.'

I noticed the curve of the woman's stomach, then. A certain fullness in her sun-kissed face. I imagined Ky preparing and then feeding me a sea urchin, me using my tongue to push its saline wetness around the ridges of my mouth, my hand on my stomach.

I could paint it for you now, that scene. All these years later, I am certain that I could pick out the idiosyncrasies of the family's individual features and render the truth of their spirits faithfully on to canvas, so that you would feel almost as though you were there, in front of those fishing huts, eating sea urchins with them. But the man I was watching them with, the man whom I had spent so long loving and picturing as the person I would make my life with? I would struggle to produce even the most rudimentary sketch of him.

Zanele Muholi, Julie I, Parktown, Johannesburg, 2016

Your naked body is curled around inflated plastic bags, pale and shining against the blackness of your skin. The contrast is turned up to render it so dark that standing there, I cannot look away from the direct lightness of your eyes as they confront me. 'The black body itself is the material,' you said. 'The black body that is ever scrutinised, and violated and undermined.'

I'll never forget standing in that room, surrounded by the intensity of your unflinching gaze.

Each self-portrait in this series – Somnyama Ngonyama *(Zulu for 'Hail the Dark Lioness') – uses different props or materials, often mundane, household ones, to tell a story. In this one, the plastic bags that you're cradling represent the fibroids that were removed from your womb during a traumatic operation. In the years since I first saw it, as my own womb plotted my undoing, this image has returned to me. Trying to tell me something, maybe.*

FEMALE, NUDE

I am happy to have lived long enough to see work such as yours given major exhibition space. Being a gay, nonbinary artist born under apartheid, facing prejudice and violence, you had to insist on a space for yourself.

Doesn't the body have so many stories to tell? I wonder sometimes if that is where writing falls down, if this act of translation is better suited to visual art than it is to writing. I have tried both, in my way, though I have not been able to make art as central to my life as I had thought I would. I have lived through the works of other artists, imagined conversations with you. The way you have lived and breathed your work never fails to inspire me.

Standing in a room at Tate Modern all those years ago, surrounded by your self-portraits, I was in awe. In one image, you lie on your back, holding up an oval mirror to the camera, giving us a sideways glance. Your small breasts are often visible, but at other times you cross your arms against your chest, blocking them from view, or wrap a bright white sheet around your waist like a sarong. Sometimes your hair is hidden, and sometimes it's exaggerated and enormous. How you represent yourself shifts and subverts.

To see them all together, all at once, made me understand that you are telling us a story about the fluidity of the self. For you, they/them is not only a way of expressing your identity, but also a way of including your family, your ancestors, your community, the universe. It's a visual polyphony.

We are all our past and future selves, but we are also made up of a multiplicity of souls, of the people who have touched us, or hurt us. I am the seriously ill woman in her fifties, but I am also the young woman on the island learning what it means to want. I am him, and her, and all of them. I am my daughter and my sister. I am all the artists whose work has changed me.

Your photographs are generous, in that they emphasise our connection to one another, and demand freedom for everyone. In doing so, you have transcended the subjective self and taken the nude somewhere entirely new.

Ninth day, morning

I remember the first time I drew a naked woman. It was also the first time that I had ever seen one, properly. I had not grown up in a naked house; my mother would cover herself if discovered undressed, and encouraged us to do the same. Our modesty was carefully guarded. She would insist we closed the curtains when getting changed, even though the house wasn't overlooked. She wasn't a prude – she spoke frankly to us about menstruation and sex and pregnancy and birth – but I couldn't tell you what her body looked like.

I was fourteen and studying for my art exam when my teacher suggested that I try a local life-drawing class. You have talent, she said, at copying from pictures, but you should start drawing from life. I still recall looking at her face when she said that. She wore bright blue eyeshadow that matched a peacock scarf she wore in her hair. Dangly earrings. You might say a bit of a cliché, but I didn't know that then. I hadn't ever met anyone arty. I found her fascinating. She gave us these impromptu art history lectures, peppered with strange and vivid details. One week, she told us how Magritte had seen his mother's body dragged from a river, after she had drowned. Perhaps that's why these nude figures are fragmented, she said, as though the flesh is rotting away. I couldn't think about drowning without thinking about Rosie, so it made me shudder, but I was also captivated. She made sure to show us the work of women artists, too: Morisot, Cassatt, Gwen John, Leonora Carrington and Dorothea Tanning. She took me outside the narrow confines of the school curriculum, setting me on a path of discovery and engagement that would come to define my life and my work.

Because I believed in everything she said, I went, dutifully, though I felt shy and common in that panelled room above the genteel pub my parents didn't drink at, a pub attended by students and university professors who lived on the greener side of town. Materials were provided, which made the steep entrance fee more worth it. I bought all my school art supplies from a cheesy chain store, where the oil paints and sketch pads were jumbled up next to cut-price paperbacks and mass-produced calendars. These were proper, though: pastels with pigments so vibrant I had to hold in a gasp when my fingers tested a line across the textured, cream-coloured paper, thick like my cousin Jennifer's wedding invitation, stuck to our fridge at home.

The model was in her thirties, I'd say, with scarlet dyed hair and heavy eye make-up. She walked in wearing a kimono and sat down on the blanket that had been put out for her comfort. The tutor pressed play on the CD player, and she shrugged off the robe to reveal herself, adjusting her pose so that her arm was resting on a nearby empty chair, her face turned upwards to the ceiling, one bent leg in front of her, the other tucked behind.

'Five minutes,' said the tutor.

It wasn't long enough. I had not learned to sketch well yet, and barely had an outline of her head and shoulders by the time she switched the pose, so distracted had I been by her breasts. They were full and quite large, but they were nothing like the ones in the magazines the boys passed around at breaktime. Her nipples were very large and brown, and one was pierced.

I thought she was stunning, but what captivated me the most was the ease with which she inhabited her body. There was a nonchalance about her that was almost boredom, and I envied it. I was finding fourteen an awkward age. I hated my small breasts and my large bum, the moles, freckles and hairs that dotted my skin. I would stand in front of the full-length mirror in my bedroom at night and try to make my figure into a shape that was acceptable. It never was.

And yet, as the class continued, with a different model every week, some male, some female, I came to view the body in more pragmatic terms. I became an observer with an artistic interest, as opposed to simply a critic. During my night-time sessions in front of the mirror, I still looked at my form through the ruthless imagined gaze of my male classmates, but instead of despairing, I began to draw myself.

I suppose that in itself was a form of fixation, but I still believe passionately that the best way to help a teenage girl understand the politics versus the reality of the human body is to send her to a life-drawing class.

These drawings continued throughout my teenage years, and by the time I came to apply to art school, I had sketchbooks and sketchbooks of them, alongside the work from the life classes, and many portraits of Rosie. These pictures turned out to be my ticket in, and were highly praised by the admissions tutor.

The portraits of Rosie were all clothed, but one day, when she was about fifteen, she used her pad to tell me that she wanted me to make a nude of her, just like the ones I had made of myself. Puberty was a hard time for her. She felt desire, as we all do, but was grappling with the realities of her disabled body. All teenage girls cry because they think they'll never get a boyfriend, but when Rosie did, it hurt my heart because I feared it would be true.

'Why shouldn't I sit for you?' she insisted. 'I want to see myself in paint.'

'Mum won't like it,' I said.

'Fuck Mum,' Rosie typed.

I told her we would wait until she was eighteen, and though she protested, I promised her that I would do it. Marc Quinn's sculpture of Alison Lapper pregnant was on the fourth plinth in Trafalgar Square the year I left school, and the media backlash at the presence of this disabled woman's nude form in a public space made me incandescent. We took Rosie to see it, and when we got home, she asked again.

Two summers into art school and home for a month as

I moved between flats, I kept my word. It remains, I think, one of my best paintings, and Rosie agreed. She didn't want it hidden at home in case our mother found it, but one day, she told me, 'When I have my own place, I will have it on the wall.' Until then, I had agreed to store it and not show it to anyone, but sometimes when Greg was out, I would take it from my portfolio in the cupboard under the stairs and look at it, and think about how Rosie had been ready when the rest of the world wasn't.

We had all gone to bed early, still tired from the boat trip, and I slept a dreamless sleep lasting more than eleven hours. The next morning at breakfast, I noticed a column of smoke rising from the distant mountainside, and Alessia turned on the radio to hear a wildfire alert. Nothing to worry about, she said. They happened all the time in summer, and the blaze was far enough away that we would not need to evacuate.

Not entirely reassured, I asked Alessia to come back to the studio, just for an hour, so that I could make some final changes. In truth, I could have made the changes without her – I already knew how the portrait would look in my mind's eye – but in order to have the conversation with her that I needed to have, I wanted her on the back foot: unclothed, surveilled. As I had been.

When had I realised that she had been watching us? I have often pondered that question, over the years, tried to unpick where consent ended and betrayal began. It is true that on the islet I had woken and I had somehow known. But how had it come to me? Had I in fact known all along?

That was Alessia's argument. I had long known that she liked to watch her partners, had known since university, when she had made a drunken, laughing admission of the fact. I also knew about her past with Ky, and suspected that they still slept together sometimes. If I knew both those things, and had been aware of Alessia's unusual keenness that Ky and I should fuck, could I really claim to have been deceived?

But that morning in the studio, deceived was how I felt.

'So – every time?' I said, once she was standing in the correct pose. 'Every time I was with him, you were there?'

Alessia held my gaze. She did not flinch.

'On the rocks, by the monastery? You lurked, like some sort of creepy . . . voyeur? It's fucked up.'

'Sophie . . .'

'In the car park? When he touched me? Where were you, in the back seat or something? This is so fucking disturbing.'

'You knew I was there.'

'Bullshit.'

'You did. You made eye contact with me.'

'When?'

'That day at the *kastro*, in the little house. I stood outside the stable door. You looked at me. You looked me dead in the eye while you rode him. You wanted me to watch.'

'I saw a shadow against a curtain! I didn't see *you*.' I threw my palette at her, and she ducked. It clattered against the stone wall, leaving a dark beige smear against the white paint. 'Is that why you asked me to paint this portrait? Is it some sort of sick power game? You're deranged.'

'You knew, but maybe you didn't want to know. On some level, you were aware. Besides, I thought it was obvious.'

'What the fuck? I did not consent to this.'

'Don't be hysterical. If you didn't know, as you claim, then how did you suddenly find out?'

She had me there. I hadn't caught her in the act, Ky hadn't told me, and, unless it had happened in a dream I'd since forgotten, there had been no dramatic epiphany. Rather, in that half-state between sleep and waking I had felt the simple truth of it as though I had always known it. It was like how, when drawing, there's a moment when the image makes itself known to you; its constituent outlines coalesce. It was not there on the page before and yet in some dim part of the artist's mind there's a feeling of recognition as she gives form to something she has always somehow intuited. Had I been aware this whole time, but too caught up in him to examine it properly? Or was she just tricking me into acceptance?

Alessia took a step towards me. I took in her beautiful body as she approached, not as an artist studies a model, but as a person experiencing desire. I was so angry, but I was also, confusingly, flattered. She paused for a moment to check she had permission, and then took my face in her hands and kissed me. It was a sweet, rather chaste kiss, that didn't try to take things further beyond that moment.

'Please don't be angry,' she said. 'It's been fun, hasn't it?'

I didn't know how to respond, so I walked over to the palette on the floor, bent down and picked it up. Had Ky, too, assumed I knew? Had he ever wanted me, or was he simply doing it to please Alessia? It had all felt so real to me, being with him.

'Let's get this done, shall we?'

For the rest of the session, I painted in silence. When the hour was up, Alessia walked over to her bag and took out a roll of bank notes. I acted as though I hadn't noticed how much money it was; far more than we had agreed. Enough, potentially, for a year of fees for a master's in fine art.

'This is for the portrait only,' I said.

'This is for the portrait only.' Alessia smiled.

'Don't you want to have a look?'

'Let's unveil it tonight at dinner,' she said. 'That way, everyone will see.'

Walking out of the studio, I could smell smoke in the air. I contemplated charging down the path to the taverna to confront Ky. I wanted to shout, maybe even to hit him. The prospect of a scene felt good; perhaps public expressions of intense emotion were more akin to my natural habitat. I had never fitted in with these upper-class people, with their containment and their politeness in company and their cold carelessness in private. Now I had someone to rail against, someone who had betrayed me so explicitly that I had a reason to abandon any sense of propriety. I wanted to launch myself at him like a wild animal, to ask him how her cunt tasted, how she sucked him off, which positions they used, if she had touched herself while she watched us, all while throwing pieces of white restaurant crockery at his head like a Greek dancer having a psychotic episode. I felt the desire for oblivion that sometimes comes with the third drink of the evening, and an acceptance of the chaos that I had had a role in creating over the course of the past days.

Let's get right to it, I thought.

I had never really felt sexual jealousy before, and the momentary propulsion of it was startling. I understood for the first time how a person could kill their lover.

But the resolve left me just as quickly. The sun was at its strongest, and an hour of painting had tired me. Walking through the olive grove, I was drawn towards the blue oblong of Alessia's father's pool. Discarding my dress as I strode over, I paused for a moment, consciously feeling the heat of the tiled rim against the skin of my feet until it became almost unbearable, whereupon I dove, perfectly, beautifully, into the cool water.

'Brava!' Helena was applauding when I resurfaced, down at the shallow end. She was splayed out on a lounger, but under a parasol, her skin as milky pale as ever. I took in the smooth jut of her hips, the outline of her ribs beneath her bee-sting breasts, as I made my way over to the bed next to her.

'See? I can be elegant sometimes,' I said. 'Give me one of those.'

She handed over a slim and a lighter, while I rubbed my hands on the bed's linen cover until my fingers were dry.

'Of course you can', she said.

I had never been elegant in my life, and we both knew it.

Smiling, I lit up and said, 'And what about you? Have you recovered from sleeping on the beach?'

'I'm enjoying the rest here. Harry's still feeling pretty rough, though.' She nodded towards the interior.

'And what about bloody Greg? Who knew he'd be such a wimp in the sea?' I knew I sounded cruel. I didn't even believe what I was saying myself.

Helena inhaled. 'I'm going to say something . . .'

'Oh, no . . .'

'He's a lovely man, Sophie. He doesn't deserve this.'

'Spare me. I know all this. Do you think that I don't feel like a total bitch? I didn't plan this. I didn't expect to respond this way to a total stranger. I didn't come on this holiday to explode my life.'

Of the three women I had come here with, Helena was the only one who really cared about me. It wasn't just that she came from a more normal background, although our shared references and our mutual experience of small-town suburbia had always bonded us, as had our lack of cultural capital. It was that she had always been interested in what I had to say. Never cruel, never dismissive. She had been as engaged with my inner life as I had been with hers, and our years-long friendship had been an exercise in mutual discovery that was almost romantic. Harry's curiosity regarding the mind of his soon-to-be wife had never stretched so far. Iris and Alessia, although I had spent many hours talking with them, had heard their secrets and their sadnesses, and had even come to know the curves and shadows and planes of Alessia's unclothed body, both remained slight mysteries to me.

In the years following our trip to the island, I came to understand something about the hospitality of rich people: for all their charm and affability, there is also always a withholding. For a person like me, raised always to say just what they are thinking, this can be enraging.

That's what I always wanted to scream at them, when we were sitting at dinner: *Just say!*

'Why did you decide to explode your life, out of curiosity?' Helena was rubbing sun cream into her clavicle, her fingers pressing so firmly into the bone that it looked a bit painful. Her eyes were fixed on me. 'Because I have a theory.'

'Oh, no,' I repeated.

'Don't get upset if I say something.'

'Never a good prelude to anything.'

'I think you're sad that I'm getting married.'

The laugh that came out of me was more of a hoot, loud enough to cause a rustle in a nearby tree as a bird took flight.

'What?' she said. 'No, listen: hear what I have to say. We've been close for years, maybe even the closest you can be, as women. That's changing. It must feel like a loss. Maybe even a betrayal. You might even be a tiny bit jealous, because you and Greg . . .'

I was still laughing, but I put a hand on her arm to show her that I didn't mean it unkindly. I have never understood those women who cling to other women with such tenacity that a romantic relationship becomes a threat. Are their interior lives so impoverished? And are their friends so willing to be subsumed by new love, rather than to allow it to expand them? I said as much now. I also said that I never wanted to get married. Not only not to Greg, which she knew, but to anyone, ever.

She said that she could see the way I looked at Ky, that it seemed to her like the making of a great love, a lifelong love, and I cut her off and told her not be so dramatic, that he wasn't the person I thought he was. I didn't go into details about why I felt he'd deceived me.

Now, I suspect that, even then, I feared that if I ever made a home with him, he would consume all of me and vice versa; that to love him would mean I would turn inwards. At the time, though, I couldn't make sense of my thoughts beyond a strong feeling that we wouldn't work.

When Helena tried to protest, I pointed out that it had taken merely a matter of days with Ky for me to act cruelly and lose sight of the kind of person I was.

'I'm going to say something now,' I said. 'It's about Harry.'
'You hate him.'
'I hate him.'
She was the one laughing now. 'Oh, fuck.'
'OK, hate is a strong word. I don't trust him. I feel like he's going to hurt you. But I do trust – and love – you, and you love him. So next month, I'm going to put on my lavender column dress – which I look ghastly in, by the way – and my fucking flower crown, and I'm going to walk down that aisle ahead of you while "Ave Maria" plays, and then I'll read "i carry your

heart with me" as you have asked me to do. And later, when we are both drunk and dancing, I'll tell you that I want the best for you. I might even cry a bit.'

'Thank you.'

None of this would come to pass, because I would be uninvited from the wedding. The sentiments expressed were true, nonetheless.

I thought about saying something else, something about the meanness I had glimpsed in Harry, a meanness that had yet to be turned on her, but that I knew would eventually come to define their interactions, probably after they'd had children. I had seen it happen to other friends. Their men had professed to care for the inner lives of their wives, had always given the impression that they believed in the value and importance of their creative and intellectual outlets. These were men far more liberal and enlightened than Harry, feminist men, men who didn't care if a woman took their last names or not. They cooked, they cleaned, they said that they would co-parent. They took the full two weeks of paternity leave when the baby came.

That is when the old scripts resurface. And oh, how hard it is to fight against the old scripts. Our mothers wrestled with them, and we thought we were different, but these stories stretch back into distant history. A child needs its mother; a father is a protector. He believes that a child needs its father, too, but mostly when it's convenient and does not interfere with the man's other activities and outlets (he does not admit this). He will deny the fact that, on some level, he believes women are there to be interfered with, that their inner lives matter less and so can be casually cast aside. She will try to express this, and he will say the woman is engaged in a bitter little battle, when to her it feels existential. She can feel herself slipping away, and no one on the shoreline is willing to help. I do not believe that a woman loses herself when she has children; it is just that if she does start to sink, no one ever seems to want to do the work of saving her.

I've always disliked that poem about not waving but drowning, but that is how motherhood seems to me.

'When my children were tiny, I kept having this feeling,' Helena would tell me, many years later, when we had found our way back to one another. 'It was a feeling of "Oh, wouldn't this be so wonderful?" – if I had not been cast adrift . . . If he had just respected me and been there. Instead, he did so little that my personality got buried in a pile of laundry. And then he told me I was boring!'

I confess, I had my doubts about her ever having the strength to leave. I didn't yet know how radicalising motherhood could be, how, although Helena's protective instincts had never been applied to herself, they would kick in when it came to her children.

'In a way, it would have been clearer if he had put his hands on me,' she said. 'I would have left immediately.' Instead, it took five years of criticism and belittlement, delivered at first subtly and then not so subtly, culminating with him spitting in her face, in the kitchen, in front of her little boys, for her to decide to run.

'I didn't want to raise my kids with a man who makes me feel like a speck of shit on his shoe,' she told me.

On the island, I knew there wasn't much that I could say to convince her, and so I didn't share with Helena the visions I had of her future. She would make these discoveries herself. All I could do was nurture the hope that she would reclaim herself, eventually.

Alice Neel, Self-Portrait, 1980

They said that you put your baby on the fire escape so that you could paint. It wasn't true, your younger children said; a myth invented by your in-laws to communicate what a bad mother they thought you were, how you were selfish, because art was always first.

After a whole life of painting others, you turned your gaze on yourself. It's a nude self-portrait of the artist, sitting in the chair in which many of your subjects posed. You're holding a brush, and your bespectacled expression is sort of severe, as though you are looking out at us, appraising us and our reactions to your ageing body. It is the body of a mother and an old woman, a body that has given birth four times and carried at least five pregnancies. Your belly and breasts droop, your skin seems to wobble in front of our eyes. We are not used to seeing this in paint. And yet the way you show it is prideful.

'In the beginning I didn't want children, I just got them,' you said. Santillana died of diphtheria before her first birthday. Then you had Isabetta, who came when you had scarcely had time to

grieve. You loved her, but you wanted to paint. Poor Isabetta; she really suffered. So did you. When her father took her from you at age two, I can just imagine the heartbreak, how it drove you to try and end your life.

Although the fire-escape story is apocryphal, I think you'd be the first to say that you weren't always a good mother to your daughter, nor to your next two babies, both boys, as you tried to raise them alone. You clearly found inspiration in motherhood, but there was a tension and an ambivalence there that I didn't understand until I had my own child. You knew that bearing and raising children was love, but also pain.

You struggled to support yourself, painted at night when your babies were sleeping. I don't know how you found the reserves to do that. I managed one painting a year, and that was tough.

There's this notion that when you have a child, all your ideas dry up. It's nonsense. I have never felt so overflowing with creativity, nor had so little time in which to paint, especially in the years before school started. I made a different choice to yours, in that I chose her the vast majority of the time. But you showed me it was possible to do both.

Your own drive was unstoppable. You did what artists do and channelled your ambivalence into your work. Some of your paintings, especially those about early motherhood, are desperately sad. In others, wriggling children struggle to free themselves from their mothers' arms while they gaze elsewhere. People hated the pregnant nudes most of all, because there's an uneasy quality to them. You capture the physical toll of pregnancy, the sheer swelling ungainliness of it, the swollen nipples, the linea negra. People weren't painting pregnant nudes anyway in those days, let alone pregnant nudes in oil of women who look pensive, uncertain – scared, even. They were too real.

To be seen as a great artist, you have to be seen to be sacrificing everything for your art. To be seen as a good mother, you have to be seen to be sacrificing everything for your children. I'm not sure a right way of negotiating that even exists. Would I have been great had I chosen art more often and my daughter less? I will never know, but in a way it doesn't matter. At times, I found fulfilment in making a person, and at times I found it in making a painting.

You had no roadmap. That you were even able to become an artist was a question of timing. 'I don't know what you expect from the world. You're only a girl,' your mother said. You were determined. You attended art school in the 1920s, at a time when women had not long been permitted to draw and paint from life. Had this not been the case, you might never have quietly become the greatest portraitist of the twentieth century.

You were seventy-four years old when you got your big show at the Whitney, the first time that you felt justified in being an artist. Six years later, after mostly painting other people, you turned your gaze to yourself. This is the body of an artist, you were saying. It is a body that has birthed children, and lived. It is a masterpiece.

Ninth day, evening

Our last dinner on the island was to be the best. Agatha had prepared a salad of figs, jammy and glistening, paired with hard, sharp sheep's cheese and the sweetest cherry tomatoes. She had topped it with balsamic Cretan rusks marinated in the exquisitely peppery local olive oil. Served alongside it was a ceviche of some sort of Greek white fish, cured in a lemon dressing and complemented with a little pile of confit tomatoes and roe. The crowning glory was a platter of courgette flowers stuffed with a ricotta-like cheese mixed with fresh herbs and lemon juice, drizzled with thyme honey. This was just to start.

I stood on the terrace, looking at the table as it was cast in the glow of the setting sun. None of us had made anything so worthwhile during our time on the island as Agatha had, not even the acclaimed Edwin. I didn't count my portrait of Alessia, which now stood facing the olive groves with its back to us, ready to be revealed. I had removed the cloth to allow my amendments, made late in the afternoon, to dry, but I had just placed my fingertip on a small corner of the canvas, and it was powdery and still damp to the touch.

When I had returned to our room after my conversation with Helena, Greg was nowhere to be seen. He hadn't been at the pool, either. His absence felt pointed, and my anxiety niggled at me until I fell asleep again and dreamed of Ky, that he was next to me in bed, though we were both clothed. It was one of those odd dreams that occurs at half speed, the action unfurling with a cinematic slowness that makes every moment hyper-focused. In it, he turned his face to me, and I looked at it in all its beauty, and then he kissed me. Whole hours seemed to pass in the movement of his nose against mine, the asymmetric tilt of our heads, the brushing of our lips, the tip of his tongue, his breath. Despite the microscopic detail, it was not an erotic dream. It was born from a deep well of contentment and feeling. That was the whole dream, almost, him just kissing me and kissing me and kissing me, except in the corner of the bed there was a baby, watching us. A bonny, bouncing baby, sitting up on its fat little thighs, laughing.

I woke feeling as though a trick had been played on me, because I was still angry, but it was as though my brain and my body were conspiring against my rage.

He had not yet arrived as I stood there, alone on the terrace, taking in the beauty of the food and the setting, so perfect that destruction seemed a pure entropic inevitability. Just look at the Athenian spritzes lined up in their delicate glasses, the sprig of rosemary in each poised at the same ideal angle that was neither too delicate nor too jaunty. What person didn't feel a flicker of temptation when confronted with such refined symmetry? Perhaps I was the only one. (There's something wrong with you, Greg would come to say. There's something *in you* that craves disaster.)

Someone had put on Bill Evans, but it wasn't right. Too wintry. So I walked over to the speaker and told it to play Beirut, wondering momentarily how much that speaker had heard over the course of the past nine days. Was some underpaid recent graduate somewhere near San Francisco trying to piece together the fragments of our conversations into some sort of coherent narrative? Was he bored, curious, aroused? Why did I imagine him as a he? It was a mystery to me why anyone had allowed these eavesdroppers into their homes.

'Take a drink,' Alessia said, appearing from the interior draped in black silk, through which I could faintly trace the outline of her nipples. She raised a glass. 'To you. And our work together.'

We took a sip and sat with its bitterness for a moment.

'The food has been laid out too early, hasn't it? But I wanted Agatha gone for the evening.' She swatted away a fly with her hand as she spoke, and I saw in the nonchalance of that gesture that she would be behaving as though everything was normal.

The others arrived, moments later, and we sat. Greg – who seemed to be studiously avoiding my gaze while performing upbeat affability with the others – was to my right. I put a hand on his knee and he shifted his legs so that my hand dropped heavily away, then blocked my questioning look with a gigantic swig of spritz. Ky was last to sit, opposite and to my left, and as he did so, he gave me a look that seemed to be trying to communicate something. It wasn't pleading, exactly, but it was a look that asked something of me. It seemed impossible that we would get a chance to speak before the evening was over, and we were due to leave in the morning.

I fixed in my mind the contours of his face and then turned to his body. Someone was passing me the salad bowl, and I served myself robotically, thinking of the night on the islet, how he had pinned me to the rough wall of that building by holding my wrists high above my head, bending his neck so that his teeth could graze my earlobe. He had had to let go for a second when he bent to my breasts, but when I had reached towards him to put my hands in his hair, he had tutted and resumed his grasp. His other hand had unzipped his fly and pulled my underwear down, and I helped by kicking my legs in a movement that made us both laugh quietly. Then he lifted my skirt and entered me in increments that made me hold my breath.

Where had she been when she was watching us? How had she even seen us in such blanket darkness?

I passed the bowl to Greg, who took it wordlessly. Iris was helping herself to ceviche, and I took the opportunity to observe how she did it. Throughout this holiday, my table manners had always been slightly off. I held my fork in the wrong hand, and crossed my cutlery when everyone else placed theirs next to their plates to reuse for the next course. Once, I accidentally wiped my mouth on the small linen pocket that held my personally designated napkin, instead of using the napkin itself. It had all been a bit of a strain. I would be relieved when it was over.

We paused to smoke after the main course. Even Greg had a cigarette, which surprised me; he was usually so hardline. He'd had two spritzes and at least half a bottle of wine. I knew he was sulking. To placate him, I lit his cigarette for him, placing both in my mouth in the manner of a matinee idol and then lighting and handing him his. This raised a complicit smile; it was an old joke of ours that I found smoking moves pathetically seductive. I noticed Ky noticing with the enhanced proprioception that seemed to strike me whenever he was around.

After we had stubbed out our cigarettes, it was time for the portrait to be turned around and revealed. Alessia stood and clinked her fork against her glass in a knowing parody of wedding speeches, and while she spoke we all laughed and made quips, even Greg. We had got through several bottles of wine already, and were all drunk.

'As I think all of you know, our friend Sophie, an extraordinarily gifted artist, has been painting a nude portrait of me.'

Wolf whistles here from Harry, and a roll of the eyes from Edwin.

'It will be the newest addition to my collection, and has taken many hours. Like you, I will be seeing it for the first time. It is acrylic on canvas, and its title is . . .' Here, she paused.

And I raised my eyes to her. '*Female, Nude,*' I said.

'*Female, Nude.* Original. And without further ado – Ky, could you do the honours?'

I watched Ky walk over to the painting, feeling my heart pounding in my chest and noticing that I actually cared what he thought. He pretended to take a sneak peek while performing a campy mime of a tourist overcome with Paris syndrome, and everyone laughed again. Then he picked up the canvas and turned it around on the easel.

Silence.

I sat there listening to the cicadas singing, waiting for someone to say something. My nerves had left me, and I was no longer thinking about the painting at all, but trying to remember something that Ky had told me about what Plato had said about cicadas, something about the wings of a soul elevated by love being like those of a cicada, and also a myth where a goddess had turned her lover into a cicada so that she could hear his song for ever. I couldn't remember the details, because as he spoke I had been looking at his mouth from where I lay next to him, and then I'd teased him about being romantic.

Ky stood there, next to the painting, taking it in, and I saw in his face that he knew I had understood everything.

Greg was the first to speak.

'It's ... you.'

'But it's also her.' Iris went over for a closer look. 'It's both of them, blending into each other.'

'It's very expressionistic,' said Harry, in the tone of someone trying out a word for the first time, having looked it up online.

'I find it sensual,' said Helena. 'I love the colours.'

'People always say they love the colours in a painting when they don't know what else to say about it,' said Greg, tipsy and honest.

'But also when they love the colours.'

'What's that in the corner? I like it.'

'It's called a kouros. It's an ancient Greek nude male statue. She's playing with the idea of the male/female gaze,' said Greg, who was frowning at the painting as one might at a particularly challenging puzzle.

'Is there such thing as the female gaze?' said Edwin. I had been waiting for the great conceptualist to speak, and give his verdict, but as Edwin waffled on about such an idea being biologically essentialist, I found that I could barely focus on what he was saying. I was busy trying to slow my breathing and, by extension, the palpitations in my chest.

'Well, I rather think—' Greg began, but Alessia, who had said nothing so far, swept out her hand suddenly and shushed them both.

She walked over to me and grabbed me by the shoulders, holding me in an embrace.

'I adore it!' Then, in my ear, sotto voce: 'You clever thing! I want to kiss you.'

'I agree, it is very well done,' said Edwin.

'In answer to your question, Edwin, I think it's not so much that there is such a thing as feminine art, or even a female gaze, certainly not an objective one. But when I, a woman, paint a female, nude, of course I am exploring the condition of living in a female body. I'm trying to translate a different language for you. There is so much baggage to deal with – can you even begin to understand what that feels like? And with so little precedent . . .' I knew I sounded frantic, but I didn't know how to stop.

'Yes!' Greg almost knocked over his glass in his enthusiasm. 'The first female nude self-portrait was only made at the beginning of the last century.'

'Well, you know, I disagree with that,' I said. 'Artemisia, the Willendorf Venus . . .'

'Let's not get into that now.'

He did that, Greg, in conversation with me. He would often dictate the terms, drawing limits on what we talked about. He wouldn't shut me down, exactly, or at least not explicitly, but he would say, for example, 'I'm not interested in having this conversation,' or, 'Can we not talk about that now?' For many years I had not noticed it, because unlike many men I had met, he did at least listen to what I was saying. What I hadn't realised, however, was that he listened to what I said, and then dismissed it, or retreated into theory rather than be forced to talk about how he was feeling. Only since meeting Ky, who was always asking me to expand, had I come to see it for what it was: a form of silencing, of exercising control. Since I had consciously decided to notice it, I had seen how often our interactions would play out in the same way. I would express a thought, and he would attempt to contain it.

That's not to say he deserved what I had done to him.

'Why?'

We all turned to look at Ky.

'"Why can't we get into it now? She was talking. Why do you not let her speak?'

'Oh, god,' I said, under my breath.

Alessia inhaled sharply and walked over to him. She tried to grab his hand, but he shook her off.

I tried to send him a look, just as Greg glanced between us, then back at the painting, taking in the watching kouros with an expression of dawning understanding.

Harry sloshed some more wine into his glass. 'Well, I think it's quite horny,' he said, abandoning any attempt to use academic terminology. 'Do you swing both ways or something?'

'Harry . . .' Helena looked mortified.

'What? We all know she likes to fuck. Well, most of us know. Greg doesn't, the poor deluded sod. I wouldn't marry this one, mate.'

So, this was revenge, for what I'd said about him to Helena earlier. Of course she would have relayed it. He was going to try to destroy me.

Ky walked over and stood directly in front of Harry, who, having sat down, now tried to stand once more, but was too drunk and misjudged the distance between them, returning heavily to his seat.

Greg said nothing, and I couldn't look at him. I felt, in a strange way, elated. It was Harry who spoke next.

'Whore.'

My recollections are dim from this point on, but I do remember that Ky grabbed Harry by the shirt, and told him to say it again, which he did.

'They all think it,' said Harry, with the wild abandon of a person excreting all their words before they are about to be hit. 'All your friends. They think you're a slut. They think you're common, and that you use your common family and your retarded sister to be all "Wah, wah, poor me, life is so hard, be my friend, take me on holiday."'

I can't remember who spoke next. I know that Ky didn't hit him, but instead pulled him upright and away from the table, towards the olive grove. I recall Helena's shamefaced look, and the fact that Greg was crying. Edwin said something about us all being fucking crazy, and went inside. I don't know what the others were doing, but I know that I asked them if what Harry had said was true.

'I don't think you're a slut,' said Iris. She said it slowly and ponderously, as though responding to a question from a tutor in a seminar. 'But I do think you're a social climber.'

That is, apparently, when I threw myself upon her.

I could make excuses for what I did. I could say that I have never been violent before. I could blame the alcohol, or my cycle. I could tell you it was the hormones. I could say that I'd had too much sun that day. I could sit here and tell you that the sexual betrayal that had been delivered upon me was traumatising, that I was a victim of a non-consensual act, a crime that had been committed against my body. I could say that I did it because I was too scared to hit the man who deserved to be hit, who had said a cruel thing about my beloved sister. I could say that I was a frustrated artist. I could admit that there had been times in my friendship with Iris when I had felt a fierce, visceral hatred towards her that had astonished me, so brimming had it been with a desire to hurt her. I could say that being around rich people for too long makes you insane; I could blame class envy, the dialectic, advanced capitalism, the housing crisis. I could say it was climate catastrophe, the fumes from the wildfires, the fact the government was collapsing. I could blame my parents. I could blame my sister. I could blame that pure, exhilarating desire for self-annihilation that we all feel when we stand at the top of a tall building or carry an infant down the stairs. I could blame love.

But I won't. There is no justification. Even years later, I am ashamed, just as I was almost instantly afterwards, when Greg pulled me away from Iris's crouched, gasping body and manhandled me into the house, and then to our room, pushing me with some force into the interior. He stood with his back to the closed door for a moment, his pale, tear-mottled face twisted in disgust. I saw a desire to hit me pass across it, before he took the key from the door and closed it quietly behind him. I heard it turn in the lock.

I am not sure how long I was in there for, or what the

others were doing. Had they called an ambulance? The police? At some point, I went to the en suite toilet to be sick, maybe twice. I sat on the bed for a while. I tried to cry, and found that I couldn't. Eventually, I fell asleep.

*Anonymous, The Woman of Hohle Fels,
between 40,000–35,000 – BCE*

Anonymous was a woman. Forty-thousand years ago, you sat down and made a model of yourself, carved from mammoth ivory. The figure has large, round breasts and a big, round belly. Strong thighs, a deep crevasse between her legs. She's almost 6cm long. There's a hole where her head should be, probably so that she can be worn as a necklace.

I picture you, this Anonymous. An early modern human, in a cave in what is now Germany, sitting in the firelight, carefully carving the fingers of the hands that rest on the figure's stomach using a sharp stone tool. A nude self-portrait, a way of saying: I exist. Look at my body, my breasts, my stomach. Look at what it can do. It creates. It is the beginning of everything.

You were a woman. Of this, I am certain.

I stand naked, looking down at my body. Illness has changed my relationship to it. I am proud of what my body has achieved during its time on this earth, and of what it has given me. I feel only tenderness towards it now it has begun to fail. From this vantage point, certain parts — my breasts, my stomach, my thighs — seem outsized, exaggerated: the same parts that are emphasised on some of those statues. In contrast, my legs seem narrow, just like those of the figurine. You will not have had access to a mirror, Anonymous. This would have been your only way of seeing yourself, unless you spent hours standing next to a pool. Is that why your figure appears to have no face?

Your figurine will be attributed to a man and given the name of a Venus. In this case, the Venus of Hohle Fels, *after where it was found. A nonsense, to call such a thing a Venus. And an outrage to name the oldest undisputed depiction of a woman's body — of a human body, actually — after a sexy goddess from the parade of sexy goddesses that were to come, thousands and thousands of years after you made this.*

Figures such as these have been found from the Pyrenees to the Don River. They have all been labelled Venuses, the Willendorf Venus, *made 25,000 years ago, perhaps being the most famous. Only relatively recently have people begun to suggest that they might be self-portraits shaped by the hands of women.*

When he came to the hospital, he kissed my dry lips, and slipped a little reproduction of your figurine into my hand. I hold on to it now that he has left. It feels smooth and cold between my fingers, shines pale in the light cast by the monitors. Ever the archaeologist, I said, when I saw what it was. I could see in his face that he was shocked by the sight of me. It doesn't matter, though. I remember how he saw me then, all those times on the island. All those times since.

It's been an honour, to be seen like that. To be loved, to be told so. He said it again when he came today. And, after all these years, I said it back. Or rather, I signed it back, in the language I used with my sister when she was small. I crossed my hands and put them to my breast, and pointed to him.

Why did he bring me this final nude? I think he understood that although I know hardly anything of you or of your hunter-gatherer life, I still feel a kinship with you that stretches across millennia. I have that same implacable drive, the need to depict myself, to be remembered. I can see you in my mind's eye, bent studiously, cast in the orange of the flickering flames, carving, etching, shaping, making. All so you can say: I am alive. I am here. I am.

Tenth day

I woke to the sound of the door closing quietly.

'Come, now.' Ky held me by the wrist and pulled me up from the bed.

'Why should I come with you?'

He shushed me and didn't answer, instead noting my suitcase and picking it up so it didn't make a noise from being pulled along the floor. The rest of the house was dark, but I could hear the tense sound of voices rising and falling from somewhere within. We exited via the rear door, cut from the side of the house that faced away from the sea. His car waited in the paved driveway.

'I need to talk to Iris. And to Greg.'

'He told me to take you. Iris is not in a condition to speak to you.'

'Alessia, then.'

He shook his head. 'She is very angry. Do you have everything?'

'Fuck, my phone. Two minutes.'

I walked around the house to the pool, next to which my

phone remained in the urn. I tried to turn it on, but it had become nothing more than a paperweight, essentially. I took a moment to stand there and look at the dimly lit pool. It was the only source of light, other than the stars, which were as vivid and as spectacular as ever. Who was it that described the night sky as a blanket punched with holes? He had obviously never been to Greece; here, you could make out far more swirling detail in the night sky than you could at home, where stars were simply individual pinpricks in the darkness, static and separate.

I looked at the still water, the refraction of the lights, pale and tasteful, like the house itself. It really was a very beautiful pool.

Ky drove with the windows down, the rush of the wind deterring either of us from saying anything. The smell of the smoke was acrid now, and I could see the glow of the fires beyond the top of the valley. Already the sky on the horizon was turning pale as the car climbed the winding road towards the capital and descended in the direction of the port. He didn't need to tell me where we were going, or that I needed to get off the island as soon as was possible. Having purchased a budget flight leaving from Athens, I had been due to get a separate ferry to the others anyway, although Greg was booked to travel with me. I assumed that Ky was going to put me on an earlier boat to avoid any trouble with the police if Iris decided to report me.

I felt strangely numb to the prospect of arrest. It was one of those unfazed reactions that you have in times of crisis. I was more concerned about my appearance, but didn't want to check the mirror and make Ky aware of that. How pathetic that I still cared what he thought of me, despite what he had seen me do. Then I thought about his behaviour, and felt a surge of outrage. He caught my glare and began to slow down as we approached the port. The sun hadn't risen yet, but it was light enough that I could see his expression.

'Sophie—'

'Save it.'

'You can't go like this. Not after—'

'After what? After you both used me?'

'I need to talk to you about that.'

'Why is she angry? What does she have to be angry about? That I spoiled her little dinner party? That I made a scene?'

'That you hurt her friend,' Ky said, and I turned my thoughts to the last thing that I had seen as I had left our room at the villa, on the nightstand by the door, placed there like an offering: a clump of bloodied, blond hair.

'But not only that. I need to explain. She was not . . . she was not always there. Not every time.'

'Not every time?'

'No. At first, yes. That was our design. But then I became . . . I felt something between us.'

I swore at him and raised my hand as though to go for him, but lacked the commitment.

He grabbed my hand and held it there.

'I wanted to be the only one to see you. That's why she is angry.'

'Not enough,' I said. I was not going to cry, I had already decided. 'Anyway, she hadn't stopped. I heard her in the undergrowth, on the islet.'

'That wasn't her, I swear to you. I made sure she was sleeping before I woke you, and she was still sleeping when we returned. I wish I had time to take you somewhere again. I wish I had the rest of my life to take you somewhere.'

It was as close a declaration as either of us would offer. I'm sure he would have kissed me had I let him. I didn't. Instead, I whispered a small, 'Fuck you.' He always said I had bad language, so I had taken delight in shocking him by swearing in jest, but this was heartfelt.

He held my fingers to his lips for a second and turned off the ignition. It was time to get out of the car. The ferry was pulling in to port and a sparse crowd of tourists was congregating with their luggage, alongside several islanders and a priest in his tall hat and black robes. Ky handed me my suitcase and I stumbled slightly while trying to pull out the extendable handle, which had a habit of sticking. My limbs seemed to have stopped working. I turned to go.

'Wait.' He walked around to the boot, opened it, and removed a large bag. 'It's yours.'

I took it without looking inside. I think I was still a little bit drunk. Only when I was seated on the ferry and it was pulling away from the island, its modest row of tavernas cast pink in the light of the dawn, did I look inside. The portrait. And with it, a letter.

In the toilet of the ferry, the smallest spot of bright red blood cast against the white cotton of my underwear. After I had finished, I soaped my hands and tried to wash the dark brown flecks of Iris's scalp from beneath my fingernails. In the mirror, my face looked slightly haggard and drawn, but not as bad as I had expected. The journey home stretched out before me, too long to contemplate. What would I do when I got back to our flat? Would I pack up immediately? I supposed that I would go to my parents'; the gallery wouldn't miss me. Some time outside of the city might be good for me. Once my phone was fully charged, I would call my mother.

Back in my seat, I turned over Ky's letter in my hands, unable to focus on its words, troubled by the thought of who, if not Alessia, had been watching us from the undergrowth that night. That it could have been any of them disturbed me, and that preoccupation made his fervent words of love and remorse even harder to digest.

Next to me sat the portrait, still wrapped in its cloth. I felt bad about the money. I would write to Alessia offering to return it, which would hurt, but was probably the right thing to do, morally, seeing as Ky had stolen the portrait for me. There was no way she had given it to him freely. She was very particular about her art collection, and had invested time and money in both me and the painting. As far as I knew, she had no plans to come to the UK anytime soon, and was set on establishing a small gallery on the island, which was becoming increasingly popular with art-world types from Athens.

They would all cut me out, of course. This I knew. I was sad to lose Helena, though not so sad to no longer be a bridesmaid. (I vowed that day to never be a bridesmaid again, and I kept that promise to myself for life. Mercifully, people do stop asking after a certain age.)

Much later, when she came to stay with us after leaving Harry, Helena would show me photos of the day. She was the perfect bride – her mother had been right about the orange-blossom headdress, to which she had capitulated – but I thought I could detect in certain photos a look of foreboding on her face.

'Walking down the aisle, a part of me was already wondering how I would get out of it,' she said. Whether or not this was true, I don't know.

It was a ghastly divorce. He tried to take the house, the children, everything. He said she was insane, took his tactics right out of the nineteenth-century playbook. You can read about it all in her most recently published work of autofiction. She captured him far better than I ever could; I have struggled to elucidate his good qualities, if indeed he had any. Some relationships are mysteries to everyone but the people in them.

My plugged-in phone finally bleeped on as we left the port of Kythnos. There was very little to look through: a couple of messages from my mother, the last one saying that a letter had arrived for me from the Royal College of Art. I had given my childhood address in the vain hope that in doing so I might fulfil some sort of geographical admissions quota. Whether or not it worked, I don't know. When I got home, I would find out that I had been offered a full scholarship.

There are events in our lives that are obvious turning points, and others that become so in retrospect. The most seismic rupture that I assumed had occurred was the loss of almost all my personal relationships. And it's true that I would not see most of those people ever again. (I would hear of Iris from time to time, rising through the ranks to become a doyenne of the publishing world. After leaving Edwin in the company of his golden lion, she never married or had children, but she did, I think, live with someone. I read a gushing broadsheet profile of her while I sat in an outpatient waiting room at the start of my treatment. In the photograph, it looked as though the patch of hair I'd torn out had eventually grown back.)

The real rupture, however, was in my artistic practice. My time on the island had cracked something open, whether through love or exploitation, or a mixture of both, I am not sure. In the aftermath, it became even more pronounced, a consequence of the shift in my physical experience, I expect. The work I produced became more embodied, its theoretical underpinnings concrete in my mind even though I painted with furious emotion for almost a year. Then, for obvious reasons, I was unable to work, despite feeling a stronger impulse to do so than ever before. The baby and I weren't just symbiotic; we operated like a single organism. Initially, I had felt a great void where all that creativity had been, but then I came to see that void as a well of feeling so primitive and intense that it could be channelled into art-making. It was once I found some spaces between us that I came back to it, and set upon the idea that would enable me to continue to paint: one or two paintings a year, made every summer: the freedom that I would grant myself, and that he would give to me, out of remorse, or generosity, or respect for my work, or desire, or love, or all of those things.

Greg appeared in the seat next to me on the plane at the last moment possible. I knew that he had hung back deliberately because he was always early. I waited for him to say something first, but when he didn't, I made a lame attempt at an apology. There was so much to apologise for that the word sounded almost comical, and the bitter laugh with which it was met felt entirely fitting.

It was an awful flight, the worst of my life. What the other passengers thought, I can only imagine. For most of the three hours and forty minutes, Greg cried. Now that our relationship was ending, I no longer saw his desire for a family with me as a pitiable attempt to trap me, but as the authentic expression of his love. I tried to explain to him that it was nothing against him, that I simply couldn't countenance a life with any man who expected things of me that would come between myself and my work. He told me that I was heartless, and that life was about more than art. I said that was something a curator and not an artist would say, and he countered with some remarks about my talent or lack thereof, which would not flatter him to recount now.

Perhaps I too was guilty of hiding behind theory, and so in the end, during yet another agonising post-mortem a few days later, I had to say, or rather shout, that I simply didn't love him, and that, in time, he would come to understand that he probably hadn't loved me, either. He certainly didn't truly *see* me. This hysterical outburst seemed to convince him, or at least reiterate in his mind that I was too unhinged to fight for.

'Oh, Soph,' he said, as he put his arms around me. 'I saw what you deigned to show me.'

He did not try to get me back, nor did I ask that of him. The violent act that I had committed, not to mention the betrayal – of which he did not want any details – were such that I had succeeded in annihilating any good feeling between us. He hated me, and I felt that I deserved to be hated. It was easier in some ways. I felt no need to account for or excuse my behaviour; I was resigned to the end of our relationship.

We slept together one more time after that. You could ask me why, and all I'd respond with is, why does anyone do anything? Years-long relations between men and women cannot be untangled overnight. In giving him my body one last time, I expect I was trying to lessen the blow of my departure, but also to make him feel that he was still a person who was lovable in the world. There had been reasons we had been together for so long, some of them good, and even though everything was horrible, I wanted this last goodbye to be a tribute to the fact we had felt tender about each other once, and could again, if only for a moment. I was also granting him some power; to let him be the one to leave. I offered him the gift of imagining that he had rejected a repair attempt on my part, that I had prostrated myself before him to no avail.

After I moved out, his mother sent me a message saying that she would never forgive me. That hurt a little. I really did like his mother.

There is no doubt that I mistreated him.

'You wouldn't have been happy with me,' I said, on the plane. 'You were never going to be happy with me.'

I had simply seen the fact of it before he had. He would quite quickly meet someone, marry, and have children. According to Helena, she was also a curator. Greg went on to curate several major retrospectives at national institutions, both here and abroad. For a while, his area of expertise – abstract expressionists, but only the male ones – went out of fashion. Poor Greg had to sit out several years of Lee Krasner and Helen Frankenthaler and Joan Mitchell shows, but the world rights its tilt eventually, and he came to be well respected, if not known for breaking new ground. In his later years, he wrote some criticism for the more staid broadsheets, the timbre of which I found surprisingly crotchety for someone of his generation. As for his wife, she went part-time after having the children. I don't know her name, so can't say what she did after that. Perhaps she had a career resurgence when the babies were older, or got a book deal, writing the sorts of mainstream art historical surveys that other curators looked down upon, but which sold many thousands of copies. Or maybe she fronted BBC programmes. I always hoped that she did something like that.

* * *

What I came to understand later in life is that the condition of having a female body is an exercise in truth-telling – even more so when you are trying to make art about it. In order to create the paintings I painted, I had to excavate what it meant to inhabit that vessel. That work had begun at university, but after that I spent a long time digging with no valuable results. It was only in Greece that the meaning of it all started to take shape. Imagine desire as being a bit like the strokes of my brush, the daubs and splatters of paint creating a form on the canvas; that is how it felt. Like I had gone, overnight, from blank nothingness to deep embodiment in a way that felt startlingly natural.

That is how I found my gaze. I had been trying to unpick it from the fact that, like many women, being watched, being looked at, was how I had been trained to interpret sex. Was that really so bad? I had never felt unconditional desire as I had felt it that summer, watched or unwatched, cognisant or not. It was so ravenous it was monstrous, almost. The shifting margins of the relations between the three of us were messy and confusing and did not bear too much analysis, but there's no doubt that I began to learn the truth of my body, that Ky and Alessia facilitated something in me that shaped the artist I was to become. I spent the rest of my life exploring what it means to live in a female body, and how best to convey that artistically and materially in ways entirely separate from the male interpretations that had dominated for so long. It made me as an artist. Perhaps that was her plan all along.

FEMALE, NUDE

Now, decades later, my memories of that time remain so detailed that it seems obvious what was happening to me. The vivid dreams, the enhanced senses, especially those of smell and taste. The greed with which I approached food and drink and sex. Sitting here in my room, writing, I can taste the salty wetness of the feta between my lips, the bursting sweetness of the peaches Agatha brought up to the house every morning. The scent of the dry pines comes to me, alongside the musk of night-blooming flowers, and the smells of lavender, thyme, the burning incense spirals that we used to deter mosquitos. I hear the cicadas and the soft murmuring of conversation somewhere only just out of reach, the way cut-glass English accents carry on a strong Cycladic breeze. His breathing – above all, his breathing – and his broken utterances gasped out so close to my ear.

My vision became sharp and heightened on the island, which is why each location appears to me even today in almost photographic form. I could draw his body and her body entirely from memory, but also the undulating outline of the little cove and the path around the headland. The squat, flat lines of the monastery, its walls bright and shining, shielding us that first time as I lay splayed on the rock while he tasted me. I could produce a hundred still lifes: the table, set for dinner; each object in that dim, dusty room; the wooden crucifix; the intricate lace work on the fluttering curtain. Many of these scenes appear to me empty, as though actors have just left a stage set, or have been transported somewhere else, out of time, leaving a ghost ship replete with uncanny remains: set-down cutlery, the smears of sauce on plates, our stubbed-out cigarettes.

I can also replay everything that happened between us, every glance, every touch, every penetrating movement of his tongue, or his dick. When I do so, it is as though I have returned there. I feel the physical effects of arousal and fear just as if I were sitting in that rusty old car near the churchyard, the backs of my thighs slick against the leather, my skirt around my waist, his fingers, my wetness. And although she is there, although I know now that she was there, watching, I do not see her.

I feel it all.

I knew so little of my body in those days. That small, red spot of blood. I assumed that his fingernail had grazed me inside while he touched me, furiously, the final time. It did not occur to me that the bleeding was from the force of the fertilised egg that would become my daughter, implanting itself, herself, into the lining of my compliant womb.

Sophie Evans: A Body of Work

Alessia Skalieris Gallery, London W1
12 April–30 May

Alessia Skalieris Gallery is pleased to announce Sophie Evans: A Body of Work, the first major presentation of the late artist's paintings. Spanning two decades, this deeply personal series of self-portraits traces Evans's evolving engagement with the female body, from desire, pregnancy and motherhood to independence and ageing. Following the artist's death earlier this year at the age of fifty-seven, the remarkable works were acquired from her daughter, Francesca 'Franny' Zikos, and will be shown together for the first time.

'When I saw them after the funeral, I couldn't help but be astonished by their intensity,' said Ms Skalieris. 'I was acquainted with Sophie Evans's remarkable talent early on. The genesis of this series took place during a summer residency at my place in Greece, a moment of artistic clarity that foreshadowed the compelling body of work to come. Though our paths diverged, I was profoundly moved to learn, after her passing, that she had quietly sustained her practice, each work imbued with an unyielding intensity and introspective depth.'

Aside from a furious period of activity in pregnancy, Evans painted sparingly throughout her life, producing no more than one or two paintings a year. Yet her work speaks with remarkable immediacy. Raw and intimate, the paintings foreground the female form in states of tension and repose, positioning Evans in conversation with a lineage of women artists who have navigated self-representation on their own terms.

'They engage with the tradition of female nude self-portraiture – if, indeed, one can call it a tradition, given its rarity,' notes curator Dorothea Wilke. 'And yet, they break exciting new ground, expanding the possibilities of the genre with a singularly expressive visual language.'

'I am thrilled that the general public are about to understand what I have always known – that my mother was a phenomenally gifted artist,' said Ms Zikos. 'She never sold or exhibited a painting in her lifetime, and I only wish that she could be here today to see them all together at the gallery.'

Evans's practice was shaped by the constraints of time and circumstance. 'When she was in her early thirties, my mother received a place on the painting MA at the Royal College of Art, and although it included a significant scholarship, she was unable to take it up as she was pregnant with me, and then the first pandemic intervened. Despite this halt to a promising artistic career, she never seemed bitter about it. She always used to say that I was the best thing she ever made, but standing in the presence of these paintings all together for the first time, I am not so sure.'

Evans painted only in the summers, and this seasonal rhythm became an essential structure within her practice, allowing for an intense, uninterrupted engagement with her work. 'We used to fly out to Greece to see my father for a week or two,' said Ms Zikos, 'and then she would go off and paint, and that seemed to give her enough creative fulfilment to sustain her for the rest of the year.'

Evans worked a range of menial jobs while looking after her daughter and visiting and assisting her sister Rosie, who is disabled and lives in supported housing. Executed on a monumental scale, these vivid, semi-figurative works balance gestural intensity with compositional restraint. *Female, Nude* (2019), the earliest work on canvas included in the exhibition, offers a striking example: two entwined female figures occupy a destabilised pictorial space, their relationship oscillating between sensuality and struggle. The identity of the second sitter is hitherto unknown. Overseeing the scene is a kouros, an archaic Greek nude male statue rendered with unsettling corporeality. Far from being uneasy at his presence or critical of his gaze, the female figures appear to delight in it.

Alongside the paintings, the exhibition presents rare preparatory drawings and archival photographs, including a series of studies of Evans's sister Rosie, a lifelong presence in the artist's work, and of Ms Zikos's father, Kyrillos Zikos, an archaeologist who lives on the island of Sifnos. He and Evans never married, but they retained an intimate friendship until her final days, and he is a recurring subject in her male nudes. The exhibition's centrepiece, *Madonna and Child* (2021), emerges from this personal archive, transforming mother and daughter into a contemporary pietà, at once luminous and devastating.

'With this first retrospective, Evans's place within the canon is undeniable,' says Skalieris. 'These paintings demand to be seen, studied and felt. They will be discussed for generations to come. I feel immense privilege at having been the one to discover her.'

List of Works

Paula Modersohn-Becker, Self-Portrait at 6th Wedding Anniversary, 1906
Francesca Woodman, From Space2, Providence, Rhode Island, 1976
Tracey Emin, I Could Feel You, 2014
Frida Kahlo, Henry Ford Hospital, 1932
Anne W. Brigman, The West Wind, 1915
Suzanne Valadon, Self-Portrait with Naked Breasts, 1931
Louise Bourgeois, Femme Maison, 1946 –47
Amrita Sher-Gil, Self-Portrait as a Tahitian, 1934
Ana Mendieta, Flowers on Body, Silhueta Series, 1973 –78
Gwen John, Self-portrait, sketching, c.1909
Carolee Schneemann, Interior Scroll, 1975
Artemisia Gentileschi, Susannah and the Elders, 1610
Emma Amos, Work Suit, 1994
Jenny Saville, Propped, 1992
Yoko Ono, Cut Piece, 1965
Lisa Brice, Untitled, 2019
Zanele Muholi , Julie I, Parktown, Johannesburg, 2016
Alice Neel, Self-Portrait, 1980
Anonymous, The Woman of Hohle Fels, between 35,000 – 40,000 BCE

Author's Note

With the exception of Sophie's painting, the artworks referenced in this work of fiction are all real, and the artists are all real. As much as possible I have tried to be accurate in terms of where in world the paintings or photographs reside, or resided at the time Sophie encountered them. Please indulge any inaccuracies as a result of artworks being on loan, in storage, damaged, or hidden away in private collections as a case of artistic licence.

I read many books, journals, articles, and other works as part of the research for this novel, over the course of many years (and indeed during my years of study), but there are several to which I owe a greater debt than most. As far as I could discern – at least at the time of writing – no one has written an art historical survey focusing solely on female nude self-portraiture, or not one that I could find, anyway. So I had to construct my own – a daunting but also thrilling prospect. I could not have done so without Lynda Nead's *The Female Nude: Art, Obscenity and Sexuality*, which I first encountered as an undergraduate and which little did I then know would provide some of the theoretical underpinning for this work. I also owe much gratitude to Frances Borzello for her great work *Seeing Ourselves: Women's Self-Portraits*, and to Lauren Elkin for the groundbreaking *Art Monsters: Unruly Bodies in Feminist Art* (especially her work on Carolee Schneemann).

I am also grateful to Jennifer Higgie for *The Mirror and The Palette: Rebellion, Revolution, and Resilience: Five Hundred Years of Women's Self Portraits*. Julie Phillips' excellent *The Baby on the Fire Escape: Creativity, Motherhood, and the Mind-Baby Problem* was a galvanising and inspirational companion as I grappled with similar questions of art and motherhood while nursing a small baby.

This novel would not exist without Hélène Cixous's *The Laugh of the Medusa*, Elena Ferrante's *Frantumaglia*, or the works of Annie Ernaux, especially *Happening*. Without these ideas I would never have attempted to take on the task of writing the female body.

I would like to thank all the museums and galleries that let me come along to see the works, and all the artists and life drawing teachers I met during my practical research phase. I'm particularly grateful to my mother, Anna Cosslett, and to Lucy Whitehead, for talking me through how it feels to draw and paint the human figure and what happens psychologically during that process. Thanks also to Hettie Judah, who helped me find clarity when I was struggling to narrow down my list of artists. Special thanks are owed to Theresa Kneppers for putting Sophie's exhibition catalogue through a 'curator-speak' filter for me.

Though there is a depressingly high body count when it comes to the female artists referenced, some are still living. I hope that, if they read this book, they feel that I have done their works justice, and that Sophie – for whom art is such a central part of her emotional life, as it is mine – has not woefully misinterpreted them. Most of all, I would like to say thank you to all of them for making such radical, inspiring work. The story of so many women artists seems to me to be one of dogged persistence in the face of hatred, violence, mockery, indifference, and exhaustion. Despite these obstacles, these artists have endured, and long may they continue to inspire us.

Acknowledgements

I owe the biggest thanks to my agent, Eleanor Birne and to my editor Mary-Anne Harrington for their wisdom, expertise and encouragement. Thank you for believing in this book before it was a book, and for supporting me during the writing of it. I wrote most of it in the period after my son was born, and while that was necessary from an artistic perspective, it wasn't always easy. Ellie and Mary-Anne, your support kept me going and *Female, Nude* could never be the novel it is – or indeed a completed novel at all – without you cheering me on.

A big thank you to everyone at Tinder Press, particularly Ellie Freedman and Alara Delfosse. Thank you to Tara O'Sullivan for an excellent and thoughtful copyedit, and to Alice Clark for her beautiful cover design.

I am profoundly grateful to Laetitia and Eric for hosting me in the Luberon, where I wrote many of the closing pages of this novel. That time and space to write, in such a beautiful place, was essential. Merci beaucoup.

I have spent many hours discussing the central questions of this novel – motherhood and identity and the tension at between them – with the many brilliant women in my life, some mothers, some not. Some are old friends and some are new, and there are too many to name here, but thank you all, your ideas, your opinions, and most of all your rants have all been so inspiring. Sarah, Holly, and Jessica do deserve special mentions though, because you have all had to listen to me bang on about this book for many years now. Your friendship means so much to me.

To my family – thank you so much for your continued love and support of me. Mum and Dad: thank you for taking me to galleries, for instilling in me the belief that art is essential, and for never allowing care responsibilities to overshadow my ambitions. Particularly Mum, because you owned books that contained paintings by artists like Artemisia Gentileschi, and you showed them to me when I was very young. And also because you painted through the chaos, and so gave me a roadmap for how to hold onto myself even when the demands of caring feel all consuming.

To my brother, who can't read this. Your love taught me the glory of what it means to care. I love you.

To my husband, for all those times in Greece, for all those islands and all those swims. Until we had our son, those were, I think, the best of all our days. And of course, to my boy: I never wept at a Raphael until I had you. Yes, you are undoubtedly the greatest thing I ever made.